UNDERCURRENT

Visit us at www.boldstrokesbooks.com

By the Author

McCall

Return to McCall

London

The Last Kiss

Laying of Hands

Wild Wales

Windswept

Innis Harbor

Undercurrent

UNDERCURRENT

by
Patricia Evans

2024

UNDERCURRENT

ISBN 13: 978-1-63679-669-7

THIS TRADE PAPERBACK ORIGINAL IS PUBLISHED BY
BOLD STROKES BOOKS, INC.
P.O. BOX 249
VALLEY FALLS, NY 12185

FIRST EDITION: JULY 2024

CREDITS
EDITOR: SHELLEY THRASHER
PRODUCTION DESIGN: SUSAN RAMUNDO
COVER DESIGN BY TAMMY SEIDICK

Acknowledgments

First, a huge thank you to Shelley Thrasher, my editor, who quite literally shaped the book you have in your hands. She's immensely knowledgeable and an absolute pleasure to work with, in addition to keeping me laughing and sane during the editing process, which is no easy feat, let me assure you.

I owe the real Trobaugh and Hooper, whom you will fall in love with again within the pages of this book, a debt of gratitude for not only their friendship, which I treasure, but also for their patient guidance concerning all things law enforcement. Fans fell in love with them for the first time in *The Last Kiss* and demanded to see them reappear for good reason, they're some of my favorite people too. In the moments I've doubted whether true love exists, their relationship is proof that it does.

Finally, thank you to Niina Heinonen, who taught me the finer points of Finnish saunas and culture and was the inspiration for the character of Wilder.

Dedication

For my muse.

CHAPTER ONE

D o you think this is funny?"
The woman at the Salem Police Department reception desk glanced impatiently back at Tala Marshall in the line behind her, then refocused her glare on the receptionist, who was leisurely folding a pink stick of gum into her mouth. "I was at the Salem High bake sale this morning, and there were cookies labeled gluten-free that most certainly were *not* gluten-free." She held a dramatic pause before she continued. "This is a life-or-death matter."

"Right." The receptionist tossed the wrapper under her desk and looked up with no change of expression. "Sounds like it."

Tala watched the muscles in the woman's jaw tense and lock, then glanced discreetly down at her watch. *Thank god other people are working to solve this case, because I may never get past the front desk.*

"What's your name, young lady?"

The receptionist rolled her eyes as she looked pointedly down to the nametag under her right shoulder. *Daisy Parker. Staff/Salem PD.* Her eyes flicked to the door as it opened again and settled back on the woman on the other side of the desk.

"Listen. If you're going to file a complaint, spell my name right. I get tired of tossing the ones from the newbies that don't pay attention."

Tala stifled a laugh a second too late as the woman in front of her buttoned her cardigan to the very top, as if it were armor. She sniffed and shifted her cream leather handbag farther up on her shoulder. "Never mind. I'll be happy to wait until an actual man of the law is available for a consultation."

"Excellent. Be sure to say 'man of the law' when you meet our chief." Daisy popped the cap off her pen with her teeth and dropped it onto the desk with a plastic ping. "She loves that shit." She paused, her pen poised over the reception log. "Now, I'm assuming your first name is Karen. Is there a last name?"

The woman stomped off toward the waiting area, and Tala waited a beat before she stepped cautiously up to the desk. "I'd ask how your day is going, but I'm afraid to know more than I already do."

"Smart move." Daisy flashed her a genuine smile as she shuffled the papers on her desk and held one up, comparing the picture to Tala. "You're Agent Marshall, correct?"

"Correct." Tala smiled and lifted the FBI badge hanging on a chain around her neck, shifting her computer bag onto her shoulder. She glanced to the left at the nearly full waiting area. Everyone there was staring back at her.

"Chief Mason is on the phone with her boss now, but you'll be first in line when she's done." Daisy glanced into the crowded waiting area to the left and snapped her gum. "Trust me, you're the only one in there she actually needs to talk to. People are freaking out about the serial killer and finding any excuse to come into the station."

Two uniformed officers walked through the glass doors behind Tala, followed by a swirl of cool fall air carrying the crisp scent of falling leaves that sifted through the long layers of Tala's hair as it disappeared. The Salem police station certainly had a small-town feel, but a thick tension hovered over the waiting room, along with the requisite acrid waft of generic coffee from the stained glass pot in the far corner of the area. Daisy motioned for Tala to roll her suitcase behind the front desk.

"I'll watch this for you until you're done with Chief Mason." She pushed the suitcase into a corner and paused, turning to look toward the double doors behind her. "Actually, that sounded like her office door, so she's probably on her way up."

In only a few seconds she appeared, tall, with broad shoulders and a pale-blond, old school fade haircut. The double doors to the hall swung shut behind her as she peered past Daisy into the waiting room. Four gold stars on the shoulder of her navy uniform shirt told Tala this was Salem's chief of police, but she wasn't at all what she'd expected. Wilder had a dapper, masculine vibe, tempered with a softness around her mouth and a quick smile as she clocked Tala on the other side of the desk. She also looked like she could lift a police cruiser onto her shoulder with one hand.

"Chief, this is Tala Marshall. She's here to see you. Tala, this is our chief, Wilder Mason." Daisy stopped abruptly and rolled her eyes as the woman in the cardigan cleared her throat loudly from the waiting room. She lowered her voice to a whisper, and Tala tried not to smile as Wilder leaned closer. "Look, Chief. I'll just give you a rundown, and you can let me know how you want to deal with this morning's selection."

"I was hoping you were going to say that." Wilder smiled and rested one arm on the desk. Tala drew in the faint scent of seawater and pine soap rising from the warmth of her skin. "Hit me."

"The cardigan that just tried to get your attention is Mary Lees. She's the new middle-school principal and has been in town only a few weeks. She's here because she's convinced someone's sabotaging the bake sale at the school this afternoon via normal cookies labeled as gluten-free. Allegedly."

Wilder caught a glimpse of her and looked back to Daisy. "Go on. Who's the group in the corner? I can smell the patchouli from here."

"That's a new-age group of—" Daisy paused, then plucked a post-it haphazardly stuck to the bottom of her coffee cup and handed it to Wilder—"'spiritual healers' from Boston who want to perform a sky-clad séance in the park tonight to help rustle up our serial killer."

Tala glanced over at the group just as one of them was scattering what looked like crushed sage in a circle around them. Wilder turned over the Post-it Note as if there might be a translation on the back. "Sky-clad?" She tossed the note into the trash under the desk. "What does that even mean?"

"Naked." Tala shifted her expression into neutral and tapped her fingers on the desk. "It means they want to do a naked séance."

"In the park?" Wilder stood and rubbed her temples for a moment, then leaned back onto the desk. "Well, the last thing we need in Salem is a naked séance, killer or no killer. The tourists think we're a bunch of witches already without adding that to the mix." She paused, then pointed to one of the shortcut buttons on Daisy's worn beige landline. "Give that one to Steele. He's the only one charming enough to send them and their incense packing back to Boston without a scene."

"Will do." Daisy jotted that request down before she continued. "See the girl taking the selfies in the far corner?"

Wilder scanned the room and nodded when she noticed a young woman in a pink, skintight hoodie who was, indeed, stretching her arm to the limit and pouting into the camera. "Yeah. Why's she here?"

"One of the units brought her in because they found her topless in front of that bronze statue in the square, doing a video for her Instagram about serial-killer witches in Salem."

"What?" Wilder shook her head, hazarding one more glance before she went on. "Why is she not downstairs being booked?"

"Well, I guess technically she wasn't naked. She had on nipple pasties in the shape of witch hats. The officer that brought her in said they even had little orange tassels on them." Daisy shuffled through a stack of papers on her desk and handed Wilder one from the top. "That's her incident report. He gave her a ticket, but she threw a fit and demanded to speak to the chief."

"Right." Wilder folded the report and set it on the desk. "I'll get to her in a few minutes. Next?"

"Just Curtis Miller in the back by the coffee machine." She leaned over the desk to scan the room. "The rest of them are random press waiting for a statement about the case." Daisy sat back down and lowered her voice to almost a whisper. "Someone slashed Curtis's tires last night." She shook her head and leaned back in her chair with a pointed glance in his direction. "If you ask me, I'd say it's the husband of the waitress he's been spending quality time with in the diner's stockroom. He wants to see if there's footage from the traffic cams across the street."

"Refer him to the next free officer and have him make a formal report. I feel for him, but that's a mile down on my priority list right now." Wilder stood, scanning the room again before she turned to Tala. "Thanks for your patience, Agent Marshall. If you'd like, you can follow me back to my office, and I'll get you briefed on what we have so far with this case."

Tala followed Wilder through the double doors and down the hall, her boots clacking against the white-tiled hallway. Wilder paused at her office door and held it open for Tala, then clicked on the lights and offered to take her coat.

"I'm okay, thanks." Tala sat down in one of the two chairs across from Wilder's desk and let her bag slide to the floor as she smiled at the nameplate on Wilder's desk. "I've got to say, you look more like a Wilder Mason than a William Barnes. Do you keep that there hoping some random police chief named William will show up and take your place?"

Wilder laughed and picked it up, shoving it into one of her desk drawers before she answered. "That hadn't occurred to me, but one can hope. I'm just the interim chief until they hire a new one to replace Barnes, but it's now been months since I've been on the other side of the desk."

Tala unbuttoned her coat and Wilder held her gaze as she sat back in her chair, which Tala noted. Most people did not.

Tala glanced around the room, bare except for Wilder's desk, the two chairs across from it, and a gray, dented metal filing cabinet in the corner. There was also a navy-blue gym bag slung in the corner. "You hate it, don't you?"

Wilder laughed and leaned back in her chair, running a hand through her hair. "Yes, ma'am. But keep that under your hat."

"You don't hide it well." Tala smiled and watched as Wilder rolled a pen through her fingers. "But your secret's safe with me."

Wilder laid the pen across the notepad on her desk and looked up at her. Her eyes were deep velvet brown, rimmed with dark gold flecks and laugh lines past the edges of her lashes. "You got the train over from Boston, right?" She picked up the phone and held it on her shoulder. "I know you're probably ready to get to the cabin and settle in, so I'll have one of my guys, Robinson, drive you over there. You're the first to get there, but everyone else should arrive by this evening."

Tala watched as she made the call. Wilder's hands were strong and square, with long fingers and a small tattoo on the edge of her left palm: two straight lines with a circle between them. Broad shoulders led to defined arms, and Tala realized too late she was staring at the diving watch on Wilder's wrist. Wilder smiled, then picked up a thick brown folder at the edge of her desk and handed it over.

"This is all the information we have on the case and the victims at this point, and I believe you got the packet they emailed us with the info on the task force?"

Tala nodded just as a smiling officer with a bushy pirate beard knocked briefly and stuck his head around the edge of the door. "Ready for me, Chief?"

"That's Robinson. He's my second in command, so he'll take good care of you." Tala stood as Wilder got up from her chair and extended her hand. "Welcome to Salem, Agent Marshall." She hesitated. "Forgive my language, but we have a serial killer on the loose and were getting fuck-all done without a profiler, so I'm looking forward to hearing what you have to say."

Tala laughed as she shook Wilder's hand, then stepped out the door behind Robinson, closing it softly behind her.

Chapter Two

The coast-guard helicopter lurched forward and dipped sharply to the left, losing altitude at an alarming rate. The sun's rays glinted crazily off the curved glass surrounding them as LJ Hooper glanced at her wife, Brenda Trobaugh, gripping her aviation headset with both hands, eyes shut tight against the endless blue expanse of sky. Hooper rested her hand lightly on her knee and leaned closer.

"You okay, Detective?"

Hooper saw the pilot glance into the rear mirror before he fixed his gaze back on the horizon. The deafening chop of the blades above them seemed to increase the cabin pressure exponentially as they tipped forward again and neared the undulating surface of the ocean.

Trobaugh finally opened her eyes, then closed them just as quickly and shook her head. "Not until we're back on solid ground, thank you very much."

"No solid ground involved, I'm afraid." The pilot spoke into his headset and glanced into the mirror again. "See that coast guard ship up ahead? We'll be landing on their flight deck in just under three minutes." He looked down to flip a chrome switch on the control panel. "They didn't tell you that when they briefed you?"

"Christ." Trobaugh shook her head, fingers white against her temples. "I'd blocked out that little detail."

Hooper smiled and leaned into the window to watch the coast-guard vessel start to loom underneath the helicopter, taking note of the much larger cruise ship in the distance.

"Brace yourself," the pilot said, turning a dial on the control panel with a flick of his thumb. "The air currents over the water are unpredictable, so it could be a choppy ride until we connect with the helipad."

"Fantastic." Trobaugh's face faded to the final shade of pale, and she dropped her face into her hands. Hooper watched the pilot suppress a smile as he glanced back, and she elbowed Trobaugh gently and directed her attention to the front. The pilot nodded toward the cruise ship in the distance and slowly pushed a lever forward with the heel of his hand. The aircraft lowered and settled into a hover, as if waiting for direction.

Hooper's headset crackled to life again.

"From there someone will direct you to a smaller boat, and we'll get you out to that cruise ship asap. I'll be waiting to fly the four of you back to the Orlando airport, but be as quick as you can. We're burning daylight, and I'd rather not do this in the dark."

Hooper squeezed her wife's hand as the pilot executed a surprisingly smooth landing between the guidelights on the flight deck of the ship. Trobaugh warily opened one eye as the whirr of the chopping blades began to slow and glanced up at the pilot, who indicated it was safe to take off their headsets. Cold air rushed in like water as the flight crew swung open the door of the helicopter and directed them down a metal ladder to a waiting speedboat. The driver nodded at two life jackets behind him as they stepped in, then pulled smoothly away from the boat into the open sea. The ocean skimmed the sides of the boat as they accelerated, coating their faces in a cold salt mist. He pushed the throttle forward, pressing them hard against the damp leather seats as they jetted off in the direction of the late-afternoon sun, a shimmering gold path to the ship that now seemed massive, just a few hundred yards in the distance.

Trobaugh zipped up her navy windbreaker and ran a shaky hand through her hair. "So, did I hear Agent Tully say at the briefing this morning that these two know we're coming?"

"Correct." Hooper pulled her phone out of her jacket pocket and scrolled through her messages. "Everything had to be organized quickly, and cell reception is spotty this far from the mainland, but they should be waiting and ready for us when we get there."

"So, they're a couple?" Trobaugh flinched as a seagull swooped just over her head. "That doesn't happen very often in the FBI, or at least it didn't in the past."

"Nope. As far as I know they've never met. Different bureaus, apparently." Hooper grabbed her sunglasses back from the wind just in time and put them on her face again. "Looks like Maren James is based in Southern California—"

"She's that agent that cracked the Riverside Strangler case in Anaheim, right?"

"Exactly. It was similar to the situation in Salem, with the body count climbing by the day, and no one could figure it out. She swanned in and solved it in time for lunch."

"I remember hearing about that." Trobaugh patted down the pockets of her jacket for her lip balm and smiled when Hooper pulled a tube out of her own jacket and handed it over. "But I also remember someone saying she's quite the character, right? She's British or something?"

"Australian, I think. She was recruited." A text notification pinged, Hooper clicked it, and both leaned in to look at the FBI headshot of a forgettably pretty woman with a slick blond bob. "We have a picture of Agent Norse," Hooper refreshed the screen and shook her head, "but so far nothing on Maren James, so hopefully she'll be waiting when we get there."

"How did they end up on the same cruise ship?"

"It's run by the Olivia Corporation, so—"

"An all-lesbian cruise?"

"Exactly."

Trobaugh shook her head and winked in Hooper's direction. "That's what I call a target-rich environment. Something tells me they're not going to be thrilled about leaving. I certainly wouldn't be."

"Reel it in, Detective." Hooper winked at her wife and tapped her knee to hers as the driver shifted down and the boat slowed and sank slightly in the water. "Hopefully we won't be on board even five minutes."

The cruise ship loomed like a silent navy glacier as they approached and pulled smoothly up to the cast-iron tethers on the side, where a vertical door lowered slowly like a medieval drawbridge. Crew in white polo shirts lashed the speedboat to the massive iron rings on the side with impressive speed as Hooper and Trobaugh attempted to find their footing. Waves rocked the speedboat, pitching it sharply from one side to the other, while club music beats and laughter filtered down from the top deck. Hooper shaded her eyes to check it out and caught several of the partygoers looking down at them, sloshing margarita glasses in hand.

The pilot stared up at the last sliver of orange sun melting into the dark expanse of the sea in the distance. "We're burning time here, Detectives. I'll be waiting, but put a rush on it. The sooner we're back in the air, the better."

Hooper nodded, zipping up her jacket as she stepped out onto the makeshift gangplank, then turned to hold her hand out for her wife. Trobaugh hesitated, then held up one finger, stepped to the rear of the boat, and threw up over the side, pausing for only a moment before standing back up and straightening her shoulders. The driver gave her a wink and passed her a bottle of water as she stepped out of the boat.

"Excellent delivery." He grinned. "Clean execution. I give it a 9.7."

Hooper laughed as staff guided both of them onto the ship and pulled up the gangplank. A member of the Olivia team was there to direct them to the Crow's Nest, an onboard espresso shop on the starboard end of the ship, where a petite blonde sat at a small table, her bags stacked neatly beside her. The chrome badge clipped to her belt glinted in the light when she stood as Trobaugh and Hooper walked in.

"Agent Darcy Norse?" Trobaugh held out her hand as she introduced herself and Hooper. "I believe you're waiting for us?"

Hooper stifled a laugh as Darcy immediately stepped back from the handshake.

"I don't touch people." She sniffed and sat back down, smoothing the crease in her pantsuit. "Holdover from Covid, I guess, but better safe than sorry."

"Wait," Hooper said, retrieving her phone from her jacket pocket. "Aren't there supposed to be two of you? Where's Agent James?"

"I wouldn't have a clue. We've never met. I just followed the directions in my briefing packet that headquarters emailed me, and it said not to be late under any circumstances." She unscrewed the top of the water bottle she was holding and slipped the cap into her jacket pocket. "I assumed she'd do the same."

"One would think, anyway." Hooper clicked on her phone and held it up to Trobaugh. "Looks like we finally got that headshot of Maren James."

A member of the Olivia staff came to the door, and Trobaugh stepped back to speak to her briefly, then squinted at what looked more like a vacation snap than an FBI headshot. Maren was leaning back on an iron railing over the sea, laughing, holding a half-empty pint of beer. She had a darker complexion and a haphazard pile of wavy black hair piled on her head, a few strands the wind had brushed across her face. Her eyes sparkled with the last shards of golden afternoon sunlight, and the wind ruffled the hem of her oversized Hawaiian-print shirt.

"Well, this should be simple." Trobaugh slid her sunglasses onto her face and headed toward the door, "She looks like every lesbian who's ever been on vacation. Also, the paperwork says she's forty-three. Why does she look like a frat boy?"

Hooper started to join her, then paused and glanced back at Agent Norse. "Are you coming?" She waited until Darcy finally realized she was serious, which took a long few seconds.

"Coming to look for her?" Darcy spun the cap back onto her water bottle and looked up. "Nope. I've been roped into this task force to hunt down Salem's serial killer, not a grown-ass adult agent who can't tell time."

Trobaugh and Hooper finally found the elevator, and Hooper pressed the down arrow. "Great. Now we have to go find her? I mean, we can go back downstairs and ask for her room number I guess, but damn."

Her wife hit the opposite arrow, nodding at the fireworks sparking and blooming a shower of rainbow colors just past the corridor window. "No need. From the look of that picture, she's going to be at that party we heard on the top deck when we pulled up. I told the Olivia staff members to pack her room while we hunt her down."

Thirty seconds later, the elevator doors opened to the pool deck, where a party was in full swing under the darkening sky. A deep-turquoise pool glittered under the amber string lights overhead, and a DJ with a pink buzzcut and loose tie spun records from behind a booth in the corner, open laptop at the ready. Dozens of champagne-laden trays floated on the fingertips of the waitstaff navigating through the crowds, most of them gathered around the pool lit from the bottom with endless flickering rainbow LED lights.

"I've said it before, and I'll say it again." Hooper lifted a flute of champagne from a passing tray and gazed longingly at the steam rising from the twin hot tubs at the far end of the pool. Trobaugh lofted an eyebrow, and Hooper reluctantly abandoned the glass on an empty table. "We should look into retiring on one of those cruise ships that sail around the world full-time. I mean, this seems like the perfect opportunity to call in sick and try this one out for size." She slowed to inspect the grilled shrimp on skewers on a passing waiter's tray. "In the interest of research."

"First of all," Trobaugh jumped to the left to avoid being drawn into a line dance and shook her head, "no one calls in sick to the FBI. And do I need to remind you that this whole task force is being put together because bodies are washing onto the shore every damn day in Salem Harbor?"

Two older women wearing hats and swilling strawberry margaritas scooted out of their path with raised eyebrows. It was clear they'd heard their conversation, so Trobaugh dropped her voice to a whisper and leaned into Hooper's ear. "As much as I love the thought of playing shuffleboard with bikini-clad pool girls while we float from island to island, we're going to have to give it a swerve this time."

Hooper elbowed Trobaugh and pointed to the opposite end of the pool. A girl in her early twenties with enough oil glistening on her body to lube a fleet of Nissans was dancing in front of someone lounging on the tiled edge of the pool. She'd just started an impressive lap dance when Trobaugh finally spotted Hooper's point. The woman she was dancing for had a Corona in each hand and a lime wedge in her mouth, which seemed to track with what they knew about Maren's reputation. They watched as she poured one of the Coronas across the breasts of the girl gyrating on her lap and dropped the lime to follow the beer with her tongue. She was also wearing an open Hawaiian shirt.

"They really aren't paying me enough for this shit." Trobaugh rubbed her temples as she started toward the other end of the pool, dodging a beach ball that narrowly missed her head. Hooper grabbed it and threw it back to a group of laughing women in the pool.

"Really?" Hooper grinned at Trobaugh and nodded toward one of them who had decided to compete topless. "Actually, I think they might be overpaying us. Maybe we should stay and put in some overtime to even things out a bit."

"Let's just corral this frat boi they call an agent and get the hell out." Trobaugh held her ears as another dance song amped up from the DJ booth. "I need my feet back on solid ground."

By the time they arrived at the far end of the pool, it was obvious they'd found who they were looking for; even the shirt was the same as the picture. She was wearing mirrored aviator sunglasses and oversized khaki cargo shorts and slapped the girl's ass with a loud *thwack* as the lap dancer turned around and started grinding into her with her arms firmly around Maren's neck.

"Jesus." Trobaugh shook her head and shifted to make eye contact with the agent, which was difficult since hers seemed to be locked on the nearly naked girl in her lap. The music pounded in the background and Trobaugh leaned back to avoid a sudden splash of pool water as someone jumped in next to them. "What's the protocol for interrupting a lap dance in progress? I'm drawing a blank on that procedure."

Hooper smiled. "In the interest of safety, we should probably just let this come to a natural end, don't ya think?" They both tilted their heads in the same direction and watched as the girl stood up slowly and whipped off her bright yellow bikini top, dropping it in the pool.

Hooper shook her head. "On second thought, that's a really bad idea." They made sure their badges were visible as they approached but shouldn't have bothered. They had to speak up twice before Maren even acknowledged them, still without so much as a glance in their direction.

"Nah, mate. I'm good on beer for the minute." Maren pulled the now-topless girl back down onto her lap, her Australian accent dripping decadence. "I'll let ya know when I need something."

"We're not waitstaff." Hooper made a gallant effort not to look at the topless girl three feet away. "You're Maren James, correct?"

"Nope." The girl on Maren's lap answered for her, her lip gloss shimmering under the lights as she spoke. "Her name is Stone Cold. She just told me."

Maren finally turned her head long enough to clock the badges, rolled her eyes, and promised the girl on her lap she'd meet her at the bar in five. Her face downshifted into an instant pout, and she kissed Maren good-bye like she was going to war. Trobaugh loudly cleared her throat until she finally got the message and dove into the pool, retrieving her bikini top as she made her way to the bar. Maren watched, then turned around slowly, pulling her sunglasses from her shirt and flicking them open with one finger.

"Look, mate. I don't know what this is about, but I'm on *vacation*." She drew out the word for emphasis while she scanned the pool area behind them, then winked at a girl by the DJ booth before she finally pulled her attention back to Trobaugh and Hooper. "As in, I'm not an agent for the next week. So, I'd appreciate it if ya'd stop harshing my vibe up in here and let me get back to what I do best."

"We're Special Agents Trobaugh and Hooper. And it's not like you didn't know we were coming." Trobaugh took the sunglasses off Maren's face and handed them to her. "Pick up your shit, and let's go."

Maren pulled out her phone and scrolled. "Are you talking about the endless emails I've been getting for the last two days?" She stopped and clicked on one of them, scanning it briefly. "Why would they even send me emails when I'm on vacation? At the very least they should assume I don't intend to read them. Like, there should be a law in this freakin' country about it. There's a law about every-fucking-thing else."

"Picking up your phone would've made this a lot easier, but we've got a serial killer amping into turbo mode in Salem, Massachusetts, and you've been assigned to a task force to help find him." She paused, choosing her words carefully. "Apparently, you have a reputation for seeing patterns that other agents miss, so this is not an option. It's an order. From both your home bureau and headquarters."

"Which you would have known if you'd answered your phone." Hooper stared as a beautiful blond crew member with warm hazel eyes wove through the crowd and leaned into Maren. The overhead bistro lights sparkled across her tan lines, and she tucked a glossy wave of hair behind her ear as she spoke. "Same place tonight? I'll text you. I get off at twelve."

She disappeared back into the crowd, and Hooper shook her head. "Well, would you look at that? You *can* use a phone."

Maren set her beer on the edge of the pool and glanced at Trobaugh. "How many bodies?"

"Three." Trobaugh held her gaze. "And counting."

Maren nodded, buttoning her shirt up over her beer-stained tank top. "In how many days?"

"Ten."

"Fuck." She sighed and dropped her cell phone back into the pocket of her cargo shorts. "Well, at least the fun-sucking dramatics make a wee bit more sense now, mate."

The three of them headed toward the elevator, only to have Maren's lap dancer spot them as they passed the bar. She popped off her barstool and headed over, still tying the shoulder strings of her bikini back together.

"Wait. I thought you said you'd meet me after you were done with..." She paused, sweeping Trobaugh and Hooper head to toe, searching for the right word, "the suits."

"No can do, love. I'm—"

"Getting arrested." Trobaugh cut in and flashed her badge. "She's going to have to come with us."

"Seriously?" Her voice dropped to a sultry purr, and she trailed a manicured fingertip down Maren's arm. "That's kind of sexy. Can I watch?"

"Fuck me." Hooper picked up a beer the bartender had just flicked the top from and downed it in less than five seconds, setting it back down on the bar with a *thunk*. "I need a leaf blower, but for people." She grabbed Maren by the shoulder and shoved her in front of them, lightly twisting her arm behind her back as she did. "Party's over, Romeo. Turns out this isn't your balcony. Now *move* it."

By the time they arrived back at Crow's Nest, a scuffed, overstuffed duffel bag had joined the pile of luggage beside Agent Norse. Hooper introduced Maren to Darcy Norse and closed the door behind them.

"That looks like my stuff." Maren glanced back at the door. "How did it get down here?"

"I asked the staff to clean out your room while we went to look for you." Trobaugh glanced at her watch and nodded in the direction of the door. Agent Norse took the hint, gathering her bags. "I'd suggest you check your belongings for your travel documents and badge, and let's go. We have a flight to Boston to catch."

Agent Norse wordlessly handed Hooper her biggest suitcase, a leather shoulder bag with fancy gold lettering, balancing her houndstooth travel pillow on the top.

"Jesus." Hooper ignored the poorly disguised snort from her wife and situated the travel pillow under her arm. "I feel like I'm picking my kids up from detention."

"Don't lump me in with this shitshow. I was the one who was actually on time." Darcy paused, leaning slightly toward Maren and wrinkling her nose. "You smell like sunscreen and cheap beer. Don't you shower?"

"Yeah?" Maren threw her duffel bag over her shoulder and returned the volley. "Well, you smell like kitty litter and regret, Agent Tightass, so I guess that means I win."

Chapter Three

A re you sure this is it?" Darcy Norse narrowed her eyes and peered out the window at the two-story, Aspen-style log cabin, floating like a dark apparition between the undulating sheets of pewter rain. "It looks...deserted."

Maren James leaned between the front seats of the patrol cruiser. "We appreciate you picking us up at the airport, mate." She glanced out the window and mentally willed the skinny, overly highlighted bitch she was stuck with to keep her trap shut. "Is there anything else we need to know?" Maren ran a hand through her hair, still damp from the mad dash from the Boston arrivals gate to the taxi, and glanced again in the direction of the cabin. Every window was dark, and the fact that a serial killer was on the loose in Salem wasn't lost on her. "It's unlocked, I presume?"

"Correct." A cell phone buzzed against the dash, and the officer glanced at it briefly before dropping it into his jacket pocket. "I unlocked it this afternoon to let the cleaners in. The chief wanted it to be as nice as possible for tonight. It's her house, but she hasn't been back much since someone started killing people in town, so I imagine there are some basics in there, but it'll be tomorrow morning before we can get you some groceries."

"That's understandable, mate." Maren elbowed Darcy, who was still glaring through the downpour at the cabin like it was Dracula's castle. "This was all last-minute, to say the least. I'm sure we'll have everything we need."

The officer zipped up his navy Salem PD jacket and jerked his thumb toward the single light glowing on the second level. "If the rest of the task force aren't in there yet, they will be soon. Everyone should be here by tomorrow, and like I said, the housekeepers should have left you everything you'll need for tonight."

"Cheers." Darcy opened her mouth to speak, but Maren reached over her and opened the cruiser door. "If you don't mind popping the trunk, we'll just grab our suitcases and get out of your way."

"Nah. You two make a run for it." The officer pulled up his hood and swung open his door, the rain instantly drenching the sleeve of his jacket. "I'll grab your luggage from the trunk and meet you up there."

Darcy tucked her computer bag under her jacket and sprinted for the porch with Maren. A single overhead bulb flickered above the screen door, the light glittering across the porch boards slicked with rain and scattered yellow maple leaves. Maren got there first and wiped her sunglasses with her sleeve before she reached for the doorknob, but Darcy's high heel slipped on the last step, and she landed unceremoniously in an awkward heap on the soaked welcome mat.

"Goddamn it!" Darcy struggled to her feet, swatting away Maren's outstretched hand. "I just had this jacket cleaned." She swiped at the drenched lapel of her suit jacket and raked a hand through her hair, somehow managing to dump more rain into the collar of her shirt.

"Christ on a cracker." Maren fished the gum out of her mouth and stuck it to the porch railing. "Who brings a suit jacket on a cruise? I didn't even bring pants."

"Adults do." Darcy took an irritated breath and opened her computer bag to be sure at least her laptop was dry. "Maybe you should look into qualifying as one."

Maren leaned to the side to check on the cop who'd been sent to pick them up from the airport, still struggling to get the trunk shut with his arms full of their luggage. "Poor bastard. This is a tough gig." The phone barely sandwiched between his head and shoulder started to slide down his arm. "I mean, only one of those bags is mine. I'm kickin' myself now, mind you. Based on your heap of bags, one needs the entire contents of Macy's to catch a fucking serial killer."

Darcy brushed at a streak of mud that covered the length of her blouse and rolled her eyes. "Listen, we were *supposed* to be packing for a cruise, not a random pop-up task-force investigation." She handed her computer back to Maren and reached for the doorknob. "And if I had any choice, I'd be spending the next week on a deck chair in the Bahamas, not in Salem fucking Massachusetts." She paused, peering up at the windows above them with narrowed eyes. "Especially at some shadowy cabin with a horror-movie past."

Maren pushed the door open, flicking on the light switch with her elbow as she passed the threshold. She dumped her computer bag and set it by the door, trying not to laugh as Darcy tied herself into knots attempting to peel off the wet suit jacket that appeared to be tighter than her asshole. She finally held it in front of her with her thumb and forefinger, rain dripping in a steady rhythm into a pool on the polished wood floor. Maren made a mental note to figure out where she was from. She wasn't listening when Trobaugh and Hooper were actively prying her off the ship against her will.

Maren switched on the nearest lamp and sensed someone else in the room for the first time, standing at the sink in the open kitchen. She almost looked like a ghost: willowy, with high cheekbones, an olive complexion, and a glossy slick of hair to her waist that moved like black water. She leaned against the kitchen counter and silently peeled a green apple with a bone-handled knife. Maren waited, but the figure didn't look up.

"Oh, thank God." Darcy held the jacket out in front of her as she shook the rain from her hair. "I'm so glad you're still here. Could you drop this by the dry cleaners on your way out? I'm afraid this mud won't come out if it dries overnight."

Maren just shook her head and took a slow step back as she watched the woman look back down at her apple, the glossy green peel curling around her hand as it fell smoothly from the apple in a single strip.

"Okay." Darcy's eyes fluttered shut as she drew an irritated breath and held it before she continued, her tone tense and thin. "Well, clearly that's too much to ask. Can you at least tell me where I can find some towels?"

The woman looked up slowly with eyes that seemed lit from behind, like gold flashing beneath a slick of black lake water. She nodded at a narrow cupboard to the left, her gaze locked on Darcy. "You'll find them on the center shelf." She paused, dropping the apple peel into the yellow farm sink as she watched Darcy open the door only to look back over her shoulder with a sigh. It was empty. "They'll be right there between white privilege and systemic racism."

The drenched officer shouldered the door open again and stepped in, shaking the rain from his jacket as he piled their dripping suitcases by the entry table. He nodded to the woman with the apple as she folded the knife and dropped it into her back pocket, then seemed to draw the sound out of the room like a vacuum and take it with her as she walked down the hall.

"Oh, good." The officer shook off his uniform cap and nodded toward the hall. "I see you met Marshall. The chief just called me and told me she was here already. She insisted on taking the train from the city, apparently."

Darcy whipped around, jacket still in hand. "Who the hell is Marshall?"

"That's Agent Marshall. She's the profiler you'll be working with on the task force." He stepped back out onto the porch and scanned the area through the rain before he turned back to them. "I'm surprised you haven't heard of her. Tala Marshall is the top female profiler at the FBI. She works out of Boston Headquarters. The chief said we were lucky to get her at all."

"Jesus Christ." Maren rubbed her temples with tense fingertips before she glanced over at Darcy. "Tala *Marshall*? Ya gotta be fucking kidding me."

The officer stepped back out onto the covered porch. "Anyway, I'll let you get settled in. The rest of the detectives should be here by morning."

The door closed after him, and the silence hardened in the air until Darcy finally shrugged and threw her jacket on the counter in a wet heap.

"Look, this all happened so fast I haven't even looked at the paperwork. How would I know who she was?" Frustration glinted at the knife edge of her words. "Thanks for the backup, by the way."

Maren walked through the kitchen and into the hall before she turned around. "I didn't say anything because she was right, mate." Maren switched the light off with the flick of a finger. "She's fucking right."

Pewter moonlight filtered through the canopy of aspens and dappled the Band-Aid-tinted Lincoln Town Car hood as Hooper squinted at the sign to the left of the winding mountain road. Trobaugh handed over the glasses from the console without a word, peeling the wrapper from a pack of butterscotch Lifesavers with her teeth.

Hooper shook her head and waved them away, still squinting at the sign that was now nearly close enough to touch. "What are those for? I don't need glasses."

"Well, the army said you do, and the ones they gave you right before we retired and went to the Bureau are thick enough to stop a sniper bullet." Trobaugh emptied half the pack of candy into her mouth and tucked the rest back into her jacket pocket. "Besides, they go with the whole 'old lady vibe' we've got going with this relic."

"Look, we're lucky we got this thing at all. It was one of the last ones on the lot by the time we got into Boston." Hooper snatched the glasses and perched them precariously near the tip of her nose. "Why was it my job to hunt down the rental car, anyway?"

"Because I'm not about to spend the next few weeks in the woods with no vehicle. Besides, I did all the packing. If I'd let you pack, we'd have a gym bag of Slim Jims, a handful of Kenny Chesney albums, and nothing else."

Hooper rolled her eyes as she took a left at the sign and headed down a narrow road lined on both sides with paper-birch trees, ghostly in the sparse beams of sheer silver moonlight.

"How do you know this is the right address?" Hooper scanned the log lodge just visible as they reached the peak of the hill and turned at a small painted sign and into a dense grove of black pines. "Do we even know anyone here yet? This could be a serial-killer training camp. Our guy could be the instructor. It wouldn't surprise me at this point."

"You're turning into quite the curmudgeon these days, Hoop."

"It's just weird. We're supposed to be on vacation next week, remember? Baking ourselves in the Florida sun as the good lord intended, not getting dragged into some random task force." She glanced out the window and up to the sky where the clouds were finally sliding back like stage curtains to reveal a swath of glittering stars.

They pulled silently up to the lodge, and Hooper cut the engine. Two windows on the second floor instantly flooded with light. Trobaugh sighed as she wedged the suitcases out of the open trunk, then bent down and yanked a duffel bag out of the far back corner.

"Well, call me crazy, but three bodies washing up on the Salem Harbor shore in the last ten days trumps that little plan. We both know that whoever it is, he's escalating, and if you didn't want to be drafted, you shouldn't be so great at your job, Agent Hooper. I'm pretty sure Orlando will still be around next time you get the itch to get sand in your shorts." Trobaugh dropped the duffel bag beside the suitcases and shook out her hand as she continued. "What the hell do you have in that thing? It's the only one you packed, and it's heavier than both my bags put together."

Hooper glanced up at her as she tossed the duffel bag over her shoulder but said nothing.

"Seriously. It's like that thing has bricks in it or something."

Hooper was stone-still, the only motion the duffel still swinging from her shoulder as it settled against her hip.

"What?" Trobaugh ran a hand through her hair and pulled up the handles on the other two suitcases. "I'm just saying, I think with your cholesterol count...."

"Babe." Hooper's voice was slow and deliberate, her gaze fixed on a point just past her wife's shoulder, at the edge of the trees. "We've got a situation."

Trobaugh turned slowly to see the outline of a bear emerging from the woods on their right, illuminated by the landscape lighting, picking up speed as his wet nose visibly twitched in the air. "Oh, holy shit."

Both women, military-police detectives turned FBI with more than fifty years of law-enforcement experience between them, instinctively reached to their belts for their nonexistent firearms.

"Yeah," said Trobaugh, slowly walking backward with Hooper, eyes fixed on the bear gaining ground by the second while still searching her unarmed hip. "I did not see this particular situation coming."

"Jesus." Hooper lowered her voice to a hiss. "You know where there aren't bears?"

The bear looked up just then, caught their eyes, and picked up his pace to a quick amble, gaze firmly locked on his target. Hooper.

"Orlando?" Trobaugh's voice was steady, but her backward gait increased as she looked over her shoulder for a possible escape route. "Well, if you'd like to make it back there, I'd suggest you join me in that treehouse behind us."

"Babe, we're never gonna make it over there. He's looking at me like I'm a pot-roast buffet." Her words slowed as they both looked down at her duffel bag. Hooper's hand tightened on the handle as she shook her head. She stopped short and turned to her wife. "If you think I'm leaving all my Slim Jims and California buffalo jerky for that monstrosity to drool on, you've got another thing—"

A fierce, guttural roar tore through the air like dry thunder, and the duffel bag dropped to the soaked ground with a *thunk* as both of them scrambled toward the rope ladder under the treehouse. The treehouse was lit from above, which meant the light also glinted across the wide back of the grizzly, who was now in a flat-out run behind them and gaining ground by the second.

"Didn't see this in the retirement brief packet, did ya?" Hooper guided her wife into a sharp left, sprinting toward the ladder. Trobaugh scrambled up to the first platform and motioned for Hooper to follow. She hesitated, one foot on the ground, looking back at her duffel like she was leaving her date at the prom.

Trobaugh shook the ladder. "Don't even *think* about it, Hooper."

They watched as the bear pounced on it, ripped open the canvas pack with one swipe of his paw, and started sorting the meat snacks with his nose, Slim Jims flying in every direction as the excitement raised a swath of amber hair on the back of his massive neck.

The bear seemed to have forgotten they were there, but Trobaugh rattled the rope ladder again anyway. "Get that sweet ass up here, and I'll personally replace every Slim Jim lost to Yogi over there."

Hooper pulled the handmade ladder up to the landing after she'd reached the platform and watched as the bear started in on the jerky, conveniently wrapped in waxed paper he peeled off with the attentive admiration of Gordon Ramsey unwrapping a filet mignon.

"Aw, man." Hooper rolled her eyes. "That's the handmade stuff from wine country. It's soaked in my favorite Tobin Cabernet."

"Well, now it's soaked in bear spit, so let it go, babe."

By the time they'd split the last of Trobaugh's Butter Rum Lifesavers on the treehouse's tiny porch, the welcome wagon had wandered back into the woods with the shredded duffel bag hanging from its mouth. Trobaugh located the firearms case in the luggage and got it out, but it looked like he was gone for good.

"Probably in an artisan jerky coma right now and sleeping it off, the asshole." Hooper muttered under her breath as she dragged the rest of the bags up the brick path to the porch. "I'm just warning you. I think I'm going to have PTSD from this little foray into *Wild Kingdom*."

"No way." Trobaugh stacked her bags and Hooper's beside the door and clicked on the pocket flashlight attached to her belt. "I've seen you handle way worse scenarios than that."

The sky cracked open suddenly, and lightning flashed through the murky clouds below, illuminating them into a gallery of gray storm ghosts watching their every move.

Hooper ran a hand along the top of the doorframe. "Didn't the officer say that he'd hidden the key in—"

"The birdhouse," Trobaugh said, pulling a set of two keys on a silver ring out of the hold in the front. "We're in. Although it's slightly concerning that anyone could have found those before we got here. As much as I respect small-town law enforcement, something tells me we're in for some culture shock."

Hooper stepped off the porch and looked up to the second-story windows. "I saw two rooms with the lights on as we pulled up, so with us, that means we're all here, right?"

"Yep. There are three bedrooms in the house, to my knowledge anyway." Trobaugh's voice was muffled as she tried one of the keys in the lock. It took some twisting and a shake at the end, but the door finally swung open. "Tala Marshall has one of them, we have one, and then Agents Norse and James are in the other." She dragged the luggage through the door and waved Hooper inside, locking it behind them and flicking off the porch light. "Although I'm going to need to see proof that Maren James is an actual agent after today. I've never wanted to ditch someone in an airport so bad in my life."

Hooper walked to the refrigerator and pulled out a bottle of water, then paused with it halfway to her mouth. The blue light attached to the door floated around her and gave the darkened split-log kitchen an ominous glow. "I don't know. By the time we left them at the airport she was growing on me. And it has to suck to be pulled out of a lap dance to solve a murder."

"Whatever." Trobaugh picked up one of the bags and threw it over her shoulder. "It happens to me all the time, and you don't see me acting like a teenage spider monkey that just broke out of the zoo."

"All the time, huh? Now there's going to be an investigation." Hooper spun the cap back onto her bottle of water and arched an eyebrow. "And it'd better come up empty."

Trobaugh laughed as she headed upstairs to search out their room. Hooper wiped down the counters with a damp sponge before she clicked off the lamp by the door and stepped out to the porch. Pewter clouds hung low and silent across the sky, the perfect canvas for the tips of the Eastern red pines silhouetted like a charcoal drawing against them. The air was crisp, like the faint scrape of gold and pumpkin-colored leaves as they skittered across the stone walk in front of her. She focused on the cedar porch railing, cold and smooth under her palm, as she tried to gather her thoughts.

On the flight to Boston that evening, while Trobaugh slept, she'd researched every member of the task force, crossing her fingers that they'd hit the magic combination of minds it would take to crack this case. They'd need some magic to stop this killer. Three bodies had been added to the Salem morgue in ten days, and they were missing the single piece of the puzzle that everything rested on. The motive. Nearly every serial killer wants to be recognized, almost admired, for their work. If they couldn't come up with the motive, this killer would remain in the shadows, and more bodies were on the horizon.

A wolf bayed mournfully in the distance as Hooper leaned onto the porch railing and rubbed her temples in slow circles. Her mind was spinning, but if she didn't get some sleep, she'd be as sharp as a headless ax in the morning for the first task-force briefing. She locked the door and deadbolts from the inside, then carefully made sure each ground-floor window was secured before she headed back to the kitchen. Sudden footsteps fell heavy in the hall, and as she turned to look, Trobaugh popped around the corner looking adorably rumpled, wearing red plaid pajama bottoms and her tortoise-shell glasses.

"I was wondering if I'd lost you to the bear." Trobaugh picked up a green apple from the bowl on the counter and nodded toward the stairs. "You coming to bed?" She stopped suddenly and picked up a small package next to the fruit bowl. "Is this what you were doing?" She smiled. "Just come upstairs, and I'll get your mind off of it."

Hooper nodded. "Be right up," she said as her wife headed for the stairs. The kitchen fell silent again as she turned the kraft-paper-wrapped package in her hand, pulling at the piece of knotted twine that held it together. She knew two things. One, a serial killer was lurking somewhere beyond the bodies washing up on the shore at Salem Harbor.

Second, she'd cleaned the counters before she'd stepped out to the porch, and her beef jerky hadn't been there.

CHAPTER FOUR

Tala Marshall rolled over in bed and stared out the window as red-gold maple leaves fluttered to the ground, filtering the first rays of crisp sunlight edging through the paper-white birch and elms that surrounded the cabin. Last night when she'd arrived, she'd found a sticky note on the door of the bedroom she'd been assigned to, and thank God, no one else was in it when she'd opened the door. She'd heard some bickering in another room down the hall, so chances were good that the woman she hadn't actually met the previous night got stuck with the blonde.

She'd loved the room the second she stepped in. It had a rustic, luxurious feel that centered around the bed, with its lush cream linens and billowy red-flannel duvet that invited her to sink into it and disappear. The bed was positioned across from a tall stone-and-timber fireplace, and to one side was a black houndstooth sofa and smoky-glass coffee table. The fireplace was charmingly scuffed, lined in chipped slate tiles with a raised black iron grate that looked to be from the last century. An antique cast-iron pan held old-school long matches and a pile of fresh pine straw and dry tinder. Split white birch logs, halved and beveled, created a library headboard above the bed, which held hardback classics, as well as some pulp fiction and local history. Tala had immediately kicked off her shoes and stood barefoot on the bed, running her fingers over the spines, memorizing the titles as the sun set.

A text ping dragged her back to the present, and she reached for her phone on the nightstand. She drew a slow breath before she read the message from her current girlfriend of three months, a twenty-something social-media influencer who rarely looked up from her phone. Lately, Tala had started to wonder why that had never bothered her.

Look, I know you said you got put on a Smartforce or whatever, but I don't get why I can't come over from Boston on the weekends. It's only forty minutes away. Unless you're doing something you don't want me to see.

She laid the phone down on her chest and closed her eyes. It was hard to explain what she was doing when technically she couldn't talk about it, but she knew that wasn't the problem. Her job was the problem. The phone pinged again.

God, you're always so intense. Why can't you just commute from Salem?

Tala felt a familiar headache start to throb against her temples. Her fingers flew over the keyboard. *Because I don't work at Whole Foods, Amy. I'm an FBI Agent.*

She put the phone facedown on the nightstand and went to start the shower.

By the time Tala had dressed, the scent of Columbian dark roast was wafting up the stairs to her nose, and when she rounded the corner of the kitchen, an athletic blonde in her early fifties was attentively adding cream into her coffee like she was pouring liquid gold. She wore jeans and a plush flannel shirt, the sleeves rolled up to reveal the white, waffle, long-sleeved shirt underneath.

"Is that pumpkin-spice creamer?"

"That depends." The woman narrowed her eyebrows and pulled the cream closer to her. The crinkles around her eyes made her look like she laughed loud and often. "Who wants to know?"

Tala laughed and chose a mug from the nearest cabinet. "Don't make me pull a gun on you, Trobaugh. I know for a fact you wouldn't drop that bottle, and I'd have a half-second advantage."

"Well, finally, I get to meet the famous Tala Marshall." Trobaugh winked and offered her hand, then handed over the creamer. "I've spoken to you so often during the last week putting this shitshow together, I feel like I might be able to profile you, instead of the other way around."

The door flew open suddenly, and a tall brunette with bright blue eyes strode in, or at least that seemed to be the plan until she tripped on her yoga mat and almost landed on the floor. She finally untangled her feet and walked over, smiling broadly at Tala. "You must be Agent Marshall. Hooper here." She flashed a smile at Trobaugh. "I've heard a lot about you. And if researching your career didn't make me wildly insecure, I probably would have done more of it."

Hooper offered her hand, obviously realizing too late that it was sprinkled with a shroud of white dust. Tala shook it anyway with an easy smile.

"Just call me Tala. And I know yoga chalk when I see it." She pulled a dish towel off the oven door and handed it to Hooper. "You do a daily practice?"

"Absolutely, but I've got to find a better spot. I'm too tall to be doing vinyasas on that porch out there."

Tala pointed out the window to the side of the cabin. "See that old barn near the fence line? I got here yesterday in time to set up my yoga mat in the empty hay loft. The entire front wall is a gate that opens to the east, so we can practice together at sunrise if you want to. I have a feeling we're not going to be getting much sleep for a while."

"Are you kidding? That sounds like a dream." Hooper accepted the coffee cup her wife handed her with a smile. "I'm pretty sure I was horrifying the squirrels out there. I sensed their plan to take me down and gave up early."

Tala poured her coffee and turned back around. "I've been following your careers since you retired from the military and joined the Bureau, and I never forgot that case you worked while you were in Italy." She blew on her coffee and took a cautious sip, leaning back against the counter. "You were stationed at NATO there, right? And a sniper was taking out male targets right and left? That first one was an American senator's son, so it was big news over here."

"Still my most interesting case, I think." Trobaugh glanced at Hooper. "Officially it was never solved."

"That's what made it so fascinating. I can tell that profile was spot-on, and the murders stopped completely, but they never landed the shooter?" She smiled and let the silence settle. "I'm not buying it."

"Damn. The Tala Marshall rumors are true." Hooper shrugged out of her hoodie and headed for the stairs. "I'm just glad she's on the right side of the law."

Tala glanced at her watch. "Do we have a war room set up yet? We've got about ten minutes before everyone's supposed to be downstairs."

Trobaugh led her into the dining room, where a log table with a milky quartz top was stacked with pens, paper, and a thick manila folder in front of each of the six chairs. A whiteboard stretched across one end of the room, and a small side table held bottles of water and a candy dish.

"Good lord." Tala ran her hand down the table and smiled. "I was just expecting some folding chairs and a couple of disposable pens." She picked up one of the pens and squinted at it. "I appreciate the effort, but I've got to get some decent pens in town. I'm picky about my ink."

"I made sure the local PD had this set up for us, and I guess they went all out." She picked up a hard, shiny red candy, unwrapped it, and popped it into her mouth. "They don't know who they're dealing with, though. My wife's going to go through this candy like a snowplow through a Walmart parking lot. Paragon of nutritional virtue, that one."

"So." Tala lowered her voice. "How long do you think it'll take to catch this guy? Are we looking at a few weeks, or…?"

Trobaugh shook her head. "None of us wants to be here a second longer than we need to, but we're going to do whatever's necessary to stop the body count and catch this killer." She set her coffee cup on the table and glanced up at the door. "Unofficially, what's your take on our guy? I know you don't have all the details yet, but—"

Darcy Norse rounded the corner just as Tala was about to answer, wearing gray tailored pants, immaculate heels that clicked a rhythmic pattern across the wood floor, and a blue oxford shirt under her matching suit jacket. The badge clipped to her belt glimmered as if it had been freshly polished, and Trobaugh and Tala watched as she chose a seat and neatly lined up the three pens she'd brought with her, pushing the ones already on the table wordlessly to the side.

"Good morning, Agent Norse." Trobaugh glanced at her watch and headed toward the door. "We still have a couple of minutes, so I'm just going to make a fresh pot of coffee. Do either of you need anything?"

Tala chose the seat directly across from Darcy. "I'm fine. I'll just get a head start on the file the local PD put together until everybody gets here." She didn't make a move toward the files. She leaned back and fixed her gaze on Darcy as Trobaugh disappeared through the door.

Darcy picked up the folders, lined up the edges, and set them back down in front of her. The silence was sharp and dense until she finally cleared her throat and met Tala's gaze. "I guess I owe you an apology."

Tala leaned back in her seat and held her gaze. A mottled red flush started to bloom at Darcy's collar, and she watched it travel slowly up her neck. Tala could see the blood pulse in the hollow of

Darcy's neck as she shifted in her seat. "Look. I know that sounded bad, but it was dark, and I—"

"Let me stop you there." Tala's gaze didn't shift from hers. "You're correct about one thing. You do owe me an apology, so I'm going to let you continue. If you can remember that an apology is different from an excuse."

Darcy swallowed hard and took a moment to refocus. Tala watched her shoulders fall and the mottled red splotches on her skin rise to cover her face.

"I *am* sorry. In fact, I'm so mortified that I couldn't sleep last night. I can't give you an excuse because there isn't one." She paused. "And I'm sorry I didn't choose better words this morning." Darcy raised her eyes to Tala's. They were a surprisingly soft grayed hazel surrounded by fine, tired lines. "I guess I didn't lead with the apology because I don't expect you to forgive me." She drew in a long breath. "I wouldn't, if I were you."

"Okay." Tala nodded. She let the silence settle before she continued, choosing each word carefully. "I believe you." She leaned forward until Darcy looked up at her. "And we all fuck up. If you're not fucking up occasionally, you're not learning anything." She paused and looked at Darcy's row of pens. "Is that a Sylth Black Noir .0275?"

"How did you know that?" A slow smile swept across Darcy's face, and she pushed one of them toward Tala with her fingertip. "I mean, no one's going to solve this case with a Bic Disposable like a damn Neanderthal." She pulled a cartridge out of the inner pocket of her suit jacket. "Keep it. And I have refills for us."

Tala accepted with genuine delight as Hooper swept into the room. She distractedly brushed her hand over her shoulder, then stopped at the mirror on the wall to stare at what Tala assumed was a tiny piece of lint stuck to the shoulder of her navy-and-white-striped sweater. She whipped a pair of tweezers out of her pocket and pulled it off, then checked the mirror from three angles to be sure the offending particle was completely gone. Tala tried to hide a smile and pulled out the chair next to her.

"What?" Hooper sniffed. "Obviously none of us is in uniform anymore, but there's no need to go around looking like common ruffians that don't travel with a lint brush."

Trobaugh came in after her, set a carafe of coffee on the side table, and rolled her eyes when she saw the tweezers on the table. "Hoop was famous for her attention to detail when it came to her uniform when we were in the military. She says she still has flashbacks from a pen that leaked in her pocket. In 2002."

"I think you'll remember," Hooper looked slightly shaken as she went on, "that it actually exploded like a remote Russian bomb. On my person. With no warning whatsoever." She sat down with a dramatic shudder. "And no. I'm not quite over it. I've been thinking some counseling might be a good idea."

All four of them jumped to their feet as a sudden deafening crack from the direction of the front door was quickly followed by another, as if the door had been kicked open and hit the inside wall. Tala and Trobaugh silently took the opposite side of the entry to the war room and pressed themselves against the wall, guns drawn. The heavy silence seemed to sink to the floor as Hooper drew her weapon and wordlessly directed Darcy to cover the east window as she approached the open doorframe. She stopped as the pounding footsteps grew rhythmically closer.

On my count. Hooper mouthed the words to Tala and Trobaugh, her gaze locked on the hall. The footsteps slowed, and they slipped into position behind Hooper just in time to see a rumpled Maren amble round the corner, wearing yet another Hawaiian shirt, although this time she had something concealed in her undershirt. Or at least she did, before she threw her hands up and what looked like the contents of the nearest convenience store tumbled out and spilled into the hallway.

"What the hell is this? I mean, damn." Tala watched as Maren took in the number of guns pointed at her. "All of you need to consider switching to decaffeinated."

Hooper looked past her down the hall and cautiously lowered her weapon, followed by Tala and Trobaugh. Half of the Twix candy bar in Maren's mouth fell unceremoniously to the floor after it bounced off the top of her open Birkenstock.

"Dude," Maren said in Hooper's direction, picking up the smudged chocolate and popping it back into her mouth. "You told me to get breakfast for everyone, remember? Like thirty minutes ago."

Darcy, gun still drawn, came through the door and stopped, instantly appearing confused. She took stock quickly and lowered her weapon. "What's going on?"

She stepped to the side as a laughing Tala and Trobaugh reholstered and made their way back into the war room, where Trobaugh reached for the carafe of coffee and passed it around. Tala leaned over the table and caught her eye. "Where's the good stuff?"

Trobaugh nodded to the small stainless-steel pitcher on the side table, and Tala grabbed it before she settled back into her seat. After she'd lovingly rescued her treasures from the pile in the hall, Maren spilled the contents of her undershirt yet again onto the center of the table and stepped back with a look of pride. A tall jumble of chips, chocolate bars, and dented corn dogs in paper boats rolled in every direction, along with a few premade sandwiches with dubious fillings and various processed meat products in shady plastic packaging. Hooper's delight was obvious as she started sorting through the loot immediately, settling on a starter collection of sour cream and onion chips and three beef jerky and cheddar-stick combos.

"Now this is what I'm talking about." She paused, grabbing a Cosmic Brownie and pulling it into her growing pile. "Breakfast of champions."

Darcy rolled her eyes and poured some coffee, poking at the pile with a single fingertip as if it might decide to eat her instead. Maren watched her for a moment, then nudged a Little Debbie snack cake in her direction with the tip of her pen. "Wouldn't hurt ya to eat a few of those, mate." She arched an eyebrow and looked Darcy up and down. "You're never going to break your dry spell looking like that. Right now, it'd be like shagging a ladder, no way 'round it."

"Jesus." Trobaugh's head sank slowly into her hands. "Maren, can you try not to be a total HR nightmare? In case you've forgotten, a killer's on the loose, and we've got shit to do here."

Tala sat back and watched as Hooper ripped the top off her chips with her teeth and Maren dug into her pocket and produced a rumpled handful of gas-station condiment packets. She carefully decorated a corn dog with two shaky lines of mustard and ketchup before she presented it to Darcy, who looked at it like it was a snake on a stick. Maren continued to hold it out, one eyebrow raised, until she gave in and took it from her.

"Okay. Now that everyone is one step closer to coronary-artery disease, let's get started." Trobaugh's phone pinged, and she picked it up. "Perfect timing. Our local law-enforcement liaison is here. They're going to run down what they know so far."

"Do you think he'll want a corn dog?" Maren pulled the stick out of the one in her hand and tossed it into the trash can in the corner. She missed. "Cause if not, I'm just gonna stack a couple of these beauties up with some cheese sticks and get down to business."

"You do you, Agent." Trobaugh almost rolled her eyes but appeared to catch herself at the last second. "Not that anyone could stop you."

As Trobaugh stepped into the hall, Tala gave in and reached for a bag of M&Ms at the edge of the pile. She poured them onto the table and started sorting them into piles by color, something she'd done since she was little. Back then she'd only cared about the brown and green colors, and she still remembered the scrape that the metal chair legs made across the scarred linoleum as she dragged the chair over to the kitchen cabinet to reach the shaky stack of plastic plates and cutlery in the kitchen cabinet. She'd carefully lay out two plates on the folding Formica table, with a fork on one side and a knife on the other sides of both. The cups and glasses were on the top shelf, which was too high to reach, so she never added those. It wasn't the important part, anyway. It was easier to pretend that there was food in the house when she had something to put on a plate.

Trobaugh walked back through the door with a woman who glanced quickly around the table and smiled at Tala.

"Agents, this is Wilder Mason, the interim police chief here in Salem, and *she*," Trobaugh glanced in Maren's direction, "will be our liaison between the law-enforcement community and the taskforce. The killer could be anyone at this point, even someone on the local police force, so it's imperative that you not reveal details of the case to anyone, even local officers." She glanced at Wilder, who nodded. "Everything goes through Chief Mason. Technically, we're on the same team, but with the body count at three already, we could get our asses handed to us if information gets leaked and tips off the killer."

Darcy looked up from the note she was jotting into her binder. "Won't that be tough, though? If we're all working the case together but can't compare notes with the detectives?"

The chief nodded, sliding a hand around the back of her neck as she answered. The muscles in her neck were tense and pronounced, like weighted cords. "With a town this size, we have only one detective, and that's been me for the last ten years. I had to step in to cover for the previous chief when he left suddenly last summer, so technically, we currently have no dedicated detectives on the Salem force. It's been eleven days since the first body washed up in Salem Harbor, and I've been pulling double duty in addition to dealing with reporters and press conferences which are only going to get more intense, so at this point, barring an arrest, we need to watch which details we share with the public."

Maren opened her mouth to speak, only to receive an elbow from Darcy, who jumped in to fill the space. "So, the task force has been formed to step in as the detectives here, and the uniformed officers are simply supporting at this point?"

Wilder nodded. "Exactly. They know how important discretion is, so keep specifics about possible leads to yourself. No one's going to be offended. After the second body was found, the national press was all over Salem, so they had a good idea of how much bigger this was getting by the second. Frankly, they're all a little overwhelmed at this point."

"Which is why we're here." Trobaugh rolled the whiteboard over to where she and the chief were standing. "Let's go over chain of command. As far as the task force is concerned, Hooper and I are heading that up, so any decisions that need to be made will go through us—"

"Seriously?" Darcy's head snapped up from the folder she'd been leafing through. "Who decided that?"

Maren rubbed her hands together and leaned back in what looked like delicious anticipation as Trobaugh and Hooper turned to answer together.

"Quantico."

"That's headquarters." Maren seemed delighted with the turn of events and whispered loudly, "You know, the big bosses."

"I *know*." Darcy spit the words across the table and returned her gaze to the files in her hands.

A hint of a smile flashed across Wilder's face as she took over again. "So everything goes through Trobaugh and Hooper. Then issues directly affecting the city of Salem will come my direction. I got my detective shield eleven years ago and was on the beat before that, in addition to being a fifth-generation Salem resident. Chances are, I can offer some insight in most situations that may keep us working under the radar for longer, but obviously there's a ticking clock on that particular advantage."

Trobaugh reached for the coffee pot and topped up her cup. "It's important to note here that the longer it takes for the killer to find out who we are, the better chance we have of gathering information that we wouldn't have otherwise. So do your best to look like a tourist." She glanced at the sunglasses dangling off the front of Maren's Hawaiian shirt. "Maren will be on hand for any questions regarding that."

Tala looked at the chief as Trobaugh continued, taking note of Wilder's fingertips turning white around the pen in her hand. Her white-blond hair, buzzed close around the sides, had looked slicked back and professional when she walked in, but she'd run her hand through its longer layers twice in the thirty seconds she'd been in the room, and they'd started to fall across her eyes.

Hooper caught Tala's eye and cleared her throat. "And that's Agent Tala Marshall's department, so we'll let her take over from here and get us up to speed on what she knows about the killer so far."

Tala opened the folder in front of her and paused, gathering her thoughts. "Three bodies in eleven days is not random. Obviously the killer is trying to tell us something. He wants to make a statement, but that's standard, and at this stage it's anyone's guess what that is."

"I went over the details in the initial reports twice." Darcy tapped the end of her pen on the table as she spoke. "But I didn't see a cause of death listed for any of the victims. I mean, I can guess, based on the details the arriving officers noted, but why is that?"

"That's just a time issue," Tala said, glancing up as she leafed through the pages of the scene reports. "The assumed cause of death is strangulation, based on the ligature marks on the bodies, but that's a guess, and we can't be sure until the medical examiner confirms it. The victims could have entered the water still alive, and when we're profiling a serial killer, that's a big difference. Comprehensive autopsies take time, and obviously, incidents of this magnitude meant they called in a medical examiner from Boston. She got here yesterday, I understand?" She glanced up at Wilder, who nodded. "I'll be on any preliminary reports as she makes them available, and I have an appointment to view the bodies this afternoon."

"At this point, we have no viable suspects." Wilder's phone pinged, and she glanced at it as she spoke, dropping it back into her pocket. "The first body was found eleven days ago, washed up on the beach at dawn, by a couple walking their dog. It was a young woman from Boston, Chesney Micheals, who moved here about five months ago. We ran images of her tattoos through the tattoo-recognition software, and a positive ID popped right up. She had a sheet for petty theft and a few relatively minor misdemeanors, but nothing obvious that would explain why she'd turn up in Salem Harbor dead. It wasn't an accidental death though. The number one was carved into the palm of her right hand."

Hooper popped the last of her brownie into her mouth and crumpled the cellophane wrapper in her hand. "What about the second victim?"

"That one couldn't have been more different from the first. Her name was Miriam Bartsmouth, and she was a respected midwife from a well-known family here in Salem. Her body was tethered to the corner of the dock at the marina, and we found a few more clues than with the first victim, although the dream would have been to have some security footage from the marina. No dice." Trobaugh walked over to the whiteboard and wrote down the details as Wilder paused and accepted a steaming coffee that Hooper passed down to her. "Her mouth was stitched shut with fishing line, and from the looks of it, it was done while she was still alive."

A stunned silence settled over the room, the only sound being Darcy rhythmically leafing through her case folder. "I didn't see those details in the initial report that we received."

"That was intentional. I didn't want to risk them getting out." Wilder stirred sugar into her coffee and set the spoon down, the clink of the spoon on the saucer ridiculously loud in the still room. "I don't know who I can trust in the department. We're going to need every advantage we can get so I'm being cautious to a fault."

"What about the third victim?" Maren wiped her hands on her shorts and dropped a handful of cellophane wrappers into the trash. "Has the killer communicated in any way, other than carving the number into the first victim's hand and stitching up the mouth of the second?"

"Well, he's clearly trying to tell us something, and when we found the first victim with the number one in her hand, I was afraid he was numbering his victims. Yet we found no visible trace of a number on the second. The third victim, Gillian Thomas, was hanging from the oldest tree in town, which dates from the early 1600s, just beyond the beach and down from the community dock. She was a college student back in town for the weekend from Boston University. I didn't know her well, but I've done a little research since, and apparently, she was well respected, known at BU for her activism around issues affecting women's rights and her political aspirations. She was going places and wanted to have an impact on the world. She was also active in the fight for LGBTQ+ rights and identified as a lesbian. You have a picture there in the folder, so you can see she was masculine presenting." Trobaugh handed Wilder a glossy 8x10, and she held it up as she continued. "I'm not sure if that's a factor at all, but at this point anything could hold the key to identifying the killer."

During a moment of quiet everyone finished jotting down the new details.

"What else?" Maren held Wilder's gaze. "There's something."

Tala watched a memory drift across Wilder's face like a storm cloud. She hesitated, and it was a moment before she continued. "She was found hanged in the middle of the night, but it looked like someone cut the rope after she died." Wilder paused. "She was found on the ground under the cut noose still hanging from a tree branch. Obviously, forensics in Boston headquarters is going over the rope for touch DNA or fibers, but at this point, it looks like the killer is a step ahead of us and wearing gloves."

"Why hang her and cut the rope, though?" Trobaugh clicked her pen closed and slid it back into her shirt pocket. "What? Is it some kind of symbolism or something?" The sound of the dry-erase marker across the whiteboard was the only sound in the room. After the names of the three victims and the details were written in neat columns across the surface, Trobaugh recapped the pen and turned around.

"I don't know what it is yet." Hooper glanced at Tala. "But there's a message in every breadcrumb he's leaving behind, and every one of those details was planned. None of that is an accident. He's telling us something."

Wilder nodded but changed tack, closing her folder and smiling at the remnants of the gas-station extravaganza that littered the center of the table. "If it's okay, let's review a few housekeeping details since we're all going to be living together for the foreseeable future. I assume everyone is okay with being addressed by their names, not their titles?"

"Whatever." Darcy wrinkled her nose and edged her uneaten corn dog toward the edge of the table with her elbow like it might be radioactive. "Let's nail this bastard so we can make this situation as temporary as possible." She glanced down the table at Maren like she was a homeless person who had just wandered in and taken a seat. "Thank God the room we're sharing has twin beds, but let's be real. Maren here looks like she just broke out of juvenile detention, so the sooner we wrap it up and get back to real life, the better." She dropped her pens carefully back into her jacket pocket and focused her gaze on Trobaugh and Hooper. "I'm still not convinced you didn't pull some random off that boat. I'll be running a background check on her ass this afternoon since we're sleeping in the same room."

"Don't flatter yourself," Maren said, one eyebrow cocked like a hammer. "Unless you've got a wet T-shirt on under that chastity belt you're calling a suit, you're not exactly my type."

Hooper gave them both a pointed look and turned back to Wilder. "You were saying?"

"To save us time, I'll have officers do our grocery shopping as well as grabbing any incidentals you may need. There's a list on the refrigerator, so feel free to add to it. I'll make sure you have plenty of supplies to put together your own breakfast and lunch. Then I thought we'd do dinner together every night, maybe take turns cooking, so we can more informally compare notes to wind up the day. I made a list of who's cooking when. It's on the fridge."

She glanced at her watch. "As for right now, let's go by pairs into town and get a feel for what we're dealing with, then regroup this evening." Wilder smiled. "Let's start with Maren and Darcy. The square in the center of town is only a five-minute walk from here. Get a feel for what people have to say about the situation, but don't give away who you are."

Hooper closed her folder and pushed it toward the center of the table. "Trobaugh and I are going to check out the sites where the bodies were discovered and see if we can find something the local uniforms may have missed. We'll take pictures to compare with the crime-scene photos and copy everyone via email."

"That leaves Tala and me," Wilder looked over at Tala and spun her pen through her fingers as she spoke. "We're meeting with the coroner this afternoon, but I thought we might start at the diner. If you're looking to get a read on the locals for the profile, that's where everything happens."

CHAPTER FIVE

Tala slid into the red Naugahyde booth with the rip down the center and turned over her paper placemat to find the menu. "I know we're here to get a read on the locals, but the M&Ms for breakfast this morning didn't really cut it. I need real food."

Wilder ran a hand through her hair and raised two fingers when the waitress looked their way. "The pancakes here are to die for. I eat here almost every morning and can count on one hand the number of times I've been persuaded to try something new."

Tala looked up from the menu. "In how many years?"

Wilder smiled, turning over both their coffee cups on the saucers. "You're the profiler. You tell me."

Tala put the menu down as the waitress filled their cups with a hurried promise to be back to take their orders. Tala looked up and met Wilder's gaze. She held it for a moment until Wilder started to smile.

"Got nothing, huh?" Wilder's eyes crinkled at the edges. "That's understandable. You just met me."

"Maybe I don't." Tala ripped the paper top off a single-serve creamer she found in a bowl next to the glass-and-chrome sugar container and set the empty cup carefully by the dispenser before she went on. "But I'd say you're around thirty-seven, and you swim in the harbor most mornings." She glanced at Wilder's defined arms and reached for another creamer. "You clearly lift weights as well, but I think you do that for your mind, not your body. You're androgynous but don't identify as butch, and you've had only one or two major relationships." She looked back to Wilder and held her gaze. "You're very sensual, although in a respectful way that flies under the radar, but being really in love feels like a weakness, so you've avoided it so far, even in those relationships."

The waitress came back just then, blowing a lock of copper hair out of her face as she reached for her pen and notepad to jot down their orders. She seemed to already know what Wilder wanted, but she carefully copied down Tala's pancake order and warmed their coffees from the pot she'd set between them. A bell dinged in the kitchen window, and she was gone.

Wilder looked slowly up from her coffee. "Damn. That was not what I was expecting." Her gaze followed Tala as she pulled her hair into a quick ponytail with the elastic around her wrist. "But I'm thirty-six, not thirty-seven, though it's fair to say that the last two weeks have probably aged me an additional year."

Tala pulled the dark length of hair over her shoulder and settled back into the booth. "And the rest?"

"The rest is spot-on." Wilder turned up the cuff of her shirt and rolled it up her forearm. "How could you possibly know I swim? I've walked to the harbor to swim every morning since I turned seven and my mother decided I probably wouldn't die."

"Your hair was still slightly damp when you walked in this morning, and you smelled like the water. The water here smells like sea salt, which makes sense." Tala closed her eyes as she tried to wrap words around the scent she'd memorized the previous day. "But it has a clean ozone top note, like the way the air smells the moment before it starts to rain."

"I'm scared to ask how you came up with the rest." Wilder smiled as the waitress dropped off a pitcher of warm syrup. "So, I guess the rumors are true. You know things."

"Yes. I do." Tala smiled for the first time. "So, watch yourself, Chief."

Wilder winked and rolled up her other sleeve. "I'm surprised you didn't tell me I'm a top."

"I would have." Tala leaned back as the loaded plates of pancakes arrived and settled with a clatter in from of them. "If that were true."

❖

Maren glanced at her watch. She'd reluctantly picked up a few pairs of jeans, shirts, and some hiking boots from a shop in town that afternoon and shoved her Hawaiian shirts to the bottom of her duffel. The chief was right about the need for them to blend into the local landscape, but she was still pissed about being yanked off the love boat.

I was robbed. That was a target-rich environment if I've ever fuckin' seen one.

She'd been on a ship full of beautiful women and endless open bars, yet somehow, she'd managed to land overnight in the farthest place possible from that dreamy scenario. Maren grabbed her leather Dopp kit out of her duffel bag and tossed it to one side of the bathroom sink, across from Darcy's side that was covered in what looked like expensive skin-care bottles, all lined up perfectly spaced and parallel to the wall. There was also a single perfume bottle. Maren picked it up but plunked it right back down on the counter. She was already familiar with its smell of sexual frustration and money. The room she was assigned to share with Agent Stick-Up-Her-Ass was nice, in a woodsy cabin sort of way, but it wasn't really her scene. She was supposed to be baking in the sun under some palm trees with a fresh mojito in one hand and someone's oiled-up tit in the other, not hunting down some folksy serial killer with tight-ass Nancy Drew for a roommate.

Maren tossed the rest of what was in her duffel into one side of the closet and headed downstairs, but she stopped at the landing, listening to what sounded like cabinet doors opening and closing in the kitchen, accompanied by cursing. She checked to be sure she was wearing her firearm but left it holstered. She and Darcy had been the only ones in the cabin when she'd gone to take a shower, and as she neared the kitchen, she recognized Darcy's voice. Sure enough, as she came around the corner, a panicked Darcy was still opening every kitchen cabinet, muttering to herself.

"What the hell's going on down here?" Maren took her hand off her weapon as she leaned into the open fridge and grabbed a bottle of water. "I heard you all the way upstairs."

Darcy whipped around, her blond bob finally a little less than perfect. She pushed an off-center lock of it behind her ear and pointed to a notepad attached to the refrigerator door. "That, obviously."

Maren glanced at it, then closed the door and leaned on the refrigerator, twisting the lid off her water. "What, the cooking schedule? Looks like you're cooking tonight, but they did the shopping, so that shouldn't be a problem."

"Yeah, if I could cook." Darcy picked up a rocks glass of whiskey from the counter and took a long sip. Her suit jacket was hanging over one of the barstools pulled up to the kitchen island, and a single button on her blouse was undone at the hollow of her neck. "I wasn't worried when the chief told us about taking turns with dinner this morning, I figured I'd just get it delivered, but I called when we got back from town, and all the restaurant deliveries are shut down. The murders have everyone freaked out, I guess." She closed her eyes and leaned on the counter. "I mean, how are people surviving without basic services?"

"Totally agree." Maren smiled, twisting the top back on her water bottle. "I can't believe they're not sending their peeps out to random houses in the dark like bargain serial-killer bait."

"It's not funny." Darcy set her glass down and rubbed her temples with tense fingertips. "I don't cook. I never cook. And there's like six of us or something."

Maren walked over to where she was standing at the sink and picked up her whiskey. "Well, this isn't helping, mate. I'm willing to bet you haven't eaten since we left the cruise, and this is the hard shit." She reached over Darcy and set the glass down in the sink. "We still have the better part of an hour before everyone's back, so let's take stock here and see what they got us to work with."

Maren felt Darcy's gaze on her as she leaned into the fridge. "What do you know how to prepare? You must have one or two things you can whip up, just like stuff you do at home."

Darcy shook her head. "I stop at the same restaurant every night after work and order the same thing. Baked fish and broccoli." She stopped, fastening the single loose button at her neck back up with shaky fingers. "Other than that, I don't eat much, I guess."

Maren looked her up and down. "Yeah. I can see that." She walked over to where Darcy was and slowly loosened the same button, her fingers warm and steady against Darcy's skin. "Just take a breath."

"But—"

Maren held her eyes, her voice low. "Take a breath."

She waited until Darcy exhaled and her shoulders dropped a bit before she nodded for her to follow and opened the door of the fridge. "It's only six people, and we've got mountains of food in here." Maren reached to the back and pulled out a container of heavy cream and handed it back to Darcy, who took it but looked at it like it might blow up in her hand. "I'm willing to bet there's some sort of pasta in the cabinets, and we've got fresh kale, lemon, and some white wine in here. And a baguette." She pulled it out and tossed it on the counter. Darcy was staring at her, still holding the cream balanced on the flat of her palm. "What?"

"I can't do this. Make dinner." Darcy shook her head and looked longingly at her glass in the sink. "I can't fake something like that. They'll know."

"Something tells me you worry about that a lot." Maren piled the heap of ingredients onto the counter and shut the door. "That people will see you."

Darcy started to say something, then paused. She straightened her shoulders and looked out the window before she went on. "You don't know what you're talking about."

"Oh yeah?" Maren pulled a box of fettuccine out of the overhead cabinet. "Well, either way I'm in the process of saving your ass tonight, so you now have to stay here and tell me anything I want to know."

Maren felt Darcy's eyes on the back of her neck as she found a red enamel pot and filled it with water, tossing in a scant handful of salt. She reached over to the oven and set it to preheat. "Darcy. What the hell are you looking at?"

Darcy cleared her throat. "I guess I just noticed you're wearing real clothes."

"Well, contrary to what you might think, I tend to look like a normal person at work, not like an—"

"Australian frat boi?"

Maren laughed, rummaging through a drawer until she emerged with a wine opener. "Okay. I'll give you that. Being jerked off the party boat mid-lap dance might not have been my finest moment." She worked the corkscrew into the bottle and pried it out, glancing at the label before she plucked a glass off the hanging bar rack and poured it. "Why were you on a lesbian cruise, anyway? Clearly, no one bothered to let you in on the wardrobe requirements before they let you on the boat."

Darcy's voice pitched up as she answered. "That's none of your business, I—" She stopped when Maren turned around and aimed a pointed glance at the pasta water. "Okay, fine." She paused. "But it's not because I'm a lesbian. I decided to take some time off, and that was the only cruise available to book on short notice."

"Try again." Maren handed her the glass of pinot grigio. "I got the last available spot four months ago. It's been booked since then. Everyone knows those cruises fill up way in advance."

"Jesus." Darcy took a sip of her wine. "I don't know. It just looked like fun, I guess."

"It *was* fun." Maren tested the water and turned off the heat. "At least the two days I got to be there. But I know for a fine fact I never saw your sensible shoes at the pool. Where were you hiding?"

Darcy jumped as the front door opened and Trobaugh and Hooper walked in, loaded down with files and, in Hooper's case, a gigantic caramel apple rolled in cracked-butter toffee and toasted almonds. The open door framed crimson leaves with crisp gold edges shifting through the air, falling gently onto the porch with a cool drift of fall air that floated into the cabin behind them.

"Is that dinner?" Hooper shut the door as she bit into her apple and shifted her words to fit around the caramel threatening to drip down her chin. "I'm literally starving."

"Ya, mate." Maren flashed her a smile. "You look like you're about ready to pass out right there from starvation, ya poor beggar."

Trobaugh rolled her eyes and dropped a load of files onto the coffee table. "How much time do we have? I need to shower and change at least, if not get my head around these new photos from today."

Maren nodded. "I know the schedule says we eat at seven, but it's going to be seven thirty tonight, so take your time."

Trobaugh and Hooper headed upstairs as Maren grabbed a handful of garlic she'd found in the pantry. She dumped the cloves on the cutting board and rifled through the drawer under the counter as Darcy pulled a chef's knife from the knife block and handed it to her.

"But if the schedule says dinner at seven, we can't just change it." She bit her lip as Maren sliced the top off the first head of garlic. "What if someone notices?"

"Jesus Christ, woman. Do you walk around this tense all the damn day?" Maren placed the flat of her knife on a clove of garlic and slammed it with her fist, then threw her head back and laughed when Darcy jumped. "You don't know it yet, but you lucked out getting stuck with me. I'll loosen ya up right quick."

There was just a hint of a smile on Darcy's face as Maren motioned her over and handed her the knife. "Now, we need to get a move on, so I'm going to let you take over here." Maren showed Darcy how to crush and peel the garlic, then dug a small ceramic bowl out of the cupboard. She filled it with several long glugs of olive oil and a sprig of fresh rosemary from the terracotta pot in the sunny west window. "Once we get those peeled, we're going to set them in the oven to roast while we make a move on the pasta sauce and baguette."

Darcy stopped, the knife lofted, until Maren looked up. "Why are you doing this for me?" She tilted her head, her next words more hesitant, as if she wasn't sure she wanted to release them. "I haven't exactly been nice to you since we met."

"Oh, look at that. You *do* have a conscience." Maren grinned, then glanced up to see Wilder and Tala coming through the door before she turned back, met Darcy's eyes, and dropped her voice to a whisper. "But it's hard to be nice to people when they look like they might fuck up your carefully constructed world."

"Oh my *God*. What smells so good?" Hooper's voice boomed through the kitchen into the war room, where Maren was packing up the folders and setting the table. Hooper stuck her head around the corner and winked. "Need me to handle anything in the kitchen?"

"Everything's done, mate." Maren shoved the whiteboard against the wall. "Yank that baguette out of the oven and whack it on that slab of wood on the counter, but other than that, I think everything's ready for transport."

"Hey." Hooper leaned farther into the room and lowered her voice. "I don't want to blow your mind here, but Darcy actually cracked a smile when I passed the kitchen and asked what was cooking."

"I don't believe that for a minute." Maren looked up and winked as she set the stack of plates in the center of the table. "But if that was true, and I'm not saying it is, I might have noticed she's not bad looking when she's not accepting the award for Ice Queen 2023."

Hooper stifled a laugh and fist-bumped her as they both walked back into the kitchen, where Maren handed everyone standing around a dish or serving bowl to bring to the table.

"God. Even the salad dressing smells amazing." Tala drew in the scent from the bowl in her hands as she walked toward the dining room. "What is it?"

"Just a little lemon tarragon dressing we put together." Maren winked at Darcy, then held a finger to her lips. "Darcy let me hang out in the kitchen tonight, and we came up with a few things."

Five minutes later, everything was on the table, and the chairs scraped the hardwood floors as everyone sat down to start passing the dishes around. Tender fettuccini tossed in a rich white wine-and-cream sauce was topped with fresh torn parsley, and the baguette had been toasted to a gorgeous brown, split down the middle, and loaded with creamy melted butter. A ceramic dish of steaming roasted garlic waited on the side, along with a platter of fresh arugula salad topped with bright, herby dressing and sliced sweet, red chilis.

"I don't want to make anyone uncomfortable," Hooper heaped her plate with the fettuccine and passed the wide pottery dish to the right, "but I need Trobaugh to know I'm now officially in love with whoever's responsible for this."

"Oh, how quickly they stray." Trobaugh started to pass the bread to Tala, then grinned and pulled it back to take another piece. "We spent a year stationed at NATO in Italy, and I had to keep an eye on her the entire time to make sure I wasn't replaced by some old Italian dude whipping up marinara at a random café."

"That's not true at all." Hooper sniffed, winding a huge bite of pasta around her fork and tucking a napkin into her collar at the same time. "I would have made sure his daughter knew his recipe and gone for her." She rolled her eyes. "It's like you don't know me at all."

Wilder served herself a swirl of pasta and placed it back in the center of the table. "So how did everyone get on in town today?" She grinned at Hooper and continued. "Once you handled the caramel-apple situation, of course."

"Dude." Hooper crunched into the bread and closed her eyes in bliss for a second before she snapped back to the conversation. "They had a stand with those little beauties, apple-cider doughnuts, and mulled, spiced cider in the park. I mean, it's just a crime to walk past without offering a little support." She nodded as she popped the buttery center of the bread into her mouth. "For the good of the community."

Trobaugh sprinkled more fresh parmesan on her salad and looked up at Wilder. "We actually took a discreet look at the scene of the hanging by the water just down from the park before I let her even glance in that direction. A few locals were trying to get on with things, but nothing like I'd imagine autumn is usually like here."

"The crime scene is still taped off, is it not?" Wilder arched an eyebrow in Trobaugh's direction. "I mean, we've gathered every shred of evidence there was, not that it amounted to much, but I wanted to keep everyone out of it until the task force could examine it."

"I think the locals are giving it a wide berth," Hooper said, elbowing Trobaugh to snag the wooden salad bowl for her. "No one even glanced in our direction, but to be fair, not that many people were even out and about."

"Better get those apples while you can, Hoop." Maren passed a bottle of sauvignon blanc around to top up the glasses, then set it back in the center of the table. "One more body and it's going to look like a ghost town."

Wilder shook her head. "That's the thing though. These people have lived here for generations. Some even have direct ties going back hundreds of years." She ran her hand through her hair and sat back in her chair. "It's not that they couldn't leave—"

"It's that they won't." Maren nodded. "I get it. Australia's the same, especially the Aboriginal communities, which happen to be my people. But sometimes that helps an investigation, though sometimes not. We have to find a way to make all that local knowledge work for us."

Tala glanced at Wilder, her fork lofted over her pasta. "Other than some seriously good pancakes, we didn't find much either. The coroner shifted our meeting to tomorrow morning. It was good to get a feel for the level of growing panic in town, but the press presence is just amping up the sense of fear that's getting bigger by the day." She spun pasta around her fork and paused. "I know we can't keep them out, but we might want to put some officers on that beat, corralling the reporters and cameramen into organized areas. Right now, they're centralized in the areas of the courthouse and police station, but no boundaries are established outside those buildings, and I have a feeling that problem will continue to grow."

Maren shoved some garlic bread into her mouth and attempted to speak around it. "Tala, you're stationed in Boston. Are you from around here or what?"

Tala shook her head, laying her silverware in the center of her plate. "I grew up on the Powhatan Native American reservation about an hour north of here. I was recruited from law enforcement, did my training at Quantico, and have been stationed in Boston since." Tala shifted in her chair and seemed to choose her next words carefully. "I'm assigned to cases all over the country, so I'm never in one place for long. I feel like I don't live anywhere."

Maren nodded, then popped the last of her garlic bread into her mouth. "I can relate. When they brought me over from Australia, I didn't realize they'd be flying my ass across the country all the time." She smiled and winked at Darcy across the table. "I mean, you know how it is. You're a goddamn hero on one case, and suddenly no one can get enough of ya, mate."

"Yeah, whatever." Darcy rolled her eyes. "I'll still need proof you've seen the inside of HQ."

"I've got some exes there that can take care of that problem for ya." Maren pulled out her phone. "Should I call 'em up, so you can get an idea of what you're missing?"

Hooper snorted into her napkin and looked across to Tala. "So, where's your family now? Back on the reservation?"

"No." Tala shook her head and started to say something, then stood and picked up her plate and wineglass. "If it's okay with you, I'll drop these in the dishwasher and look again to see if I missed anything in the initial reports."

Tala walked out before anyone had a chance to answer, and Maren shook her head, leaning back into her chair. "What'd I do?" She looked around the table. "I wasn't even hitting on her. I swear."

Darcy stood and gathered everyone's plate as she walked around the table. "All the subtlety of a backhoe."

Wilder looked at Trobaugh and tilted her head, hesitating before she spoke. "I feel like I'm missing something here."

"I feel like I'm missing a shot. With a damn shot for a chaser." Maren sighed and downed the rest of her wine. Darcy slipped out and had made it almost to the door before Trobaugh said her name.

"Darcy." Trobaugh tapped her thumb on the table lightly as she spoke, her words hanging in the air like sunlight. "If you had a tip for communicating with—" She simply nodded toward the hall and dropped her voice. "What would that be?"

"What? Why are you asking her?" Maren looked confused. "Why would Darcy know?"

Hooper elbowed her into silence, and they both turned to listen. Darcy paused in the doorway, the stack of plates balanced on her fingers. It was a long moment before she spoke. "Just don't step into her space. She'll close the gap when she's ready."

CHAPTER SIX

Just don't step into her space. Wilder muttered to herself as she climbed the stairs a few hours later. She'd worked in the war room until she was so tired she had to sleep, but unfortunately, that itself was the problem. *Fuckin' fantastic.*

She knocked lightly on the door and stepped back. Light crept onto the wood floors in a golden strip from underneath the door, and she could hear shuffling in the room. Wilder looked down the stairs and thought again about the couch, but sleeping alone in a downstairs room surrounded by bay windows was just begging the killer to add an easy fourth body to the count overnight. They had officers on duty around the perimeter, but tempting fate had never really worked out for her in the past.

She knocked again, and the door swung open slowly to reveal Tala standing on the other side in a Yale sweatshirt, barefoot, with a yellow toothbrush hanging out of her mouth. "Little late, isn't it, Wilder?" She leaned against the doorframe and looked at her watch, pulling her toothbrush out of her mouth. "What do you want?"

"Look," Wilder said, glancing again at the stairs. "I should have told you this sooner but—"

Tala opened the door and stepped back. Wilder walked in and hesitated, suddenly unsure of where to stand. "I was up most of the night last night at the station, so there might be some confusion, but there are six of us and only three bedrooms, so..."

Tala shut the door and took a step back. "You're saying that you're expecting to sleep with me?"

"God, no!" The room suddenly felt hot, and Wilder shrugged off her jacket, draping it over the arm of the couch. "I mean, not like that, anyway."

Tala leaned against the door, her expression blank and eyes narrowing by the second. "What exactly *do* you mean, then?"

"Jesus Christ." Wilder raked a hand through her hair and tried to push back the headache that made her heartbeat echo against her temples. "Never mind. It's my fault. I should have said something sooner." She picked up her jacket. "I'll just be downstairs."

She was headed for the door when she saw the stack of sheets and a flannel comforter folded at the foot of the bed.

"Relax, Chief." Tala flashed her a smile like sudden sunlight and locked the door behind them. "Trobaugh broke the news that we're roomies this morning."

"Jesus. I see how you are." Wilder melted in relief, and she sank onto the couch. "That little stunt was impressive. I was about to go sleep down there in full view of our killer."

"Well," Tala said, crouching next to the fireplace and pulling a pocketknife out of her sweats. "None of us know shit about Salem but you, so I'd say you're worth a spot upstairs." She chose a stick of birch kindling from the copper kettle beside the fireplace and started peeling back the bark with the blade in even strips, curling it in a downward direction from the core of the wood until it resembled a pinecone. "And I happen to know that you own this place."

"I do." Wilder leaned back into the couch and crossed one foot over the opposite knee, loosening her boot laces as she spoke. "This is my bedroom, in fact."

"Why did you put me in with you?"

"I didn't." Wilder looked up as she pried one boot off and set it down, already working the laces of the other. "Trobaugh did. She chose for all of us and had one of the officers put Post-it notes on the doors before she ever got here."

Tala nodded, placing the stick on the fire grate and reaching for another. Wilder tried not to watch but found her impossible to look away from, like a secret scrawled on the wall in a dark room. A flash of Tala naked underneath her on the bed whipped across Wilder's mind. She shoved it out of her thoughts but still watched the hair that fell like darkness around Tala's face as she deftly carved thin, intentional layers into the soft-core wood. She wore faded navy FBI-issue sweats and what looked like a plain white T-shirt under that sweatshirt, but it was the way her hair curved around the delicate angles of her shoulders that made Wilder not care that she was staring. Tala's skin was warm, glowing like dark, amber resin brushed with firelight that didn't yet exist. Everything about her looked like warmth.

A rush of flame drawing the air from the room into the fireplace pulled Wilder back into the present. The two carved sticks flared to life, the thin, airy edges of the wood igniting with a *whoosh*, already reaching for the kindling she'd stacked in a grid on top of it. Wilder watched Tala lean into the hearth, blowing steadily under the grate, pulling her hair over one shoulder as she coaxed the flames under the logs from saffron yellow to an undulating deep crimson that flamed into blue sparks, taking over the first log like a translucent ocean wave.

"That's not your first fire."

Tala looked up, taking a seat on the hearth as she stashed her chrome Zippo back into her pocket.

"No, ma'am," she said. "It's not." She paused, then nodded toward the copper bucket holding the kindling. "I like that you don't have a gas starter for the fireplace."

"You noticed."

"I notice everything."

Wilder held her gaze as she laced her fingers behind her head and sank back into the couch cushions. "And what do people notice about you?"

"Nothing, I hope." Tala pulled the sleeves of her sweatshirt down over her hands. "But if they do, they're not brave enough to tell me." Her dark eyes flickered with the reflection of the firelight. She had the lighter out of her pocket now and was turning it through her fingers. "What about you? What do you see?"

Wilder smiled, then leaned back until her eyes caught on the pitched log ceiling. "That's a loaded question." Sap crackled in the flames, the sound a sharp, hollow echo against the stone walls of the fireplace. Wilder drew in a breath that burned like wildfire chemistry and looked back to Tala. The fire flickered in her eyes like gold dust blown across dark glass. "Maybe I will someday, but I have the good sense not to tell you right now."

"Here." Tala handed Darcy a pair of latex gloves from the box on the steel table beside them. "You ever done one of these?" Three bodies covered by white sheets were lined up on stainless-steel exam tables across the span of the room. Ordinarily, they'd be at the medical examiner's office, but in a town this size, the only option was the tiny morgue area in the basement of the local hospital. Fluorescent strip lights buzzed overhead, one of them flickering as if threatening to black out. A small black spider crawled slowly up the white cinder-block wall behind the bodies, and the sickeningly sweet scent of formaldehyde hung thick in the air. Tala felt it sinking into her pores, changing the scent of her skin. She hated that smell.

"Truthfully? No." The loudspeaker in the hall jerked to life, and Darcy jumped. "I haven't had to see many dead bodies in my career. It's not really been—" Darcy swept her gaze along the line of bodies with no change of expression "an occupational hazard, given my area of expertise."

"What is your area of expertise, anyway?" Tala checked her watch and looked around the room for the clock. After yesterday's cancellation from the medical examiner, no way was she going to miss today's appointment. "The bios we read on everyone before we got here were detailed, but yours pretty much just listed your years of service as an agent."

Darcy didn't answer, but Tala noticed that her face was a shade paler than normal as she looked around at the autopsy instruments. The room was cold, which Tala had expected. She'd worn a charcoal merino turtleneck with some black jeans and thrown a mid-length camel coat on top of it. She also wasn't surprised to see Darcy in another forgettable but painfully appropriate suit.

"Here." Tala shrugged off the coat and offered it to Darcy, who waved it off. Tala continued to hold it out. "Seriously. If we're looking at three bodies with the coroner, we're going to be in here a while, and the sweater I'm wearing is wool. I'll be fine."

Darcy hesitated, then took the coat, sliding into it with a little shiver. Tala watched as she drew it around her, but then she paused, holding her breath.

"Is that better?"

Tala waited, then decided against asking again when she saw Darcy's eyelids flutter closed and her fingertips graze the left side of the coat. Whatever was happening was odd, but so was Darcy. There was something about her that Tala couldn't get a read on, and that was rare, but over the years, she'd learned it didn't help to throw words at it when that happened, and she didn't plan to start now.

"Great. If we're all here, let's get started." A tall, beautiful Black woman with intricate braids to the middle of her back strode in, and the temperature seemed to rise. She flashed a wide smile and snapped on a pair of gloves she'd pulled from her pocket. "Agent Marshall and Chief Mason, correct?"

Tala started to extend her hand and remembered too late they were both already gloved up. "I'm Tala Marshall, yes, but a situation with the press popped up at the station, and the chief had to go handle that early this morning." Tala turned to Darcy and gently touched her elbow, which seemed to snap her out of it enough to turn around. "This is Agent Darcy Norse, one of the members of the task force who was kind enough to step in. I'm sure you'll meet us all eventually."

"I appreciate the thought, but hopefully none of us will need to be on the case long enough for that to happen." She smiled and nodded to the embroidery on her white lab coat. "I'm Dr. Lynvee Ard, and I'm stepping in as the medical examiner until we figure out how to nail this bastard." She seemed to catch herself a second too late and winked as she walked to the first of the tables and motioned them both to follow. "Or something that sounds a bit more professional."

"No need." Tala flashed her a smile. She liked Dr. Ard already. "You were right the first time."

She watched as the doctor gently lifted the sheet placed over the first body and folded it down to chest level, then glanced in Darcy's direction. "Listen, if you start feeling woozy, don't be embarrassed. Most likely it's more the smell of the chemicals than the actual situation, so if you need to step out, don't hesitate. We all need to take a breath sometime."

Darcy nodded silently, the last of the color draining from her face. Tala returned her attention to the body. The head was resting on a standard white plastic neck support, and she was young, maybe early twenties, with acne scars, dank, bleached hair, and bare lashes that still looked wet. Wide bands of reddish bruising were also visible around her neck.

"This is our first victim, Chesney Micheals." Dr Ard picked up a stack of transparencies on a side table and clipped them to the lightboard above the body. "She was found in the harbor in the early morning, and because of her tattoos, we were able to quickly identify her."

Darcy pulled her gaze away from the body to look up at Ard. "The chief said she had a few priors?"

"She did, but nothing that really stood out as to why she might have ended up in the harbor." Dr. Ard slipped another transparency onto the lightboard. "Until I ran a tox screen. That's when it really got interesting."

"Damn." Tala leaned in to study it. "That's quite a list. Her tox screen reads like a dark-web shopping cart."

"Well put." Ard flashed her a smile. "And she was probably taking most of it daily. But the last one on the list is a tranquilizer that packs a punch and is almost impossible to access."

"Something else is going on here," Tala muttered to herself more than anyone else. She nodded to the other two bodies in the row. "What did their reports say?"

"Same." Dr. Ard pulled the transparencies off the lightboard. "A potent tranquilizer was present in all three bodies, although in the next two, it was the only drug in their system. Regardless of the differences in how they were found, all three were strangled before the killer staged the scene."

Tala watched as Ard pulled the sheet back up over Chesney's face, then uncovered one hand, turning it gently up to expose a long cut carved into her flesh. "One other detail you may have noticed in the reports—"

"The number one carved into her hand?" Tala leaned down to look closer. "What do you think that's about?"

"I wouldn't know, and we can't be sure that's even what it is. It could just be a laceration. But I can tell you that—"

"She's a transwoman." Darcy's words landed with a hollow thud on the stainless-steel table. She turned to look at Tala. "Yet the carving isn't about that."

"How did you know that?" Dr. Ard tucked Chesney's hand back under the sheet. "And you might be right about the cut not being an intended message. I was almost expecting a pattern, but the third victim didn't have anything similar, except for this…" She popped another transparency onto the lightbox. "Four vertical scratches on her lower abdomen. Honestly, though, there are several different reasons they could be there, and they could all be accidental. The edges of each wound are too jagged to have been done with a knife, which seems the obvious choice if the killer is making a statement, so maybe not." She thumbed through her transparencies as she continued. "With the second victim, however, the one with her mouth sewn shut, I encountered something I'd literally never seen before."

"I'm almost scared to ask." Tala glanced down the row at the gurney containing the third body. "But hit me."

"When I opened her mouth, I detected some trauma. It took a while to put it together, but her tongue had been cut out and sliced into three pieces. I found them in her throat." She paused, looking up at Tala and Darcy from the lightboard. "You two are the experts, but I'd say those placements mean something." Dr. Ard returned to her transparencies but didn't seem to find what she was looking for and distractedly asked them to wait while she pulled up the photos.

Tala took a step back and motioned for Darcy to follow. "What are you talking about? How do you know she's a transwoman? And that the number didn't have anything to do with it?"

Darcy tensed, and she glanced back at Dr. Ard, who was now firing up a computer across the room and cursing at the screen. "I can't tell you. I just know. And I know it's not about her being trans. The murder itself may be connected, but the number is something else."

Tala took a slow breath, lowering her voice. "Look. We don't have time to mess around here, so I'm going to be straight with you, and I hope you'll return the favor."

"Jesus Christ." Darcy bit her lip. "Seriously? We have to have this conversation here?"

Tala chose her words carefully. "I asked about your career this morning because I have an idea why you're here. You don't have to tell everyone your business. In fact, I'm the last one to advise you to do that shit." She paused, then decided to just tell the truth. "But you have to let someone know, or we're going to start missing things that could blow this case wide open."

"And you want to be my person?"

Tala shook her head and looked to the ceiling, both gestures warmed somehow with genuine affection. "I can't believe I'm saying this, but yes."

Darcy smiled, and for the first time, light glimmered behind her eyes. "Fine. Let's get down to brass tacks here, because I'm guessing we don't have long." Tala and Darcy leaned to the left together to glance at Dr. Ard, who was now feeding paper into the printer and smacking the side of it with the heel of her hand. "Okay?"

"My thoughts exactly." Tala said. "What do you need from me?"

"Not much. Just nod." Darcy lowered her voice. "And know I'm not trying to get into your business here. I wouldn't do that."

Tala arched an eyebrow and waited. Darcy looked down, and Tala watched her eyes flutter shut again, although she turned and tried to hide her reaction, maybe out of habit. When she opened them, her voice was a whisper.

"You have a tattoo, wrapping around your left rib cage—"

Tala's mouth dropped open. "How would you—"

"It's a tribute to Aponi Standing Deer. Something happened when you were...small."

Tala felt her jaw clench and fought the tears that burned the back of her eyelids for a long moment before she spoke. "Holy shit."

Dr. Ard ripped the paper out of the printer tray and started to walk toward them from across the room. Darcy looked back at her and whispered the next words, low and soft, like a secret. Because they were.

"She's your mother?"

Tala nodded finally, blinking back tears that slipped down her cheek before she could catch them. Darcy had turned to return to the tables when Tala grabbed her hand. Darcy stopped and turned back.

"Thank you for speaking of her in the present tense." Tala caught the last tear and felt it melt under her fingertips. "It makes me feel like she's still here."

"That's because she is." The room seemed to warm around them, and time slowed to match Darcy's words. "Who do you think told me?"

CHAPTER SEVEN

B ut how did Darcy know she was trans? I've seen her in the crime-scene photos, and I was there in person when the body was found. That detail wouldn't have been apparent to anyone until the autopsy, so that's literally sometime in the last three days." Wilder paused to look at Tala. "It wasn't in any report she received. I know that for a fact."

Wilder reached to the top of the hearth in the living room for the matches and handed them to Tala. The fireplace took up most of one wall and was topped with an aspen mantel that held her collection of handmade wooden boxes. She'd been collecting them since she was a kid, and when she got older, she started making them in her woodshop, learning how to craft a dovetail joint and a soft-close lid, and line them with scraps of velvet she sourced from antique shops.

"Yeah. I know." Wilder watched Tala run her fingers over one of the boxes, crafted of ash and dyed a brilliant blue that accentuated the grain. "But I didn't ask her, either. Something tells me that's not the way to go about things with Darcy."

"Well, I'll take that cue from you, but I'd like to know how the hell—"

Tala caught her eye and nodded toward the doorway.

"Are we done for now, Chief?" Maren popped around the corner of the doorway with a ponytail holder in her mouth. She scraped her hair back and piled it on her head, most of it falling out before she got the elastic around it. She blew a piece out of her face and buttoned up her jean jacket as she spoke. "Hooper's gonna show me the yoga ropes or some shit out in the barn, but just between you and me, she doesn't look like a yogi, so if I'm not back in an hour, send in the troops." She flashed a grin that made Wilder smile despite herself. "And by troops, I mean Trobaugh."

"You're safe this time." Tala shrugged out of her cardigan, leaving just a black tee shirt as she sank down on the couch, the matches still in her hand. "I've done yoga with her a couple of times now, and she's way better than me, so chances are she really wants to teach you something."

"Seriously?" Maren glanced down at her watch. "Dammit. I thought 'yoga' was code for something that's actually fun."

"Try it. You might like it."

"And yes, we're done for the night, by the way." Wilder kneaded the concrete muscles in the back of her neck with one hand. "It's like ten thirty, for Christ's sake. I have no doubt we'll get this bastard, but it's not going to be tonight."

"Copy that, Chief."

Tala smiled as Maren loped down the hall, and she handed the long matches back to Wilder. "We've been over every single piece of evidence in those reports and every word of the autopsies a thousand times now. I'm just having a hard time getting the pieces to fit together in the profile. I don't have any idea what the killer is doing this for, you know? There's no sexual assault, yet all the victims are women, and they were all strangled, yet staged to look as if there was a different cause of death. They appeared obvious at first, but not one of them actually died by drowning or hanging."

"Yet all three were either found in water or soaking wet, hanging from a tree." Wilder looked up from the fire. "So what is it, symbolism?"

Tala just shook her head. "I wish I knew. I feel like I'm missing something obvious."

"Would it help to talk about it? Or do you need to just let it fall into place in your head?"

"No offense, but we've been doing nothing but that since we got here. I'm missing something, and I just have to let it come to the surface somehow."

"You've been shaping the profile since day one." Wilder twisted the grocery-coupon insert from the *Salem Times* into a loose log shape and laid it on the iron grate in the fireplace. "And don't bother telling me that's not true. You're famous for keeping your cards close to your chest, apparently, but I've been watching you do it from the moment I walked into the war room."

"What?" Tala lofted an eyebrow and passed Wilder the copper cauldron of kindling. "That doesn't sound like me at all."

"That sounds exactly like you." Wilder arranged a few sticks of fatwood on the paper and added some twigs from the cauldron. "You'll find I pay attention more than you think I do, Agent Marshall."

"If you're so great at it, why do I know all about your ex-wife that you split up with four years ago? And you know next to nothing about me?"

"What?" Wilder turned to look at Tala, the first split log still in her hand. "How is that even possible? I'm not on social media, and apart from our wedding pictures in the paper a decade ago, there's nothing to find." She grinned, tossing the log on the fire and holding the lighter under one corner of the newspaper. "I call bullshit."

Trobaugh cleared her throat, and when Wilder looked up, she was standing in the doorway in her plaid robe holding a steaming mug of what smelled like hot chocolate. "Just wanted to let you know I'm down for the count. Darcy just went up too." She took an appreciative sip and nodded in the direction of the window. "Maren and Hooper are in the barn, and I took the liberty of notifying the officer assigned to that quadrant of the property so he could keep an eye on them. Hoop wanted me to come, but I want no part of what's going down out there."

"I should have thought of that, actually." Wilder stepped back as a rogue spark made a grab for her. "Thanks for taking care of it."

"Those two are armed, of course, and I don't think anyone in their right mind would mess with either one, but better safe than sorry. I saw Hooper queuing up her Kenny Chesney playlist after dinner, so if I had to guess, I'd say she's getting ready to teach our Australian to two-step, and I'd rather not be a part of that. After five minutes, I'd be the one with PTSD."

Tala tilted her head, confused. "Is that a euphemism for something, or are you seriously saying they're country dancing out there?" She stopped, appearing to consider her options. "Because if that's really going down, doesn't it seem like someone should be secretly videotaping that scene for future blackmailing opportunities?"

Wilder threw another log on the fire and raised a hand. "I'm going to pretend I didn't hear that, but if I had, I'd agree."

Trobaugh headed upstairs as the scent of burning cedar glazed the air with warmth, the crackles and pops of green twigs Wilder had found in the tinder cauldron the only sound in the room. The living room had always been Wilder's favorite space in the house. The thick, chinked maple logs made it nearly soundproof, and the soaring Aspen-style ceiling made the room feel more like a freestanding one-room cabin in the woods. The expansive bay windows framed the black night sky like a wall of gallery paintings, but since Salem's nightmare started, Wilder had spent her evenings staring into the darkness without seeing it, willing the killer to walk by like a New England apparition, hovering in the murky darkness.

Wilder shook her head to clear it and brought herself back to the present. "So, you met Miranda?"

"Yes, ma'am, I did. She owns the fudge shop in town, right?" Tala tucked her bare feet underneath her on the couch and shook her hair out of the tight bun it'd been in all day. "She clocked my weapon under my jacket and put two and two together that I might know you."

"I'm almost afraid to ask what she said." She paused. "No one cheated on anyone, by the way. We just realized it wasn't going to work." Wilder hit the lever beside the hearth that controlled the chandelier and dimmed it to a soft amber that brought out the colors of the fire. After a moment she went on. "Or at least that's what she convinced me of at the time. We came through it eventually, at least enough to live in the same small town and be cordial, although it was dicey for a while. Especially when I found out she was dating one of the male patrol officers the week after she moved out."

"Damn. I can't imagine how that must have been in such a small town." Tala stared into the flames, then flicked her gaze back to Wilder. "And I know how that feels. When everyone knows your business."

"You grew up on the Powhatan reservation, right?"

Wilder coaxed a fallen log back onto the grate and turned back to Tala, who nodded, then looked slowly into the fire again. A crow glided past the window at eye level, her golden eyes following them as she sailed languidly past and out into the inky night sky. The room was starting to warm, and Wilder unsnapped her navy uniform shirt, leaving just her white tee, then draped the shirt over the back of the couch. She'd planned to change out of her uniform and take a shower before dinner, but the growing press presence had been a nightmare most of the afternoon, and she'd barely made it back to the cabin in time for dinner and the evening debrief.

"So," she said, tucking the front of her tee behind her leather belt. "Tell me more about that."

Tala looked up, her dark eyes sparkling. "What? How it was to grow up on the reservation?" She smiled, then took the fire poker from Wilder's hand and lifted the side of a fallen log back into place. "Um…no."

Wilder barely suppressed a laugh and winked in her direction. "Just…'no'?"

"Yeah." Tala slicked her fingers through the glossy length of her hair and leaned deeper into the lush, emerald-green velvet sofa. "You look like you may not hear that word much, but I think you'll find that 'no' is a complete sentence."

"I'm pretty sure I shouldn't," Wilder said, trying to hide a smile, "but I'm going to take that as a compliment."

Wilder rehung the poker on its hook on the hearth and opened the mahogany cabinet to the left of the door. She poured two fingers of amaretto liqueur from a decanter into a square whiskey glass, then chose a dark blue bottle with rafia twine at the top and gold hand lettering.

"What the hell is this?"

Wilder heard the alarm in Tala's voice and whipped her head back to see her standing by the hearth. She was holding up a wooden skewer from the pile next to the cauldron like it might decide to spring to life and stab her.

Wilder brought the glasses to the coffee table and took the skewer she was holding gingerly with two fingers. "Those are fire starters. I bought one of those old wooden cheese molds at an antique store, and then I fill it halfway with dryer lint—"

Tala made a face, dropped the skewer into Wilder's hand, and scooted back to her spot on the sofa.

"And pour the wax leftover from my candle jars on top." Wilder winked and tossed it back into the kindling cauldron. "I add a wooden skewer or twig, whatever I have, and I've got the perfect fire starter from stuff that would've gone to waste."

She handed Tala her glass as she picked up her own and sank back into the sofa. It'd been a long day. More than ten of them in a row, although it felt good to be surrounded by women who she knew were the best in the business. Their presence lifted the pressure somewhat, but something told her the body count was about to go up, based on the killer's past pattern and timeline. She felt the vague pressure of a growing headache behind her temples and pressed it with her fingertips, willing it to fade.

"This smells delicious," Tala put the glass Wilder had poured her on the coffee table again, "but I don't drink."

Wilder took a long sip of the almond liqueur from her glass, savoring the dry burn at the back of her throat that rose like fire into her nose. "I know. It's non-alcoholic. I've noticed you don't drink wine at dinner, so I picked some black-cherry cordial for you in town. Apparently, it has a 'hint of pink peppercorn and a daring splash of frightful black tarragon,' according to the shop assistant."

Tala picked it back up, was silent for a moment, then held up the glass. Firelight flickered on the dark glass as if coming from within. "What are we toasting to?"

"To your kickass profile." Wilder smiled, raising her glass. "And, of course, to—nailing the bastard."

They spoke almost at the same time and laughed. Tala held on to her glass, sitting cross-legged on the couch, tracing the rim of the etched crystal glass with her finger. It was easy to assume Tala was bigger than she really was. Her presence was impactful, strong, and undeniable in a forged-steel kind of way. Tonight, though, she rubbed her eyes with the heel of one hand, and the other shook slightly as she set the glass down on the coffee table again.

"Give me your weapon."

"But." Tala looked up, her hand instinctively drawn to her holster. "Aren't we supposed to be armed, even in the house?"

"Technically, but," Wilder held out her hand until Tala unholstered and handed over her firearm. Wilder set it on the coffee table between them and handed her the cashmere plaid throw from the back of the couch. "You are armed. You have me with you."

Burning wood dropped suddenly into the grate and split into glowing crimson coals with black edges. Wilder got up to toss a new split fir log onto the fire and waited until it settled into the flames before she added another.

"So," Tala said, still gazing into the slick, obsidian surface of the cordial as she spoke. She rolled the glass in her hand and watched the luminous darkness coat the sides of the crystal. "Tell me about Miranda. Why did it end?"

"It had been building for a while, I guess. I got shot in the line of duty early on in our marriage, and I think she always assumed I'd quit the force afterward." Wilder stood and laced her fingers behind her head. "If anything, it strengthened my resolve to become a detective. I wanted to be a voice for the victims that weren't as lucky as I was, the ones who didn't live to tell the story, especially women." She met Tala's gaze and held it. "I knew I had to be the one that could put the pieces of that story together and tell it for them."

"And she didn't understand that?"

"God, no. She'd always hated me being on the force. When I didn't quit and then went on to get my detective shield, that was the beginning of the end." Wilder bent down to blow the coals into flames, then hung up the poker and sank into the couch. "Also, she'd always been somewhat conservative, but she started to step back into the closet as the years passed, instead of the other direction. I never really understood it."

"Was her family supportive?"

"Always, so that wasn't it. I started to wonder if she was really gay, and I guess she did too."

"That's right. She ended up with a guy, correct?"

"Yep. A few of them." Wilder dampened the resentment in her voice and looked up from the fire. "She married a doctor a couple of years ago. He works out of Boston but comes back to Salem on the weekends. He bought her the fudge shop to keep her busy, apparently. She volunteers at Salem High as well."

Wilder lifted the empty glass of cordial out of Tala's hand to refill it. She uncorked the bottle, poured it, then handed it to her as she sat back down, doing nothing to throw words at the silence between them.

Tala looked up as she took the first sip. "What?"

"Nothing. Just waiting for the complete recounting of your love life that you owe me. Start from your first kiss and move through every detail to the present." Wilder winked. "No pressure."

"I owe you exactly nothing," Tala said, although her eyes sparkled for just a moment as she spoke. "But if you must know, a little romantic drama might be why I look so tired this morning."

"Yeah. I saw you leaving with your phone last night. You were out in the hall for ages."

"I thought you were awake." Tala smiled. "And not just because that couch fits only two-thirds of you."

"Accurate." Wilder sipped and kneaded the back of her neck with her hand. "Go on?"

"It's nothing that's breaking my heart or anything." Tala slid her phone out of the back pocket of her jeans and pulled up a picture, then turned the phone around and handed it to Wilder. "I saw the writing on the wall."

"Holy shit." Wilder took her time zooming in and reluctantly gave the phone back to Tala. "That was not what I was expecting. She looks like a model."

"She is, kind of. She's an Instagram influencer."

Wilder's eyebrows narrowed as she leaned over for another look. "Okay. You got me. What the hell is an influencer?"

Tala threw her head back and laughed. "I know, right?" She dropped the phone back into her pocket and shook her head. "I guess they do advertising for different companies on their social-media sites, promoting products and 'lifestyles,' whatever that means."

"Oh, God. Like Gwyneth Paltrow and the 'Yoni Eggs'?"

"What?" Tala reached for her phone again. "What the hell is a Yoni Egg?" Her fingers flew over the keyboard, and then she leaned in as if she were examining photos of a bloody crime scene. "You've got to be freaking kidding me. They sell egg-shaped stones to put in your—"

"Trust me. You don't want to know more than that. Some of those things cost more than what I make in a year." Wilder waved the phone away when a laughing Tala turned it around again. "Oh no. Believe me. I don't need to know anything else about the Yoni Egg."

"Let me guess." Tala clicked the phone off. "Miranda was a fan?"

Wilder nodded. "I don't want to talk about it. I've developed excellent skills for repressing those memories."

Tala laughed until she looked down at her watch. "How is it so late?"

Wilder picked up Tala's gun and handed it back to her. "We'd better go now so we can grab a few hours before we're due back in the war room. We've got the medical examiner coming tomorrow morning, right?"

"Not so fast, Wilder." Tala nodded but didn't budge. "I have a few more questions, but we'll do them in a speed round."

Wilder laughed and stood, at least until she realized Tala wasn't kidding. "Oh. You're serious about that?"

"Sit." Tala pulled out her phone again and set a timer for thirty seconds. "I'll rapid-fire some questions, and you give me the shortest answer possible." She looked up, her finger poised over the button on her screen. "Got it?"

"Wait. I get to ask questions, too, right?"

"That's a negative, Chief." Tala clicked the button and set the phone on the coffee table. "What's your family background?"

"Dad left, single mom. She retired five years ago and moved to Europe."

"This cabin is gorgeous and right on the water. How did you buy it on a detective's salary?"

Wilder laughed, sliding a hand around the back of her neck while she decided if Tala was serious. Tala pointed at the timer with the sharp arch of her eyebrow.

"Oh, damn. That's a real question." Wilder glanced out the window toward the lake that it was too dark to see. "I was a childhood chess champion. I rose to Junior Grandmaster, and Mom invested every penny."

"Damn." Tala smiled. "That's not what I was expecting."

Wilder nodded in the direction of the rapidly spinning timer. "Tick-tock, Tala."

"Fine. One more." Tala settled her gaze on Wilder's and leaned in slightly. The silence dropped between them, and Wilder held her breath. "Do you still love Miranda?"

Wilder held her eyes, then shook her head. "No." The timer dinged dramatically, buzzing against the surface of the coffee table. "Do you still love the model?"

Tala smiled. "Never started."

Both looked up suddenly when Hoop cleared her throat. She and Maren were standing there watching, propping up opposite sides of the doorframe, matching beef-jerky strips in hand.

"Oh, no," Maren said with an enthusiastic glance in Hooper's direction. "Don't stop on our account. That shit was just getting good."

CHAPTER EIGHT

The phone buzzed and spun the handset in a slow circle on the coffee table in front of Wilder's couch. She picked it up to check the time, then wished she hadn't. She'd been asleep for exactly two hours.

"Hey, Robinson." She sat up and swung her legs over the side, trying to clear the cobwebs of a dream from her mind. Sergeant Robinson had stepped in as her second-in-command at the station when she had to take over the Chief position the previous summer. The acting chief had been caught buying some narcotics over the dark web and been immediately terminated, but in a small-town station like Salem, that came with an immediate shuffle of responsibility. Robinson had stepped up to the challenge and been promoted to sergeant when Wilder took over as chief, which was admirable, considering the seven children he had at home with his wife, Sophie. "Hit me. What's going on?"

"Hey, Chief. I'm just getting to the scene now." Wilder listened to the hollow sound of wind whipping around the phone as he stepped out of the cruiser and shut the door behind him. "I just got a call from dispatch that a motion alarm was triggered at one of the buildings downtown, so I'm going to check it out. I put a hold on any other officers coming to the scene till we know what we're dealing with. I know you're trying to be careful about who knows what right now."

"Great, but I don't want you anywhere by yourself at the moment, so let's check it out together." Wilder grabbed a pair of jeans from a top shelf in her walk-in closet by memory and stepped into them, switching the phone to her other hand and nearly dropping it in the process. "Just text me the address and stay put until I get there."

Wilder threw on a tee and black wool sweater, or at least what she hoped was that combination, then pulled on her boots in the dark. By the time she'd stepped out of the closet, her eyes had adjusted to the dark enough to see that Tala had pulled her shirt off in her sleep and pushed the duvet to the side. Cool, silver moonlight drifted across her bare back like fallen smoke, illuminating every curve as if she were a painting in a museum, the length of her hair draped over the side of the bed like a bolt of dark silk. It was easy to think Tala was larger than life because of how she carried herself, but her frame was classically feminine and far more delicate than Wilder expected.

The phone buzzed in her hand and jolted her back to reality. It was Robinson. Wilder carefully replaced Tala's comforter, looking away as she rolled into it and onto her side.

"Yeah." She reached for her holster and slipped it on one shoulder. "I'm almost out the door."

"I hate to ask, I know we're short-staffed as it is, but—" Out of the corner of her eye, Wilder saw Tala lift her head off the pillow and put a silent finger to her lips, hoping Tala would take it as a hint to go back to sleep. She did not. Wilder just shook her head and tried to listen to the rest of what Robinson was saying. "Could I get one of the unis to park outside my house and just keep an eye on it while I'm not there? Sophie's mom is staying with us until we catch this guy, but they're both asleep right now, and I'd just feel better with another set of eyes on the place until I get back."

Wilder turned toward the door to give Tala a chance to grab her shirt. "Of course, but let me send one of the task force, if you feel comfortable with that, okay? Until we catch this guy and know for certain he's not one of us, I'd rather be safe than sorry."

"That'd be amazing. You know my address."

Wilder heard the click at the other end of the phone and turned around to find Tala dressed and reaching for her holster. She slipped her flashlight into the strap and handed Wilder hers as she pulled on her boot with one hand. "What? Trying to sneak out of here without me after you stole my shirt?"

"I did *not*. I—"

Tala flashed her a smile. "I'm kidding. I'm famous for pulling my clothes off in my sleep." She bumped Wilder's shoulder with hers as she passed. "You can catch me up on where we're going on the way."

Wilder rolled her eyes and opened the door to the bedroom for Tala. "Fantastic. I'll just be duct-taping my eyes shut tonight."

❖

"So Trobaugh and Hooper are just camping out in your sergeant's living room until we get done with the scene?"

The door slammed against the dark silence as she slid into Wilder's black Jeep. "I met Sophie briefly when I rolled into town. I came to the station, and she was dropping off his lunch, so we chatted for a minute while he was on the phone. She's going to love those two." Tala pulled her hair into a quick ponytail and fastened her seat belt as Wilder pulled onto the road into town. "Can't say I blame you for not wanting to send one of the units though. This killer could be anyone at this point."

"Exactly." Wilder clicked on her fog lights as the cold mist they'd encountered on the way out the door turned to rain. The wipers' steady rhythm filled the Jeep, and she dialed up the heat, flicking the air vents in Tala's direction. "Dispatch is contacting me and Robinson directly with anything out of the ordinary, and we'll pull them in if we need them, but something about this call already doesn't feel right."

"So, what was the call? A triggered alarm?"

"Yeah, which sounds like no big deal, but that almost never happens in Salem, especially on the square." Wilder held her fingers up to the air vents to warm them. "And right now, everything is a big deal until we find out it's not."

A buck leaped out of the darkness suddenly, and Wilder swerved, the back end of the Jeep fishtailing for a few tense seconds as she got back out onto the rain-slicked road. The spatter of the black rain against the window turned steadily into a hard, silver sheet, and Wilder had to slow down; the center line was an edgeless blur until they reached the square in the center of town. She pulled in slowly and took a left, then parked next to Robinson's patrol car just as he stepped out to meet them. He pulled up the hood of his rain jacket and nodded in the direction of the massive red Gothic windows across the square.

"I waited to go in till you got here, but this seems a little too random to be random, Chief."

"Yeah. I was just saying something like that." Wilder nodded, clicking the locks on her Jeep and dropping the keys into her pocket. She took a long visual sweep of their surroundings. At least the press wasn't camped out yet, although if they needed to call in CSIs, the scanner would alert them, and they'd undoubtedly descend on the square like a flock of vultures. She realized suddenly her mind was spinning and pulled her attention back to Robinson. "Sorry. I'm distracted. You two know each other, correct?"

Robinson flashed Tala an easy smile, visible even under the Viking beard that almost reached his chest. He was closer to seven feet tall than six and had a look about him that made you think he had a schooner in Salem harbor and a night job as a marauding pirate.

"Yes, ma'am. She showed me how to disable the seat-belt alarm on the cruiser when I drove her to the cabin. You know I hate that endless beep when I'm trying to get situated in the car." He winked at Tala and laughed. "Yanked that sucker right out."

"Really?" Wilder flashed a smile in Tala's direction as they started toward the north end of the square. "I hadn't heard. Hard to imagine she left that part out."

Tala rolled her eyes, then spotted the crime-scene tape and reached for her flashlight. "So, what is the building we're looking at? The set for some Halloween slasher movie?" She squinted, aiming the beam at the neon red lights outlining the carved wooden sign over the door. "Is it a church or a museum?"

"Both." Wilder pulled up the hood on her jacket as the rain intensified and wet leaves blew across the slick asphalt. "It's the Salem Witch Museum. They built it in a renovated cathedral, and now it's a major part of the tourist draw for the town. It's usually booked for the month of October a year in advance."

They crossed against the red light and hurried to the door, dodging the cold shards of rain. The building was imposing but undeniably beautiful, with tall, arched, Gothic doors painted a glossy bloodred, hammered black hardware, and strategic lighting behind the ancient stained-glass windows. A flickering electric candle shone in the corners of each window frame, somehow simultaneously bringing the colors to life and shrouding the thick leaded glass in a haunted, villainous vibe.

The rain beat a staccato rhythm on the pitched front-entrance roof and fell dramatically around them, splashing the outside of their boots. Wilder used the end of her flashlight to pull one of the imposing Gothic doors the rest of the way open. It was already cracked about a foot, with no sign of forced entry. The door resisted, creaking and scraping against the darkened marble floor, the hinges stiff with cold.

"So, what tripped the alarm?" Tala stepped in and spun her flashlight around the entry-hall area of the museum. "I don't see a sign of forced entry, so either it was open already or someone had a key."

Robinson slid out of his jacket and shook the rain off it. "I'm guessing it was the interior motion detectors they installed last month. I called the manager, and she's on her way, but tomorrow's Sunday, so she'd already left today to go to Boston to see her new grandson. I told her to wait till morning and take her time. It's going to be a while before we can release the scene anyway."

Wilder leaned around the corner of a narrow hall that led to the gift shop, tucked into the west corner of the entrance area.

"Good call. She'd be risking a speeding ticket just to have to sit in the diner across the square all morning."

"That's what I told her, but from the sound of it, she'll more than likely show up sooner rather than later. At least we're getting to see what's going on without the inevitable shitshow of looky-loos that'll be here in the morning when word gets out." Robinson flicked on the row of electric light switches near the door. "I took a look from the outside when I got here, but I waited for you to clear the interior of the building."

Warm, amber light from electric wall sconces flooded the room, which still had the bones of a Colonial stone cathedral, and the chiseled limestone walls served as frames for images of the local Salem Witch Trials theater productions over the last two hundred years. Solemn black-and-white photographs lined the walls of the foyer, each with a small brass plate underneath that included details about both the actors and the real citizens involved in the famous witch trials of 1692.

It took only a few minutes for the three of them to clear the building, and Wilder wasn't surprised to find it deserted. Whoever had tripped the alarm had been in and out in a flash and, from the look of things, hadn't taken anything, which worried her more than if it had been a simple robbery. The cash register in the small gift shop also looked intact, and nothing else was disturbed. If theft was the motive, that would have been the obvious first target.

"I don't see anything out of place." Tala stuck her head around the doorframe of the gift shop. "But I did find the lights for the main exhibition room if you want to take a closer look in there."

Wilder glanced around again and joined her. The main open area of the cathedral was organized in rows, each lined with historical exhibits and relics from the actual Salem Witch Trials, and Wilder knew them all by heart. Her mother had taken her to the museum countless times when she was a kid, which was handy now that she was looking for something out of place. She passed the glass case with the initial decree of execution preserved in the center, surrounded by etched-glass drawings of the first four women accused of witchcraft. Tituba, a young native South American slave that was accused of spectral magic, Sarah Good, Sarah Osbourne, and Bridget Bishop, who was the first woman to be executed for the crime of witchcraft in Salem.

"Wilder." Tala's voice was tense. "You're going to want to see this."

Wilder spun around and followed the sound of Tala's voice, weaving her way through the exhibits until she turned a sharp corner and saw her standing by a smashed glass display case. Broken glass crunched between Wilder's boots and the stone floor, and the air was suddenly vacant and still as she looked at the exhibit she'd seen a thousand times, now strangely naked without the protective sheets of etched glass surrounding it.

"I'm guessing this wasn't originally part of the exhibit?" Tala snapped on a pair of latex gloves from her pocket and handed another set to Wilder.

"Want me to get CSI on standby, Chief?" Robinson clicked the button on his radio and looked at Wilder.

"Yes, but make sure they know not to come in until they get the word from one of us. And call it in from your phone. Don't use the radio."

"Copy that."

Robinson walked back up the aisle to the front of the museum, and the sound of the front doors closing behind him faded as he stepped outside. Eerie silence echoed around the stone walls as Wilder and Tala stared at the single weathered board that used to stand behind glass. Tala dropped her gaze to the patinaed brass plate on the base of the exhibit.

"This is the only part of the gallows that remains today?"

Wilder nodded, pushing the larger glass shards to the side with her boot, looking for the missing component of the exhibit she knew should be there. A looped length of the handmade rope used to hang the first of the accused witches, Bridget Bishop, should have been attached to the rescued wood from the gallows, but it was gone. In its place a delicate gold ring dangled from an antique square, iron nail driven at a steep angle into the plank. Wilder pulled a pen from the inside pocket of her jacket and leaned closer, sliding it onto the tip. The ring was gold and obviously antique, the etching of vines worn almost smooth over time. In the center was a single glassy, black stone. Tala crouched down to look at the inscription on the inside of the band.

"What does it say?"

She stood, looking around the room that had suddenly grown cold, as if a sharp wind had swept around the silent stone walls and solidified around them.

"Nothing." Tala's voice fell to the floor and faded among the shards of glass. "Just two initials. *R.N.*"

❖

"Look. I can't get behind this if I don't have a clue what's happening." Wilder rubbed the back of her neck as she slid into the Jeep, glancing over as Tala clicked on her seat belt. "I don't know why you can't just tell me."

"Because I can't." Tala pulled her phone out of her jacket pocket, her fingers flying over the keys. "I know that on this project you outrank me, but you're just going to have to trust me on this one."

Wilder shook her head, reminding herself to soften her tone. Her lack of sleep was heavy and cloying and was making her feel worse by the minute. She gripped the steering wheel, concentrating on the brittle, cold leather under her hands and letting it drag her mind into focus. Sometimes you had to dig into your gut about someone, and as much as this little stunt chapped her ass, she felt like she could trust Tala.

"Fine." She glanced at the glowing blue screen of Tala's cell phone and leaned back in her seat. "Robinson left about ten minutes ago, so he should be back here with her soon."

"Now that we've settled that, let's move on to more important priorities." Tala looked around the square, turning to squint at the main road behind them. "I'm literally starving right here in your Jeep. Does Salem have anything open at this time of night?"

Wilder smiled despite herself and hit the door on the glove compartment with the heel of her hand. An assortment of granola and protein bars fell out onto Tala's lap. Her face lit up, and she dug through it, then looked up like someone had just stolen her purse. "Where's the good stuff?"

"I hesitate to ask for a definition of 'the good stuff,' but it's hard to get better than that." Wilder rifled through the rest of the pile in the glove box. "That's high-quality fuel right there, all organic protein and grains. I keep them in there for after the gym."

Tala held one of the bars up by the corner with her thumb and forefinger, then let it drop back in her lap with a dramatic *plop*.

"Look. I'm not arguing with the results." She squeezed Wilder's bicep for just a second too long before she seemed to pull her focus back to the subject at hand. "But I can't live on snacks made of papier mâché and wallpaper paste." She glanced at her watch. "I need real food, like the kind I have to reach through a car window to get and unwrap before it hits my mouth."

Wilder laughed, running a hand through her hair. She still felt the heat of Tala's hand on her arm, but when she glanced back over to the passenger's seat, Tala was staring back at her with the stoic gaze of a newscaster reporting the aftermath of a natural disaster.

"Okay, okay. I get it." Wilder looked up into the rearview mirror and saw Robinson's lights pull up behind them in the darkness. "There's one all-night pizza place for the college students that we can hit on the way home. I'll make sure you get loaded up with whatever you want."

"And Darcy?"

"Of course." Wilder opened her door and nodded behind them to remind Tala that they had company. "I don't know where you two are going to put it, but I'll buy you all the slices of processed junk you can handle."

CHAPTER NINE

"Seriously?" Wilder looked up at the three-story, Cape Cod, clapboard house as the wind whipped around the car with an earnest whine. The rain had stopped temporarily, shapeshifting itself into a smoke-like, swirling mist, which seemed to be the only thing she had going for her in this situation. "We just walk up to the Davis house in the middle of the night and…knock?"

Wilder glanced into the backseat at Darcy, barely visible wrapped up in Robinson's oversized duty jacket. She'd obviously managed to put on some jeans and a sweatshirt before she left the cabin, but somehow the concept of a coat, any coat, in forty-degree New England weather had escaped her. The three of them left Robinson at the scene with a couple of trusted officers to manage the CSI unit and the inevitable press that was sure to show up at dawn. Wilder had taped off a wider area around the museum before they'd left, but even with that precaution, the combination of townspeople and reporters when word got out in the morning was guaranteed to be a nightmare.

Thank God for Robinson. Wilder made a mental note to put in for some bonus time off for him after they'd wrapped up the case. She rooted around in the console for the Altoids tin of Advil she kept in there and swallowed three. *Assuming we do actually find this guy. At this point we have a better chance of catching a ghost and pinning the whole damn thing on him.*

"Wilder?" Tala was waiting with her hand on the door handle. "Don't you think we should actually get out of the Jeep at some point?"

Wilder got out and opened the door for Darcy on her side, and by the time they'd reached the walkway, lined by miniature pumpkins and potted mums, Tala was already waiting on the porch. The Davis house was one of the nicest on the block, painted a soothing latté brown with white trim and shiny black shutters. Four potted ferns hung from the roof of the white wrap-around porch, dangling in the freezing night air over a row of wooden rocking chairs. The chairs were all rocking slightly, each in a different rhythm. Wilder decided not to look too closely at them and just hope there was a sensible reason they'd be moving like they held a row of porch-sitting Southern Baptists on a Sunday afternoon. She'd lived in this town long enough to know you didn't go looking for answers you didn't want to find.

"I'll just let you two take the lead here." Wilder reached for the heavy brass knocker on the door and clapped it against the carved plank door twice. The sound echoed across the empty porch. "Since no one's told me jack shit about this fun little FBI spin on trick-or-treating we're doing." She cleared her throat and glanced back at the Jeep. "Or however I would have phrased that question if I wasn't so sleep-deprived."

"Look. All we have at this point is the ring." Darcy paused. "I don't know anything I haven't told you, so we're all on the same page at this point. Except for why we're at this house." She focused back on the door as the sound of shuffling footsteps grew louder. "And I'd share that little tidbit, but I don't want to."

Wilder could tell she was trying to make light of the situation, but both of her fists were jammed hard into the pockets of Robinson's jacket, and the fine lines around Darcy's eyes were deeper than usual, although it was strangely satisfying to see her looking a little more human and a little less like Detective Barbie.

The door opened just a crack, and a middle-aged woman with kind blue eyes appeared. Wilder recognized her right away as Marjorie Davis. She always dressed modestly and wore her hair in a single braid, and besides being present for church functions, all anyone in town seemed to know about her was that her life seemed to revolve around her husband and daughter. Not so with her husband. Roger Davis was the reverend of the only evangelical church in Salem and kept the police department on speed dial for complaints about the influx of the Salem Witch Trial tourists.

"This is unexpected." Marjorie pulled her robe tighter around herself and looked out at the sky that was suddenly threatening to dump an additional deluge of rain. "How can I help you, Chief Mason?"

"I know it's late, Mrs. Davis, and I apologize. But would it be possible for us to talk briefly inside?" Wilder introduced Tala and Darcy, silently wishing Darcy would replace her intense expression with one that had an outside chance of not scaring Marjorie into slamming the door in their faces. "It's urgent, or we wouldn't bother you in the middle of the night."

"You brought FBI Agents? Can I ask what this is about?" Marjorie glanced behind her and pulled the door closer, dropping her voice. "Roger is in the basement working on his sermons, and I'd hate to disturb him."

"No need to do that at the moment." Wilder flashed her most reassuring smile. "And I'm sure it won't take long."

Marjorie opened the door, putting a finger to her lips. "My daughter Jessa is upstairs as well. She's home from Boston University on fall break. This doesn't have anything to do with her, does it?"

She didn't wait for an answer, just showed them through the hall to the main living room, which was decorated in several Victorian styles at once, with floral lampshades trimmed in finely knitted lace, white doilies on the backs of the chairs and sofa, and multiple bowls of faded mauve potpourri on each end table. The pink taper candles in brass holders on the coffee table were still wrapped in dusty cellophane, and one even sported a faded price sticker near the top. She switched on a lamp on either end of the sofa and gestured for all three of them to sit, then carefully lowered herself into one of the floral chintz chairs on the other side of the cherrywood coffee table.

"I'd offer you some coffee, but I'd rather not wake my daughter." She folded both of her hands into her lap as if she'd just slid into a church pew. "Now, how can I help you?"

Wilder hated not having a fucking clue what was going on, and at almost four in the morning, her patience was wearing thin. She sat back on the sofa and stared pointedly at Darcy, who ignored her.

"Marjorie." Darcy flashed a surprisingly charming smile that seemed to relax the entire room like a warm swath of late summer wind. "May I call you that?"

Marjorie's face melted into her first genuine smile. "Of course."

"You mentioned your daughter was home from college. May I ask how old she is?"

Wilder waited for the silence to settle, but it was a long moment before Marjorie answered. "She's just turned eighteen. She graduated a year early." She jumped at the sound of a phone ringing in the basement before dragging her attention back to Darcy. "She's our only child and such a good girl. Whatever this concerns, I can assure you it has nothing to do with her."

Wilder shifted in her seat and glanced at Tala, who turned discreetly and told her without speaking to keep her mouth shut. Darcy's hand tightened in her lap, and it occurred to Wilder that she must have taken the ring they'd let her hold out of the evidence bag. Wilder had to stop herself from rolling her eyes. They'd dusted it before they left the scene and found no prints, but there could have been touch DNA on the gold or center stone. *Darcy knows better than that.* She shifted her attention back to the conversation, trying to bring her annoyance level back down to a low simmer.

"Jessa really struggled her first year of college. She kept wanting to come home every weekend, and when she did, we'd barely see her. It was like she was still stuck here somehow, not really embracing the college life like I'd hoped she would."

Darcy leaned forward slightly, completely focused on Marjorie. "And how is she doing so far this year? She's a sophomore, right?" "Well, she stayed on campus over the summer to work as a lifeguard at the university pool, and because of her schedule, she couldn't come home as frequently as she used to. Before she got here this weekend, she hadn't been back to Salem in six weeks." Marjorie dropped her voice to a whisper and leaned forward in her chair. "Which is the way it should be. I want her to experience a little of the world before she gets married." She paused before she went on, as if she wasn't sure she would until she heard her own words. "Although I don't say that around my husband."

"Mom, what's all the—" An athletic teen with bright blue eyes and wheat-blond hair to her waist ambled around the corner of the sitting room and stopped, crossing her arms over her chest when she saw who was on the couch. "Dad's gonna hear you and be upset. The sun isn't even up yet."

"I know. I just…" She stopped and gestured for her daughter to sit in the chair beside her. "Jessa, you probably recognize Wilder from town, but she's stopped by with some…" She paused, as if auditioning several words before she found one that was acceptable. "Colleagues, and they were just about to tell us why they're here."

The silence was heavy, pendulous, like waiting for a wounded redwood to fall in the forest. Finally, Darcy looked up and smiled, turning the ring in her fingers just out of Marjorie's sight. "This might be delicate, Marjorie, but could we have a few minutes alone with your daughter? She's not in trouble of any sort, but she may know something about an important case we're working on."

"Oh no. I think I should be here for this. We're very close and I may be able to help—"

"Mom, go ahead and get breakfast started." Jessa managed a tight smile with a maturity Wilder suddenly realized shouldn't be there. "Dad's going to be up in a few minutes, and we should get whatever this is wrapped up before that happens, don't you think?"

Marjorie got up with a single nod, smoothed her robe with her hands, and disappeared around the corner to the kitchen. They all sat, listening to the coffeemaker gurgle to life, until Jessa spoke, her voice low. "I know why you're here."

Tala spoke first, shrugging out of her jacket and handing it to Jessa. "It's cold in here. Put this on so you don't freeze to death while we talk."

Jessa took it without a word and nodded toward the wide stone fireplace in the corner. "These old houses are so drafty. I always started the first fire in the morning when I lived here, but Dad never does it." She pulled on the coat and wrapped it around her like a shield.

"I can start one while you guys talk, if that's okay?" Tala ran her hand along the top of the mantel. "Where's your lighter?"

"We use those long matches." Jessa nodded at the copper sleeve bolted to the side of the fireplace. "Dad says lighters are borrowed hellfire from Satan." Which could have easily been a joke had they not been talking to Roger Davis's daughter. "And the chimney still needs to be swept for the season, so just expect the draft to pull from the left. The right is dead."

Darcy switched to the chair next to Jessa, and Wilder watched as Tala started a beautiful fire out of thin air. Airy pine kindling sank swiftly to fiery embers, then climbed and ignited the split maple logs Tala stacked in a cone shape around them. Velvet smoke rose and languidly pulled to the left, just as Jessa had said, and Tala shifted the log distribution to offset it. Red splotches had started to appear on Jessa's neck, and she pulled the sleeves of the jacket Tala had given her down over her fingers, twisting them into her fists before she crossed her arms in front of her again.

Wilder leaned forward and pulled a field notebook out of her jacket, clicking open her pen. "So, Jessa. You said you think you know why we're here. Why is that?"

"I've just been expecting it, I guess." She looked at the ceiling as the redness climbed to her cheeks. Her voice cracked when she continued, and when she finally looked down, her eyes were already shimmering with tears that spilled down her cheeks. "You can't do what I did and get away with it."

Wilder glanced at Darcy, but she was watching Jessa. "Can you tell us a little bit more about that?"

Jessa swallowed hard, as if she might be sick, and tensed as she looked back at Wilder. "Do I have to?"

"We can take this at your own pace." Wilder gave Darcy a pointed glance, willing her to take over. She hated going into a situation blind, especially an interview. Jessa clearly had something on her mind, and getting her to lay it out on the table was going to take more than just experience.

"Jessa," Darcy said, locking her gaze onto Jessa's as she laid the small gold ring onto the table between them. "What can you tell me about this?"

Tala turned and sat on the hearth, poker in hand, and raised an eyebrow in Wilder's direction. The only sound in the room was the crackling of dry aspen logs as they hissed and spit, flames taking over in a *whoosh*, as if trying to fill the silence. Jessa reached out slowly and picked up the ring, tucking a wave of hair behind her ear that sprang back to brush her cheek as she slipped it on her finger. She shook her head, the tears falling from her chin now onto the collar of the jacket. Wilder pulled two tissues from a box with a dusty macramé cover the color of a Band-Aid and handed them to her.

"I thought this was gone forever. I mean, I'm so glad to have it back, but why would he give this to *you*?" She shook her head and dropped her voice to a whisper with a glance in the direction of the kitchen. "Does he hate me so much that he couldn't just meet me and give it to me in person?"

Wilder moved quietly to sit on the hearth beside Tala. Whatever Jessa was struggling with was a lot, and she knew from experience that those kinds of memories needed space to unfold and soften enough to read the story written across them.

"I mean, it's not like he even cares anymore, I guess. I heard he's replaced me now anyway." She turned the ring on her finger as she spoke, then set it silently down on the table between them. "I gave it to him when I left for college, and he wore it around his neck for like a year. I know he did. I saw it in his social-media pictures."

Marjorie came around the corner with a tray of coffee cups, sugar, and a chipped ceramic cream pitcher shaped like a white lily. "I don't want to intrude." She put the tray down on the coffee table and smiled at Wilder. "I just know that if you're up this early you probably haven't been to bed, and coffee is the cure for that."

"Thank you, Mrs. Davis." Wilder reached for a cup and dumped a teaspoon of sugar into it, then two more. "I didn't know I needed it until you made it, but this might just save me."

Marjorie smiled and walked back into the kitchen as Darcy picked up a cup for herself and Jessa, who quickly handed hers over to Tala.

Darcy lifted the hand she'd put over the ring when Marjorie walked in. "Your mom doesn't know about him, right?"

"God, no. I couldn't do that to her. Dad wanted her to keep homeschooling me through high school, and it was a battle, but thanks to her I got to go to regular high school. I wasn't going to rock the boat after that." She stared into the fire. "As far as I know, no one ever knew about me and him before I opened my big mouth, even when I was in his classes. I talked to my roommate about it this summer, you know, just to get some perspective, and last time I was home I told an older friend at church. He was right. I should have just kept my mouth shut."

"He's a teacher?" Wilder took a second to steady her voice to a casual tone. "One of your university professors?"

Jessa's gaze didn't shift from the fire. The room had started to shimmer with undulating waves of warmth from the now-roaring fire, but she just wrapped the coat tighter around herself. Wilder watched goosebumps rise on the back of her hands and wrists. "That's why you're here, right? He always told me I could ruin his career if I ever told anyone. And I believed him, but it just got to be too much after a while. I felt like if I didn't tell someone why I was so sad, I'd go crazy." She finally dragged her gaze away from the fire and looked at Darcy. "Am I going to jail?"

"Did he tell you that?" Darcy's voice was soft. "That you'd go to jail if anyone ever found out about you two?"

"He said that it was illegal and we'd both be in trouble, yeah. I should have just kept my mouth shut." Her voice cracked, and she tried to fight back the tears, glancing toward the kitchen more than once as she dabbed at them with her sleeve.

Darcy didn't answer, and Wilder watched her consciously shift her expression into neutral. "Can you tell me a little about that ring, Jessa? It looks old, like maybe something that was passed down to you?"

"It is old, and I'm not even supposed to have it. That's why I was so worried about getting it back. And it's even worse than that," she lowered her voice to a rushed whisper, "because Dad thought Mom got rid of it years ago. It's evil, apparently. But I don't think it's evil at all." She picked it up off the table and slipped it back onto her finger. "My mother loved it. And she doesn't even know I took it, so now I can just put it back where I found it."

"Why does your dad think it's evil?" Tala leaned in and poured a bit of cream into her coffee from the ceramic lily. She stirred it with the tiny silver spoon on the tray. The clink of the spoon against the cup seemed unnaturally sharp in the quiet room.

"I don't know, but it was one of the only times I heard them fight. He was screaming at her in their room. I was about ten then, I think, and I heard him say that it was bringing evil into our home, over and over, like if he said it enough times, she'd just believe him." She looked into the fire, and Wilder watched as she pressed her thumb into the palm of her other hand, hard enough to leave an angry, red mark. "He made us get into the car, and he drove us to that covered bridge outside of town." She looked up at Wilder. "Do you know the one I'm talking about?"

Wilder nodded. She wanted to ask a thousand questions, but this was not the time. She knew enough that if you tell someone's story for her, she'll never feel heard, even if you get it right.

"I remember Mom was crying the whole way out there." Jessa stiffened at the sound of silverware shuffling in the kitchen. "He was driving but didn't say a word until he pulled up by the water. Then he just got more and more amped up as he walked her to the edge of the river. He was, like, waving his bible around and stuff." She paused so long Wilder started to think she might not go on. When she spoke again, her voice had sunk to a whisper, almost as if she was speaking from behind a door. "She must have told him to give her a minute, because at one point he kind of stepped back, and I watched her throw it into the water. By that time, I'd gotten out of the car and was just sitting by the door on the side of the road. I still remember the plinking sound when it hit the water, and I watched her sit down on the rocks and cry." Jessa shook her head. "She hid her face in her hands so I wouldn't see the tears, but I knew."

Tala's voice was soft. "But she didn't really throw it?"

"No. I asked her about it a few years later when I found it by accident. She'd hidden it in one of her little boxes in the attic. She made me swear I wouldn't tell my dad, but she told me she'd thrown a coin into the water and slipped the ring into her hair after. She always wore one of those tight buns back then." Jessa sighed and leaned back into the chair, as if she'd just put down an anchor that had been slung around her neck since that moment. "Dad never noticed, and she just learned to hide it better."

Wilder cleared her throat. "We'll need to talk to you at some point about—"

"How you're doing and maybe get just a few more details." Darcy interrupted smoothly as she walked over to pluck another handful of tissues out of the box. "But you're not in trouble, Jessa. He is."

Wilder took the hint and let Darcy take the lead, not that she had a choice. It was an odd feeling to work with someone who could hold a ring in her hand and know the background of a story. It was like starting in the middle of a book that someone else knew by heart.

Jessa shook her head, her face flushed and damp as she took the tissues from Darcy. "But he told me we'd both go to jail if I ever told anyone." She shoved them into her pocket and straightened her shoulders. "I guess I just hoped I could get the ring back and no one would ever know, but I guess I was more messed up about it than I realized. I just couldn't carry the whole secret anymore, especially when I heard he's talking to another girl. She's just a kid. A real kid."

Darcy's face was a careful balance of intensity and kindness as she handed Jessa the tissues. "And how old is she?"

A dense silence hung in the air before Jessa bit her lip and looked up. "It's going to get out anyway. I heard she'd already told someone, but I don't want to be the reason why. I never did want to get him into trouble. I just wanted my ring back." She looked up. "This girl is fourteen though. Like, her birthday was last Sunday. He met her at drama camp last summer. I mean, obviously I was more mature than other girls, he told me that, but this girl wasn't, so I tried to talk to him about it. I'd show you the texts, but I lost my phone a few days ago. When I was at church on Sunday, I think." She twisted the tissue in her hand, wrapping the damp end around her thumb as she went on. "I'm still hoping it'll turn up."

None of them heard the footsteps come around the corner until they saw the reverend staring at them. Thirty seconds later the three of them stood on the sidewalk wincing at the echo of the door slamming behind them. Wilder looked up to find the rain clouds had cleared, and ochre-yellow dawn was rising through the burnished maple trees that were giving up their leaves with the slightest gust of wind. Crispy crimson leaves with verdant edges skittered across the path to the Jeep, blowing like fire across their boots. The air smelled cold and clean, with a hint of the wood smoke that curled out of the Davises' chimney and wafted up to the awakening sky.

"Hey." Tala climbed into the Jeep and pulled her seat belt across her chest, leaning around the seat to look at Darcy. "What did Jessa say to you as we left?"

She said, "Don't tell my dad. He'll kill me."

Wilder ran a hand through her hair as she fired up the engine. "Something tells me she meant that literally."

CHAPTER TEN

Maren lifted the stainless-steel bowl of mussels down into the sink and settled it into the crushed ice. A pile of fresh, velvety, gray shrimp was already waiting there in another bowl, and the scallops were chilling in the fridge. Maren checked her watch, mumbling as she looked out the window. "Right on schedule, if everyone gets their asses here for dinner on time."

"Talking to yourself again? You've really got to get some friends." She looked up to see Darcy leaning on the log doorframe of the kitchen, wearing faded jeans and a black cashmere hoodie. Maren knew it was cashmere because she'd seen it in the closet the day before and almost had an orgasm while running her hand over it. Seemed a little decadent for Darcy's taste, but she was starting to realize that bitchy waters might run deep. "So where is everybody?"

Maren turned around and leaned against the counter. "Wilder rocked up looking like the mutt's nuts this morning, as you know, and passed out on the couch in the living room going over crime-scene photos. I think Tala took a nap at some point, and Trobaugh and Hooper drove into town. I'm the only one who wasn't up all night, so I went down into the harbor to get some seafood."

Maren peeled the skin from two scallions and picked up a chef's knife, holding it out to Darcy. "Look. If you want to stand there and talk about my imaginary friends, you're gonna have to make yourself useful."

Darcy took the knife with a smile that made Maren think she might have been waiting for the invitation. "How do you want this cut?" She picked it up and gave it a wary sniff. "This is a warped little onion, right?"

Maren edged a small prep bowl over to the side of the cutting board. "Kind of. It's a French onion, or shallot. With what I'm making tonight, I want a more delicate, gentle flavor that won't overpower the saffron. Just cut it so it ends up in pieces. Nothing is ever exact in this dish."

"Saffron?" Darcy looked up and nearly took the tip of her finger off with the knife. "That's a spice, right?"

"That it is, but watch what the hell you're doing there." Maren nodded toward the knife. "This dish is all about timing, and I didn't plan out a window to be taking you to the ER."

Darcy smiled and started to slice the shallot into both thin slices and alarmingly asymmetrical chunks. "Every time you're in the kitchen I think about you getting dragged off that boat in flip-flops, and it's hard to reconcile the two images."

Maren turned the dial on the oven, peeking inside before she closed the door. "What? You're surprised I can cook?"

"Actually, yes." Darcy finished the first shallot and moved on to the next, pushing up the sleeves of her hoodie to her elbow before she picked the knife up again. "Or maybe it's more accurate to say I was shocked to find out you can cook like you do." The knife slipped off the slick edge of the shallot and hit the cutting board at just the right angle to stick. "Why is that, by the way?"

Maren edged Darcy over to one side with her shoulder and retrieved the knife, curled her fingers over the rounded top of the shallot, and sliced it into razor-thin, perfect half-moons, the knife moving so quickly it looked like a silver blur even to her. She winked in Darcy's direction, using the flat of the blade to scoop them up in one swoop and deposit them into the prep bowl.

"That's because I went to culinary school right after high school and worked my way around Europe and Asia in random kitchens. I'd build up enough money to travel to my next destination and just disappear." Maren smiled. "Like vapor."

"I don't believe that for a second." Darcy narrowed her eyes as if they were suddenly in an interrogation room. "How the hell did you get here then? And don't give me some bullshit answer because I've done enough research to know the FBI recruited you after you cracked that crazy case here in the States, and that almost never happens."

"By the time I was twenty-four, I'd shagged and chefed my way around the globe a couple of times, and even I had to admit it was getting old. I woke up hungover on the beach one day and just decided it might be time to do something more meaningful, which thrilled my poor mother to no end. She was convinced I'd end up being as useless as an ashtray on a motorcycle." Maren pulled a huge cast-iron pan from one of the lower cabinets and settled it on the burner, turning the heat up with a flick of her wrist. "My old man was a copper, and I'd always secretly thought about it, so I traveled home to Perth and went for it."

"Pretty successfully, I hear." Darcy stuck her head in the freezer and pulled out the vodka, uncorking it with a pop. "Didn't you make detective before you were thirty?" She pulled a rocks glass out of the cabinet and poured. "That's impressive, no matter how you managed it."

Maren turned down the flame under her pan and opened a bottle of buttery chardonnay she plucked from the door of the refrigerator. She poured two glasses, switching one of them for Darcy's vodka before she could protest and dumping it down the sink with a splash.

"What the hell?" Darcy said, watching the last of her vodka disappear down the drain in a swirl. "I was drinking that."

"If you tell me why you were drinking straight vodka, I'll give you this glass of California chardonnay. Which is considerably more nuanced, by the way."

"You want me to tell you why I drink the hard stuff?" Darcy shifted, looking everywhere but at Maren. "I don't have to do that."

"You certainly don't, and if you really want the vodka, I'll pour you another one right now." Maren handed her the glass of pale-gold wine, already hazing the crystal glass with condensation. "But you have a reason."

Darcy reluctantly balanced the glass on two fingers as she leaned against the counter. She looked pale, suddenly, and a bit off balance. Maren found something else to look at, giving her space to breathe, and waited.

"I guess it just takes the edge off." Darcy set the wineglass down and, surprisingly, met Maren's eyes. "Which sounds like a generic answer, but for me, it's exactly what happens." She hopped up on the counter to sit, her fingers tangled together like a knot in her lap. "I feel things. And sometimes I just need to not feel everything as it happens. It gets—"

"Overwhelming?"

"Yes, exactly." Darcy let out a slow breath. "How did you know that?"

"I may have had a conversation with Wilder today about what happened last night."

"Seriously?" Darcy bit her lip. "It's not like I'm hiding it, but sometimes it seems like it's just a drop in the bucket. I mean, yeah, now we know about Jessa, but I don't feel like we're any closer to the killer."

Maren took a sip of her wine and glanced back at the door to make sure they were alone before she continued. "Darcy, you're the reason we even knew where to look. Whoever left that ring in the display is absolutely connected to our case, and she's connected to that ring. None of us would have had a clue where to go from there if you hadn't been here."

"I just wish I could have gotten us more." Darcy's voice was soft as she let Maren's words sink in. "But I still don't know why you dumped out my vodka."

"I dumped it," Maren stepped up to where she was sitting on the counter and laid both palms lightly on Darcy's knees, "because

I like you." She paused, holding Darcy's gaze before she went on. "And I want to get to know you. The real you."

"Really?" Darcy smiled, picking up her wineglass. The reflection of the gold wine sparkled in her eyes. "Say more things like that."

Maren threw her head back and laughed. "Look. I can't imagine how it feels to be you, and if there was ever a good reason to hit the hard stuff, that has to be it." She paused. "But maybe lean on me a little, instead."

"I'll think about it," Darcy said, laying her hand over Maren's as she peered over her shoulder. "But let's keep that pan from bursting into flames first."

"Shit." Maren looked over her shoulder at the smoking pan and rushed to turn off the burner, holding the pan aloft to cool. "Hey. My jacket is hanging on the hook by the door. Dig around in the pocket until you find a bottle, and then bring it here."

Darcy gingerly reached into the jacket pocket and produced a tiny glass bottle. "Is this what you're talking about?"

"Exactly." Maren put the pan down on a different burner and poured some hot water from the kettle into a measuring cup on the counter. "Okay. I think we're ready for it."

"Is this the saffron?" Darcy held it up. "Maybe it's just the way you said it before that makes it sound sexy, but this looks like red thread in a bottle."

"It's just my accent, or so women tell me. Come here." Maren carefully started the flame underneath the pan again and stepped back. "Stand in front of me."

Darcy hesitated, then stepped between the stove and Maren. Maren held an open hand over the iron pan. "Put your hand about four inches up, like this." She held Darcy's hand under hers and positioned it over the empty pan, leaning down to whisper in her ear. "Now tell me when it feels a little intense, but not too scary hot."

"Okay." Maren felt Darcy hold her breath for a few seconds before she nodded. "I think...now."

Maren pulled out four tiny red strands of saffron from the bottle and dropped them in the hot pan. Instantly, the threads relaxed against the hot iron, and the aromatics warmed and deepened, the rich, spicy scent filling the room like a sudden haze of sultry Moroccan heat. Maren felt her breathe in as Darcy's shoulders relaxed against her.

"That smells amazing. How can something that tiny make such a difference?"

"That," Maren leaned down until her breath touched the slope of Darcy's neck, "is exactly my point."

Sudden loud footsteps started in the hall and skidded past the open kitchen door. Maren just caught who it was and stepped back, shifting the hot pan over the fire until Wilder realized she'd passed the kitchen and reappeared, out of breath and holding onto the doorframe.

"Hey, buddy." Maren smiled and picked up her wineglass. "Where's the fire?"

Wilder went straight to the dinner roster posted on the fridge and followed the calendar list down with her finger.

"Shit! I knew I was forgetting something. I'm cooking tonight." She stopped, looking around as she noticed the pan on the stove and the spices warming the air. "Wait. What's going on?" She leaned to the left to look past Maren to the sink full of cleaned seafood and rubbed her eyes. "I feel like I'm missing something."

"You're not missing anything, mate." Maren clicked off the heat and carefully slid the toasted saffron threads onto her knife blade, dropping them into the steaming glass of water on the counter where they instantly turned into a swirling kaleidoscope of sunset colors. "You were up all night, so I made an executive decision and grabbed some seafood to make a Spanish paella."

"Dude, seriously?" Wilder ran a hand through her hair, looking mesmerized by the saffron magic in the glass. "I could kiss you right now."

"Please don't." Maren laughed and dodged as Wilder made a joking play for her. "Just go grab a shower, or whatever it is you guys that look like fucking models do every day. Dinner is in forty-five minutes, and don't be late, or I'll send the heat after you." Maren looked pointedly at Darcy, then back at Wilder.

"Damn. Can't have that." Wilder winked at Darcy and disappeared down the hall. "I'll be back five minutes early."

❖

"So, I know there was no school today because of SAT testing." Wilder tore a slice of garlic bread off the crusty loaf in the center of the table and dipped it into the garlicky, rich wine sauce from the paella she'd just refilled her bowl with. "I'll go with you guys in the morning and see if we can get a lead on this alleged pedophile."

Hooper paused to squeeze a lemon over her pile of shelled mussels and popped one in her mouth. "Maren, this is literally the best meal I've eaten in ages. What the hell was it again?"

"Spanish paella. It's usually a bit more of a refined dish if you get it in a restaurant, but I tend to go rustic with it."

"*This* is rustic? It's gorgeous." Tala speared a shrimp and looked down the table. "And how'd you jam all that flavor in the seafood? When I make anything remotely similar, and by that, I mean plain shrimp and rice in the microwave, it tastes like I literally boiled it in boring." She bit into the tender shrimp, and her eyes fluttered closed. "And this is a world away, thank sweet baby Jesus."

"It wasn't complicated. We seared the shrimp in some chili oil and a Malden salt crust for just a few seconds, and the scallops I basted with butter and tarragon in a cast-iron pan." Maren edged two more scallops onto Darcy's plate. "Most people make paella all in one pan from start to end, but I cook the seafood and add it in just in the last few seconds to finish so it stays buttery and delicate."

"Well, I'm in buttery, delicate heaven." Hooper picked up her wineglass. "A toast to the dynamic dinner duo."

Everyone smiled and raised their glasses toward the middle with a flurry of clinks, but by the time the glasses made it back to the table, the doorbell had dinged twice, followed by a loud, impatient knock. Everyone froze when the front door slammed against the wall and footsteps started in the direction of the war room. Trobaugh and Hooper reached for their weapons and stood, along with Wilder, but by the time they'd gotten to their feet, a tall woman with a blond ponytail and too much makeup was striding toward them.

"She's fine," Wilder said, reholstering her gun with a quick glance around the table. "I'll take care of this."

"It's a little late for that, Wilder." The woman tossed her ponytail over her shoulder and shot her an icy stare. "I just heard what happened at the museum last night. My shop is on the other side of that building, and you couldn't even bother to give me a heads-up? What the actual fuck?"

Wilder closed her eyes for a second as if searching for composure and stepped away from the table. "Guys, I need to handle something. I'll be right back." She started to walk away, then paused and gestured at the woman in the doorway. "Everyone, this is Miranda Mason, my ex-wife."

Miranda gave the table a sweeping, disinterested glance until she caught sight of Tala, and her gaze intensified. "And what the hell is *she* doing here? I knew you had something going on with that one." Her voice pitched up to a level that could have shattered the wineglasses. "The very least you could have done for me is—"

"Nothing, Miranda. I owe you exactly nothing." Wilder took her by the arm and guided her down the hall. Everyone leaned in to watch as they rounded the corner and, from the sounds of it, stepped out onto the porch. The front door closed more gently this time but retained a definite slap that told the story.

Hooper pushed a plate of empty mussel shells the size of her head toward the center of the table. "That's what I love on a Friday night. A heaping plate of rustic paella and a shitload of dyke drama."

"Good God." Trobaugh squeezed Tala's shoulder and refilled her water glass. "What's her beef with you? Have you guys met in an oil-wrestling ring you haven't told anyone about or something?"

"If that's the case," Darcy stared down the table at Tala, "my money's on you. Not Godzilla in yoga pants out there."

Tala shook her head, tapping her fork on the edge of her plate. She started to say something, then reconsidered, placing her cutlery over her plate and glancing up with a tense smile. "Ignore her. She took one look at my badge when I walked into her little shop the other day and started putting together a story that doesn't exist."

"Doesn't exist, huh?" Trobaugh smiled in her direction, clinking the ice in her water glass for emphasis. "Wilder watches every move you make, and something tells me it has nothing to do with the case."

"True story. I've noticed too." Maren busted out two Snickers bars from her jacket pocket and tossed one across the table to Hooper, narrowly missing the open bottle of pinot grigio. "But last I heard, she's single. If the blond Amazonian makes another appearance like that again and sets her sights on you, I can tell you the rest of us won't be so polite."

Tala smiled despite herself, and everyone looked toward the door at the sound of footfalls headed back from the porch. Wilder came in and took her seat, reaching for the last piece of bread in the basket. She paused then and took a breath before she turned to Tala.

"Tala, I'm sorry about what she said to you. That was unacceptable. And I let her know it." She buttered one end of the bread and looked around the table, holding it aloft as if only then noticing the silence. "What?"

Wilder's phone she'd set beside her plate started to ring in response, vibrating in a winding circle on the wood tabletop like some sort of medieval serpent. She dropped the bread onto her plate and sighed, clicking on the phone halfway to her ear.

"Mason here." She was silent for just a few seconds, then shot up and grabbed the jacket on the back of her chair. "No. Don't do anything, and more importantly, don't say anything until we get there." She lowered her phone as she went to click it off and changed her mind, raising it back to her ear. "Hey, Robinson? You said it was the staff that called it in?" She motioned for everyone to get up, and they all grabbed their jackets in the same motion, checking weapons and badges as if it were a carefully choreographed dance. Wilder zipped up her jacket and looked around to find everyone locked, loaded, and waiting for her direction.

"Confiscate those phones. I don't want anyone else to know what's going on until we get there." Wilder paused, then looked back at the table. "What do you *mean* it's too late?"

CHAPTER ELEVEN

Wilder and Tala pulled into the parking lot of Salem High first, followed by the rest of the task force in Trobaugh and Hooper's Impala. Fortunately, they had the good sense to park a reasonable distance away when they saw Wilder had been spotted, then hung back. Wilder had planned to stay low-key, but the road to the high school was jammed with civilian vehicles and news trucks, and she'd had to slap her siren onto the roof of the Jeep and force her way in. Somehow, half the town had gotten the memo before them, and news trucks from Boston were already setting up in the parking lot.

The air was pitch-black and ominous around the artificial bubble of parking-lot floodlights, blinding yet still hazy at the edges. Someone had switched on the lights over the football field to the right for the news trucks that were setting up there, and a few onlookers were standing on the top level of outdoor bleachers with binoculars and cell phones recording exactly nothing. The temperature had dropped twenty degrees since noon, and the air held the crisp scent of snow lurking just beyond the lights.

"Well, so much for anonymity." Tala pulled on her hat as she nodded in the direction of a reporter running awkwardly toward them in heels, microphone in hand. A cameraman was close behind, and Wilder looked past them to see more reporters picking up the scent and following their lead. She leaned her head back in the seat and savored the last few seconds of silence.

"This is the understatement of the year, but I need to see if I can get a judge to sign a gag order for the press. Like, yesterday. We can't do our jobs if we have press tripping us up every two seconds." Wilder opened the door to step out of the Jeep, and the same reporter shoved a microphone in her face.

"Chief Mason? You are the acting chief of police here in Salem, correct?"

Wilder nodded, gesturing for her to give them space as they walked to the entrance. She almost reached back for Tala's hand but stopped herself just in time.

"What can you tell us about this horrifying situation here in Salem?" She pushed the microphone closer to Wilder's face and arched a painted-on eyebrow. "There are those terrible rumors on social media, but what can you tell us right now about what's going on in there?"

A quick glance over the reporter's shoulder told her several others were on their way, pushing through the crowds and trailed by cameramen. Groups of Salem residents standing around holding travel mugs and talking had now noticed she'd pulled up as well and started toward her. She spotted Robinson at the entrance to the gym and several police cruisers arriving from the other direction. She spun her hand in a wordless circle for him to have cars surround the building and turned back to the reporter.

"We do not have an official statement at this time, but we may be holding a press conference in the future." She clicked the lock on her Jeep and motioned for Tala to walk ahead of her. Four more reporters had reached them in the time it had taken for her to get an initial read on what they were dealing with, and she didn't trust them not to get too close to Tala from behind. If they did, Wilder ran the risk of losing her cool, so she decided to avoid that situation, at least temporarily. The press had their place, and she understood that the public had a right to know when there were facts to report, but Wilder had never had much patience for them.

Darcy, Trobaugh, and Hooper had already discreetly reached the door of the gymnasium, where Robinson let them slip in, but to anyone paying attention, their badges were clearly visible.

"So much for anonymity," Wilder muttered as she and Tala walked as quickly as possible to join them at the door. She paused when they got there, letting Tala go in first, hanging back to get the scoop from Robinson.

"Do we have Steele on scene yet?"

Steele was the officer she always brought out if a crowd was threatening to get out of control. He had a level of patience with the panicked citizens that Wilder did not, which had come in handy more than once in the last few months. He was handsome in a California-soap-opera kind of way, and smooth as silk in front of the camera. All of that was of no use if he wasn't someone she could rely on, but they'd joined the force the same year, and by this point, she would trust him with anything.

Robinson pushed his beard aside and spoke into the radio on his shoulder, then just as quickly clicked it to silent. "He's just pulling up."

"Have him take over out here. You were first on the scene, and I need you in there with us."

"Copy that, Chief." He scanned the parking lot over Parker's shoulder. "I see his cruiser now, so I'll brief him on what's happening when he gets past those reporters." Two massive news trucks turned into the parking lot as they spoke, and Robinson rolled his eyes. "Give me a minute to make sure everything's secure out here, and I'll see you in there."

"Before I go, do you have any idea who leaked this?"

Robinson glanced out at the growing crowd. "Obviously Salem PD has given out only minimal details, but some locals created a Facebook page after the first body was found so they can help find the serial killer from their couches, apparently. The janitors got here a couple of hours ago and, instead of calling the police, tromped all over the crime scene and posted a picture immediately."

"On *social media?*"

"Correct." Robinson held out his arm to deter a group of locals that looked like they were headed for the gym entrance, then turned back to Wilder and went on. "By the time they called 911, most of Salem had seen it, and then of course the press got ahold of it, and all hell broke loose."

Wilder waved away a new reporter headed for the door. "Before that happened, when was the last time someone besides them had been in these buildings?"

"We're going to have to take a look at the security footage, but according to the witnesses, the gym and auditorium had been locked up all day."

Wilder paused. "Okay. Can you get someone to collect that footage sooner rather than later?"

"Yes, ma'am. I'm already on it." Robinson waved Steele over to the door. "And I have CSI en route. Boston is lending us their top units for this one."

Wilder walked into the gymnasium, at least as far as she could before she felt a hand on her shoulder from behind and spun around. A reporter was behind her, but he must have found an alternate entrance and had some damn good timing because Robinson certainly wouldn't have let him sneak in. He was paunchy, with steely eyes and a forgettable face. He also needed to get that damn hand off her shoulder.

Wilder looked pointedly down at his hand and stared until he dropped it and yanked a rumpled notepad out of his shirt pocket. Reporters usually went everywhere with a camera when the news was this big, so seeing him walk up with just a notebook struck her as odd. Wilder glanced around to check if someone might be lurking in the background, but she saw only the rest of the task force standing around under the far basketball net, waiting for her.

"Chief Mason, Howard Banyan here from the *Boston Globe*. Can I ask you some questions about what you're walking into here?"

"I appreciate that you're just doing your job." Wilder kept her voice even. "But I have to get in there and do mine before I can give you any information at all."

"But what about the fact that the information leaked on social media has compromised your investigation?"

Wilder glanced over at Trobaugh and Hooper and barely resisted the urge to roll her eyes. "Our investigation is ongoing, and that's all I'm going to say."

Banyan nodded and started to head for the door, but just as Wilder was turning around, she heard him stop. "These murders are looking more and more like a part of Salem's past they'd rather forget." He paused, scanning the gym as though memorizing it. "Hopefully the killer doesn't feel he has to make that similarity clear with additional murders."

Wilder watched as he left, then locked the door behind him. Something wasn't setting well with her about that guy, but she'd have to come back to it. She turned around and walked toward the others, breathing in the familiar scent of the varnished wooden court and the hint of leather and scuffed rubber that always hovered in the air of a high school gym. One of her officers was talking to two middle-aged women in the glassed-in coach's office on one end of the court, but besides them and the task force, the gym was empty and eerily silent.

"Are we here for a pickup game, or what? I mean, I know you wanted to wait till we got here to give us the lowdown, but..." Hooper looked longingly at the rack of basketballs to the side of the court. "Is there some action here?"

"I'll let Robinson give us the details when he gets in here, but let's check the locks on the other two exits. The last thing we need is more civilians getting in here and muddying up evidence, if there is any."

"I already left them open, with a sign that says PRESS ENTRANCE." Trobaugh grinned in Wilder's direction. "I'm kidding. We checked them first thing when we walked in. You're hating the crowds, aren't you?"

"How can you tell?" Wilder rubbed her temples as she spoke, glancing back at the side door to the gym as the door swung open. Robinson stepped through and locked the deadbolt again as soon as it shut. "I'm a detective. I'm supposed to be in the background, not the spotlight."

Robinson's boots squeaked at a ridiculous volume across the court as he approached, which broke the tension somewhat. He strode past them toward the back exit of the gym without even glancing back.

"The auditorium is connected to the gym." Wilder thought out loud. "It's not even in here. Robinson did that to throw off the press."

"What is 'it'?" Hooper looked confused as they filed through the door and down the hall. "When do we find out what's going on here? I feel like we're walking around on the set of *Law and Order* or something."

Robinson opened the final door at the end of the hall and let the task force go in first. The auditorium itself was dark, empty, and cavernous, a sudden switch from the chaos they'd just come from. Every footstep echoed against the walls as they walked down the center aisle toward the matte-black main stage. Robinson stopped at the lighting control panel. A deep click of the stage lights stopped them, the silence reverberating around and slowly sifting to the floor as the body hanging above the stage appeared like a ghost out of the darkness.

"Holy shit." Trobaugh led the pack as they walked cautiously down the aisle, stopping about ten feet from the edge of the stage. "It's safe to say that whoever our killer is, he's turning up the heat."

Tala's gaze was steady and locked onto the man hanging from the lighting scaffolding as she pulled out her phone, found a picture from the previous night, and turned it around to Wilder. Except Wilder didn't need to see it. She knew the museum by heart, and the only thing stolen from that exhibit was the length of rope from the noose for the witch-trial executions. It was a very distinctive handmade rope, over three hundred years old, but as thick as her wrist and still as strong as it would have been during the witch trials.

Robinson went to answer a knock at the door as everyone snapped on one of the pairs of latex gloves they kept in their pockets but hoped they wouldn't have to use.

Less than a minute later Robinson stuck his head through the door and looked back at Wilder. "Chief. CSI and the coroner are here. Do you want me to send them in?"

"Have them give us a few minutes, okay? Just brief them on the situation and emphasize the need for discretion." Wilder looked back up at the stage. "And in the meantime, will you work your magic with the lights and flood the stage with everything they've got?"

Robinson went to work, and Wilder turned to Darcy. "What do you need from us to help you…do what you do?"

Darcy smiled. "I don't think anyone has ever asked me that before." She paused, with a glance at Maren, who nodded in support. "Maybe just some space. I'll need to walk around by myself for a minute if I have a hope of getting anything that will help, and there's no guarantee."

"I understand that. Just let us know what you need, and we'll make it happen." She turned to Tala. "What about you? What do you need to get a handle on this guy? What can we do to support you?"

"Maybe some paper and a pen?"

Wilder grabbed a sheet off a clipboard on the sound booth, smoothed out a practice schedule and turned it over, then handed them to Tala with the pen from her jacket pocket. Wilder ran both hands through her hair as she took a breath, then flashed Trobaugh and Hooper a smile. "Okay. Now that the FBI superstars have what they need, how about the three of us mere mortals check it out?"

"I don't know why, but I feel like that's a compliment, mate." Maren started toward the stage stairs. "I'll be a mere mortal with you lot any damn day."

Tala and Darcy went in their own directions, so they carefully climbed the stairs at stage left and right, then onto the hardwood. Robinson hit every stage light at once, and the beams glinting off the polished boards were blinding for the first few seconds as they examined the scene for anything the killer might have left behind, either as a message or a mistake.

"What I want to know," Trobaugh sounded thoughtful as she looked up to the noose that was knotted on the scaffolding. "Is how the killer got him up there. His feet are a good three feet off the ground, and he has to weigh around 165, maybe even more."

Hooper shaded her eyes and looked toward the ceiling. "Don't these catwalks at the top move around so the lighting techs can adjust the lights during a production?"

"Yeah. I think I remember that from my high school years. They aren't super high tech, but I believe that main arm above us swings over to the ladder at the back of the stage." Wilder pulled the handle she found just enough to move it an inch. "And two people can definitely fit on that catwalk."

"Still, though, our killer has to be one hell of a big dude to drag a body up there, over a hundred fifty pounds of dead weight, and get him into that noose. Unless this one is different, and hanging was the primary cause of death." Trobaugh stepped closer to look for obvious injection sites. "We won't know until the coroner's report, I guess, but how did the killer lure him out here and get a noose around his neck? It doesn't make sense."

Darcy climbed the stairs onto the stage and walked over to the body, keeping her hand only an inch away. Her eyes were closed, and the stage fell silent. Well, except for Hooper, who leaned in Maren's direction. "She took her glove off, man. What the hell is she doing?"

Maren stepped back, as did the others. "You'll see. Just let her work."

It was a long minute more, but finally Darcy put her hand back in her pocket, her eyes still closed. "Check his left pocket for a—"

Everyone but Darcy jumped when a phone rang, the sound echoing back and forth across the stage like a demented racquetball, going on for what seemed like forever before Maren stepped up, gingerly reached into his left jacket pocket, and pulled out the vibrating phone.

Wilder nodded in answer to her silent question. "Answer it."

Maren hit the button to answer and put it on speakerphone, holding the handset on the flat of her hand.

"Why haven't you been answering your phone?" The voice on the other line was emotional and thin, with an undercurrent of barely suppressed panic. "I've got the ring. Can you pick me up?"

Tala's head snapped up as she walked to the center of the stage, her gaze fixed on Darcy.

"Hello?" The voice on the other end of the line trailed off, and she sighed. "Scott?"

Wilder stepped up and took the phone. "Hi. This is Wilder Mason. Who am I speaking with?"

There was silence on the other end of the line for the space of a breath. "Why are you answering Scott's phone?"

Wilder looked at Darcy and held her gaze. The three of them had last heard that voice only a few hours ago.

❖

"Dude. If those reporters don't chill, you're gonna have another murder to look into." Maren squeezed into the back of the Jeep with Hooper and slammed the door shut, which didn't do much to muffle the media still shouting on the other side of the windows. "Although at least I don't have to be photographed in the spinster mobile over there. Lucky for us it got a flat and I was saved."

"I told one of the officers to just return it to the airport after she changes it, if that's okay with you, Trobaugh." Wilder started the engine and revved it a bit for good measure to clear the human roadblocks. "We'll all be safer getting places either in my rig or a cruiser at this point."

"Yeah. No point pretending they don't know who we are now." Trobaugh looked at her watch and relaxed her head back onto the headrest. "God, it's late. Will Tala and Darcy be okay getting home?"

"Robinson's going to drop them off himself, and I've already radioed back to the officer at the cabin entrance to stop the press at my property line if they decide to camp out there." She flipped on her lights and pulled carefully through the crowd and back onto the road. "I mean, I get it. They're just doing their jobs, and it's not like I thought we could keep a lid on it forever—"

"But *damn*." Maren rolled her eyes. "Those reporters could all be Miss Universe finalists, and I'd still want them to fuck off a little bit."

Trobaugh pulled a pack of butterscotch lifesavers out of her jacket pocket and peeled off a chunk of three. "So, what's the plan for the rest of the night? I don't mean to be a snowflake here, but I'm shattered."

Hooper nodded enthusiastically from the back seat. "And hungry. I may literally starve before we get back to the cabin."

Wilder rubbed her eyes with one hand and smacked the glove-box door with another. "I get it. It's after one a.m., and as much as I want to track this guy down, we've got to get some rest, or we won't be worth anything."

Trobaugh tossed a power bar over her shoulder to Maren, who let it drop beside her like someone had flung fresh roadkill in her direction. "I thought I heard you on the phone earlier. You called a counselor to pay a visit to Jessa in the morning?"

"I did, and I've got a unit outside her house as well. I don't know what's going on inside with her father, and it's better safe than sorry. The social worker at Salem High plans to give her a ring in the morning and hopefully meet her away from the house. She's not in trouble. She was fifteen when this started, and none of this is her fault. And to be fair, she doesn't have to talk about it now. I'm just concerned about her."

"We can't do anything, really." Maren lowered her window and leaned out into the night air. "It's not like there's anyone to prosecute at this point."

Wilder and Trobaugh both turned to look at Maren in the back seat.

She picked the power bar up by the corner of the package and flung it back into the open glove box. "What? I'm just sayin'."

Wilder turned into the all-night pizza drive-thru and rolled her eyes. "But who knew about that ring and decided to go vigilante to make sure it got returned instead of making someone aware of his possibly ongoing behavior with the younger girl?"

"Yeah. Didn't you guys say she told someone at her university and a friend here in Salem who goes to her church? We should check them out if she'll identify them, as well as check with Darcy for her take on this, but I have a hard time thinking that Jessa is involved here." Trobaugh lowered her window a few inches and took a deep breath of the cool night air that swirled into the Jeep. "From how you described that conversation, she seemed genuinely upset that he didn't return the ring himself, right? And he was already dead at that point, we think. So that doesn't make any sense."

"And what the hell is the point they're making with the Witch Trial Museum rope?" Maren lowered her window the rest of the way and leaned out of the Jeep to get a closer look at the flickering neon pizza menu. The rich scent of bubbling cheese and oregano wafted toward them from the open kitchen door in the back of the pizzeria. Gold light spilled out onto the concrete slab outside the door, and a skinny guy in a knit beanie and a stained white apron wandered out as the Jeep idled. He shook a cigarette loose from a pack of them and sat down on a red milk crate, leaning back against the brick wall and watching the gray twist of smoke from the burning end of his cigarette rise into the darkness. "I mean, there's a reason they broke into a glass case in the museum and not the local hardware store."

After Maren had ordered her weight in whole pies for the cabin, they made their way carefully back, each of them staring at a different mirror to be sure they weren't being tailed. The energy in the Jeep was silent and watchful; even Maren wasn't digging into the pizza boxes on her lap. Whoever this guy was, he was making a point of bringing in the witch trials, and Wilder didn't want to revisit anything about them. Anyone with even a perfunctory grasp of history knew this situation was bad enough without dragging in that element.

As they approached the cabin, the moonlight sifted through the maples lining the drive, landing in pale pewter slices on the gravel below. When Wilder opened the door, her breath froze and hung in the air, and she looked up as an owl swooped past and landed on one of the attic eaves facing the car. It turned its head slowly from the direction of the lake to stare at them as the rest of them piled out of the Jeep, then shot out a piercing hoot that sent the pizza boxes flying into the air until Maren managed to catch them all in a wild stack just inches from the ground.

"Little jumpy there, aren't ya, cowboi?" Trobaugh laughed as Wilder double-checked the Jeep locks. "I thought you'd be used to all the scary beasts from hanging out down under. Looks to me like you just about had a heart attack over a little fluffy owl."

Maren handed the pizza boxes to Hooper and playfully punched at Trobaugh. "Call me crazy, but spending the night hunting a serial killer will do that to ya."

Tala opened the front door and peeked around the edge. "Are you guys coming inside with those boxes, or do we have to draw you a map?"

By the time they made it through the door, Tala and Darcy were already carrying plates and parmesan into the war room, where they just pushed all the binders and stacks of paper to one end and dove in. Trobaugh and Hooper loaded up their plates and headed upstairs right away, saying something vague about date night, and Maren smiled when Darcy slid a second slice onto her plate. After a couple of pieces, Wilder leaned back gingerly in her chair and winced.

"What's wrong there, twitchy?" Maren winked in her direction and reached for another slice of pepperoni. "I thought gym rats like you were made of stone."

"I slept wrong last night, I guess." Wilder rubbed her neck with the heel of her hand. It felt like running her hand across the steel bumper on an antique car; nothing she'd done to stretch it out during the day had helped coax the muscles to let go of their grip. "I usually go to the gym most days and sleep in an actual bed, so I think my body is just having trouble adjusting."

Darcy looked up from cutting her slice into tiny squares with her knife and fork. "What do you mean 'sleep in an actual bed'?"

Tala popped a crispy slice of pepperoni into her mouth and smiled in Wilder's direction. "Wilder's been nice enough to let me have the bed. She's slept on the couch since we've been here."

"What?" Maren arched an eyebrow. "You guys scared you can't keep your hands off each other?" She folded up her next slice end to end and looked at Wilder. "I mean, no offense, but we're going to be here for a damn minute, so ya gotta work that out, mate."

"Not to veer away from this fascinating topic that's none of our business." Darcy threw Maren a look. "But what did the surveillance footage at the high school tell us? Anything yet?"

"I've got two tech guys on it now, and I had the officers send the digital files to Boston headquarters, where they have better equipment. They've been going over every minute of it since we got there tonight, but nothing useful's coming up yet." She dropped the crust from her last slice onto her plate, staring at it for a moment before she went on. "I mean, Salem High doesn't exactly have a high-tech system, to be fair, but we should be able to get something useful, and they're going over yesterday's footage now." Wilder cracked open another bottle of sparkling water and refilled the glasses. "The actual high school students are low priority to me as far as suspects, unless you guys think I'm overlooking something. This is a pretty sophisticated killer, and the historical undercurrents here are deep. The killer is bringing in the witch trials, and I just don't see an eighteen-year-old kid pulling it off."

"Yeah. Besides the actual strength it would take to get the bodies into the positions we've found them in." Maren unzipped her fleece jacket and shrugged it off, tossing it over the back of the chair beside her. "So, they're going to send you stills of the adults going in and out of the entrances for the last three days? At the very least maybe we can see if our drama teacher arrived with anyone." Maren shook her head, pausing in a way that made her voice sound suddenly thin. "I don't know, just *something*."

Wilder nodded. "A camera is pointed at the parking lot of the auditorium, but there are so many ways to get between the buildings without going outside in view of the cameras. Our perp could literally have walked into any part of the high school and made his way into the auditorium without the few cameras that pick him up outside. We just have to hope he didn't."

"What did the coroner say to you tonight about time of death?" Tala pushed her plate toward the center of the table and closed the empty pizza box closest to her, dropping it on the end of the table. "I mean, I know she can't be exact at the scene, but did she give you an idea?"

"She did. She thought he was probably killed in the early hours of Wednesday morning. The auditorium was locked at that time because of the testing the next day, so that puts us at about forty-eight hours, give or take, since the murder." Wilder's phone pinged four times in quick succession, and all four of them stared at it until Wilder picked it up. She turned it around to the table. "These are the stills. I told them to put a rush on the ones from that period."

Maren leaned in. "Damn. Could it be any grainier? I can barely see their faces." She looked up at Wilder. "Do you recognize any of them?"

"Well, the first one is a no-brainer." Darcy pointed out the jacket on the first man to walk up to the auditorium entrance from the parking lot. "See his jacket? The left cuff was turned up there and also when we found him. That's Scott Fardulis, our victim."

"Hang on. That could be anyone." Maren pulled a pair of readers out of her pocket and plopped them on her face. "Obviously the glasses aren't mine. I borrowed these from an actual old person, but this deserves a closer look."

"She's right." Tala pointed at his shoes. "One of his shoes was untied when we found him. I remember because it looked odd just hanging down between him and the stage." She pulled the phone closer and pointed near the bottom of the grainy footage. "Look. The laces were trailing behind him when he was walking up to the door."

"And just at a glance, the rest of the clothes fit what he was wearing when we found him too." Wilder fired off a text to the techs that had sent the photos, then sat back in her seat and wrapped her hand carefully around her neck. "I'll take a closer look, but I sent the techs a photo of Howard Banyon that I got from his vague-as-hell LinkedIn profile. He's that reporter from the *Boston Globe* that accosted me on the way into the gym that night. I'd like to know what entrance he used and how long he'd been there, but he doesn't show up anywhere." Wilder shook her head. "Let's move on though. Anything else come to mind?"

Darcy looked at Tala, and they both leaned back in their chairs. "Call me crazy," Darcy said, taking the last sip of her water and raising an eyebrow in Wilder's direction as she pointed at the second still photo on the phone. "But isn't that the blond nutjob that charged in here earlier when we were eating?"

"You know." Tala tapped her thumb on the table and met Wilder's gaze with the barest hint of a smile, her words landing between them one by one. "The one you were married to?"

Wilder squinted at the photo and nodded reluctantly. "Maybe. But from the date and time stamp, this is Wednesday, and she has cheerleading practice with the varsity squad every week." She looked around the table and waited, but no one said anything, so she went on. "She went to Baylor on a cheer scholarship and was a captain then, so she's always volunteered to coach the high school team." She paused, her voice slightly higher when she continued, as if someone might be squeezing it. "They went to nationals last year."

The silence lingered, and finally, Maren looked around the table. "Who's gonna say it?" She waited a few seconds, then answered her own question. "Me? Fine." She shifted her seat and looked down the table at Wilder. "You married a blond, cheerleading captain who makes fudge for a living?"

"You've got me there." Wilder almost laughed, then winced as she held the side of her neck. "But that's not nearly as interesting as the fact that the FBI had to send Trobaugh and Hooper to yank you off a cruise where someone with their tits out was giving you a free lap dance."

"Well, that's just a blatant lie, mate." Maren laughed, then glanced at the nonexistent watch on her wrist and stood up, stretching both arms toward the ceiling with a leisurely yawn. "It was certainly *not* free."

"Wait. Don't tell me anything else about that little scenario." Darcy stacked the plates and headed into the kitchen. "I'm barely living with her now."

Wilder caught Tala's eye and nodded toward them a few seconds later as the two of them walked down the hall to the staircase, Maren's hand on Darcy's shoulder, pulling her closer. At least one good thing was coming out of this investigational shitshow.

Wilder put her phone down on the table and clicked it off. "Okay. They're going to enhance all the stills overnight and try to match them with the license plates from the cars in the parking lot." She sighed, rubbing her temples with the pads of her fingers.

"We probably won't be able to catch all of them, depending on the angles when they drove in, but I'll have them work with the staff there at the high school to see if we can get a better lead on who's who. If we can narrow down the pool of adults, at least we might have a start."

Tala started to get up and paused. "Your neck is really hurting you, isn't it?"

"Nah." Wilder straightened up and gathered the remaining glasses with one hand. She stood, motioning for Tala to hit the lights on the way out. "No. I'll be fine. I just need a good night's sleep without a robbery or body popping up."

CHAPTER TWELVE

Tala stepped out of the shower and wrapped herself in a towel, swiping her hand across the hazy mirror. She pulled on the hoodie, underwear, and sweat shorts she'd taken into the bathroom with her, then dug in her toiletry bag for a small amber bottle that had migrated to the very bottom. She poured a small pool of the fragrant palo-santo oil into her palm, then ran her fingers through the damp length of her hair, letting it drop down her back in a loose twist when she was done.

Her phone buzzed against the counter, and she picked it up. It was Takoda. A picture of his new barracks in Alaska. The phone pinged again, this time with a text. *Don't think I've forgotten that this is because of you. Love you, sis.*

Tala bit her lip. Takoda had been more her child than a sibling, and when they put them into foster care on the reservation as kids, she'd walked the three miles between their separate houses to stand under his bedroom window and see him every day. Every night when she went to sleep, she told herself that she'd shielded him from the truth of what happened, but she knew it wasn't true, even though he refused to talk to her about it afterward. He'd never said one word, asked one question, or even acknowledged what happened to them. It was like he'd directed all his energy into pretending that night had ever existed.

He'd struggled with alcoholism after he'd barely graduated from high school, drifting from one minimum-wage job to another, until Tala drove back to the reservation and pulled him off someone's stained, dank couch in the middle of the night. He reeked of bottom-shelf vodka and wasn't wearing a shirt, just dirty jeans that hung off his hips and looked like they didn't belong to him. A childhood friend had called her late the night before and told her she needed to get back to the reservation and find Dakota, but wouldn't say why, just hung up and didn't answer when she called again. She'd grabbed her keys and driven to the airport, shoved him into the car as red dawn spilled across the reservation dirt, and didn't speak to him again until she pushed him through the door to her Boston flat. She didn't speak because she had nothing to say. They both knew it didn't matter what happened. It mattered what you did in spite of what happened.

That night had hovered between glittering gray sleet and snow, when she was ten and he was three, waking to the gunshot and its echo ricocheting around the walls. Then running, her bare feet pounding on the bare plywood floor, the nicked steel nails scratching the soles of her feet. She launched herself at the crack in his door and fell through it, but Takoda was still asleep in his bed where she'd left him, tangled in the mismatched sheets, his fat baby hands twitching with every soft breath. She exhaled every bit of air in her lungs, and they filled back up with a cool expanse of relief she knew she'd do anything to hold on to.

Tala lay with her cheek against the rough shag carpet in his room, listening to his breath move, somehow light and rough at the same time, in and out of his lungs. By the time she got up, pale yellow dawn was tinting the frost on the inside of the window in Takoda's room. She left quietly and watched one foot fall in front of the other as she made her way down to her parents' room at the end of the hall. The doorknob was jarringly cold under her palm as she inched open the hollow, wood-paneled door. The acrid sting of gunpowder still hung in the air like evil, and black blood pooled underneath them, seeping into the carpet in uneven trails. Her hand fell from the doorknob and bounced against her leg. She felt frozen, breathing in the sharp gunpowder air and cloying iron scent of blood that stuck to her skin. The air was too warm, too close, and she watched herself vomit onto her feet, as if it was happening to someone else. She shut the door and sank down in the hall.

No one found them for eight days. She fed Takoda the remaining food in the house, tucking him into bed every night, making up colorful stories about the sudden trip their parents had to go on in the middle of the night. Finally, someone from her school knocked on the front door. She knew it was the end, or at least her body did. Every muscle gripped the one beside it until her body felt like stone, but she didn't answer. Then it was the police, and a battering ram was coming through the door, shards of cheap, thin wood flying like arrows around them. She curled around her brother and stayed that way until they dragged him away.

A knock at the bathroom door stopped her heart and jerked her back into the present.

"Tala, are you okay in there?" Wilder's voice was gentle. "Is it okay if I open the door?"

Tala nodded, and Wilder opened it at that second, as if she'd heard her. It wasn't until her forehead touched Wilder's chest that the tears came, and Wilder didn't speak, didn't ask or try to make it go away. She just stood there, in the windstorm of memory with her until it faded and fell around their feet. Tala reached up and wrapped her arms around Wilder's neck. Wilder picked her up, carried her to bed, and turned out the lamp.

"Stay."

"I'm not going anywhere." Wilder's words were as soft as ash in the darkness. "I'll be right over there."

Tala turned over to face her. Just enough moonlight was streaming through the window for her to find Wilder's arm, and she brushed her fingertips across her wrist. Wilder tangled her fingers slowly into Tala's and waited.

"Stay here with me."

❖

"Wake up, people." Maren tried the doorknob which was, thankfully, locked. "I'm making breakfast, and we've got a killer to string up." She paused. "I mean catch."

Tala turned in Wilder's arms, and Wilder pulled the duvet back over them. The room was flooded with sunlight, a golden backdrop for the dust motes floating in the air as if the light was slowly moving river water. She felt Tala's fingertips across her shoulder and the warmth of her breath in the hollow of her neck.

"Um... Wilder?"

"Yes?"

Wilder felt her smile. Tala already knew the answer, but she asked the question anyway. "Why is neither of us wearing a shirt?"

Wilder reached over to the side of the bed and hooked Tala's hoodie with her thumb. "Because you pulled yours off in the middle of the night, so I did too. I didn't want you to be the only one when you woke up."

Wilder's breath caught when she felt Tala's hand, as light as breath, across her nipples. She dropped the hoodie onto the bed and trailed her fingers down Tala's naked back, feeling her heart speed up against her chest. "You're holding your breath." Wilder traced the shape of her lips gently with her thumb. "And here I thought you only did that for blond Instagram influencers."

Maren knocked again. "I better hear you two rustling around in there, or I'm going to pick the lock."

"Give us five to throw some clothes on." Tala sat up and pulled on her hoodie, and Wilder rolled out of the covers, sniffing the air. "Do I smell bacon?"

"No, dude. You smell salted maple-butter crepes with peppered hickory bacon." Maren sniffed. "Whole different beast."

Tala's face lit up. "Is this a good time to mention that we're in love with you? Both of us?"

"No need." Maren laughed, and they listened to her footsteps down the hall. "I already knew."

Five minutes later they had pulled themselves together enough to go downstairs, and Wilder closed the door to their room behind her as they headed for the stairs.

"Wilder?" Tala stopped at the first stair and turned around. "I feel like I should tell you what I—"

"Tala." Wilder slid her hand around Tala's waist and pulled her close. "You don't have to explain anything."

"But I don't want you to think that I..."

"That you what?" Wilder whispered into her ear. "That you're human? That you might have normal reactions to fucked-up situations?" Wilder smiled as she felt Tala's head against her shoulder. "All I know is that I was lucky to be there." She paused. "That you *let* me be there."

Tala melted into her for a few long seconds before she followed Wilder down the stairs, where Darcy was sitting on the counter, contentedly nibbling a slice of thick, crispy bacon. She was wearing Maren's jeans with the rip in the knee, and Wilder considered teasing her about it as she pulled a stack of plates out of the cupboard, but Darcy had looked so happy in the last few days that she thought better of it and went to set the table in the war room.

Trobaugh and Hooper were already there. Trobaugh was setting out rocks glasses with a pitcher of fresh orange juice and had placed a tiny dish of melted butter with a silver spoon in the center of the table, which was a stark contrast to the haphazard pile of cluttered cutlery dropped in a basket beside it. A rogue spoon lost the battle with gravity and pinged onto the table, as if to underscore the injustice.

"Let me guess." Wilder passed out the plates. "Hoop was in charge of the silverware."

"One job." Trobaugh rolled her eyes to the ceiling and closed them in defeat. "I gave her one job."

"And I did it in five seconds." Hooper sank into one of the chairs and stretched one arm out languidly, then the other. "I believe that's what we call efficiency, kids." She yawned, pushing up the sleeves of her fleece in anticipation when Maren rounded the corner with a warming dish of crepes and an overflowing platter of bacon. "The first lesson is free, but you'll have to pay for any further expert instruction."

Five minutes later, everyone was digging into gorgeous, buttery crepes so light they melted the second they hit your tongue. A decadent salted-maple glaze glossed the tops of the crepes Maren folded onto everyone's plates and lazily crept to the edges of the crispy bacon slices on the side, giving them a uniquely sweet and salty crunch. Even Hooper was unusually quiet as she communed like a blissful yogi with her personal pile of bacon.

"This meal is so beautiful I hate to ruin it with shop talk." Tala reached over to the side table and plucked out her notebook. "But I think yesterday gave us some important clues about the psychology of our killer."

"Yeah. That I've been barking up the wrong tree. I assumed this was someone targeting women," Hooper used her knife to push a translucent amber river of syrup onto her last bit of crepe. "And now it's obvious that it's something deeper than that."

"Hit me with the shop talk." Trobaugh nodded, picking up a slice of bacon off Hooper's pile and dropping it onto her plate. "Because I'm not ashamed to say this last victim threw me for a loop."

"You're not the only one," Tala smiled across the table and opened her notebook. "I know I'm supposed to be the profiler, but I think it's going to take all of us to get a handle on this guy."

Wilder nudged her plate toward the center of the table. "Listen. I've been thinking about this rope that was stolen from the museum and then later used to hang Fardulis. Why go to the potential risk of breaking into the building and shattering the exhibit just to use that rope if you're not making a major statement there?" She leaned over to the stack of notebooks behind her and grabbed a pen as well. "He obviously wants us to connect these murders to the witch trials, but why?"

Hooper topped up her glass of orange juice from the pitcher. "Weren't men executed too, back then? Not just women?"

Wilder nodded. "That's right. A lot of people think only women were involved, but one man, Giles Corey, in 1692, was one of the last to die."

Darcy gathered up everyone's plates with Maren and stopped before she reached the door. "If only one man died back then, maybe we're looking at the same pattern now." She shifted the plates in her arms and nearly dropped the syrup pitcher before Maren tucked it into the warming dish she was carrying away. "How many people died in the witch trials?"

Everyone looked at Wilder, who leaned over to the whiteboard and wrote the number at the top.

"Holy shitballs, mate." Maren took a step back, plates balanced on both arms. "Seventeen?"

Maren and Darcy left to put the dishes away, and Hooper wiped the whiteboards clean except for the ominous number at the top. "Listen. I agree with Darcy. For whatever reason, this bastard is mirroring the trials, and apparently enjoying the ride. I think the Fardulis murder was the tip of the iceberg there, and he'll start killing women again."

"Let's strip back here and go over everything we know about our victims. They have to be connected to our killer somehow, and right now they're all we've got." Tala caught the dry-erase marker Hooper tossed her and walked over to the whiteboard. "Trobaugh and Hooper, you guys have been digging up everything you can find on them, correct?"

"Yep. We've done a deep dive on their social-media accounts, talked to family and friends, and basically searched for everything that might be useful." Hooper looked up at Tala. "Fair warning though. I don't think we uncovered any bombshells. And it hasn't been immediately obvious how they're connected except that they all have deep ties to Salem."

"Okay," Wilder tapped her water glass with her thumb as she spoke. "Let's get some details on the board. Maybe something will pop out at us once we're all looking at the same thing. Let's start with the first victim, Chesney Micheals." She watched as Tala wrote her name on the board. "She's the only one that had a minor arrest record, but nothing major, no felonies."

"I think the most serious issue was a ticket for solicitation, so we know she may have dabbled in sex work." Hooper licked her thumb and paged through her notes. "And when we checked the second victim's work records, Miriam Bartsmouth—"

"She was the midwife?" Darcy looked up from the paperwork in front of her.

"That's right. The manager at her practice, Nina Watts, was kind enough to cross-check some records for us, and we found that Chesney Micheals was listed as a patient of hers. Of course, we don't have any other details, but at least we can assume they've crossed paths."

"I know Nina. Her husband is one of the two vets in town. She and my ex, Miranda, were close." Wilder looked up, pen spinning slowly through her fingers. "Was that appointment recent?"

"She hasn't been back in Salem for that long, so probably, and we barely got that information out of her. She'd tell us only that it was within the last month."

Hooper got up to grab the coffee carafe and anticipated the next question. "She wasn't pregnant, though. We called the medical examiner to be sure, so I'm not positive why she would have been there."

Wilder nodded. "Miriam has been known to unofficially see patients in the past who didn't have insurance if they had a concern she could help with. She asked me off the record a few years ago if she could potentially get into trouble doing that, and I told her to err on the side of caution. Knowing her personality, though, it wouldn't surprise me if she'd still offer advice if she could, and Chesney probably knew that."

Tala finished jotting that point on the board and drew a line to connect Miriam and Chesney. "That could be a coincidence, but maybe not."

Wilder leaned back in her chair. "Look. I've got something else that may or may not be important. The morning we found Miriam in the park, I asked her husband Matthew to come in so we could ask him some questions, which is standard practice. He was my obvious first choice, and we all know anyone is capable of anything, but I didn't see anything that day but shock and grief. He's also a police dispatcher, and he was on shift when Miriam was murdered. I confirmed with his logins and even the security surveillance."

"It's hard to get a better alibi than that." Hooper paused. "But I'm guessing there's something else?"

"Yeah. It gets a little more interesting at this point." Wilder pushed her cup over to Trobaugh, who was holding the coffee carafe. "Miriam was having an affair. Matthew got wind of it and tracked the guy down, and there was an altercation at his house about two weeks ago. No one got hurt, but everyone in town heard about it within an hour." Wilder paused. "Other than that, Miriam is the most unlikely victim I can think of. Everyone loved her."

Tala jotted down the affair detail under Miriam's name and turned back around. "Okay. What about Scott Fardulis? What do we know about him?"

"He was the typical young drama teacher that everyone likes." Hooper glanced over at Trobaugh, who was warming up her third cup of coffee from the carafe. "But from what we gathered just from talking to a few people in town with kids in Salem High, he's pretty close with the girls. He coaches girls volleyball and seems to be a magnet for drama."

"I don't like that the first thing they mentioned was that he was close with the female students. I mean, whatever, he was a handsome guy, I guess. Typical knob jockey." Maren grabbed her jacket off the back of her chair and pulled a handful of Slim Jims out of the pocket. "But what did he do to make someone want to string him up from the scaffolding?"

Tala recapped her marker. "Remember the break-in at the museum?"

"Yeah. You guys found a ring or something, but the focus was the exhibit that was broken into, correct?"

Wilder nodded. "That's what we thought too. It seemed like the major clue at the time, but Darcy here led us to the reverend's house in town, and it turns out his nineteen-year-old daughter was home from college. It was her ring. Well, technically her mother's, but she'd taken it and given it to Fardulis."

"Why would she have done that?" Hooper grabbed one of the Slim Jims and ripped into it. "And I wasn't aware you knew anyone in town. How did you know what house to—"

Trobaugh gave her a pointed look and waited until she saw Hooper make the connection.

"Oh, she's the..." Hooper paused, index finger hovering in the air like it was waiting for someone to land on. "She's the one who knows things she shouldn't. I remember now."

Darcy laughed and smiled down the table at Hooper. "That might be my favorite way it's ever been described."

Maren brushed Darcy's hand with hers and smiled as Tala tapped the whiteboard with her marker. "Anyway, we found out that the very conservative family she belongs to has no idea she'd been sleeping with Fardulis since she was fifteen."

"Allegedly." Wilder looked up suddenly. "We haven't interviewed her yet, so we don't have confirmation, but it certainly looks that way." She paused. "I believe her, for the record."

"Well, that sounds like a pretty good motive to me." Hooper folded the last of her Slim Jim into her mouth. "Was the reverend privy to that little fact? I mean, I know he's supposed to be a man of God or whatever, but it sounds like he's got an agenda, to say the least."

Darcy looked at Tala, who shook her head. "We don't think that's the case, or at least Jessa, his daughter, was pretty sure it was a secret."

Maren took a sip of her coffee and shifted in her chair to look at Darcy. "And what do you think?"

Darcy started to speak, then bit back her words in a measured moment of quiet before she said anything. "Someone knows. I'm not sure if it's the reverend, but someone knows, and I think that situation is connected. But how?"

"He certainly was in a hurry to get us the hell out of the house." Wilder nodded in the direction of the whiteboard, and Tala handed her the marker. "The second he saw me he couldn't get us out of there fast enough, and we've never had bad blood. It was odd."

Tala slid into Wilder's seat. "What makes you think someone else knows?"

"It's hard to explain, but someone else's energy was in that ring." Darcy stopped, glancing at Tala, who nodded in support. "I felt Rebecca's energy, of course, and I felt the energy of Jessa and her mother, but someone else was there." Darcy spun a small silver ring on her thumb as she spoke. "Someone who didn't belong."

Hooper raised her coffee cup to her lips and stopped. "Anyone want to fill me in on who the hell Rebecca is? You guys gotta stop talking when I go to the bathroom. I feel like I'm missing things." She mock rolled her eyes. "Damn."

Everyone looked at Darcy, and Tala handed her the marker. She wrote the answer across the top of the whiteboard.

Rebecca Nurse. Executed June 1692.

"She was hanged at the age of seventy-one. Jessa and her mother are her direct descendants."

❖

By the time they'd gone over every scrap of evidence, it was late afternoon, and everyone was stir-crazy. It had been seven hours since any of them had even stepped foot out of the war room. Everyone wrapped up their notes and drifted out to decompress until only Tala and Wilder stood staring out at the afternoon light already starting to fade outside the iridescent glaze of the windows.

"I need some fresh air." Wilder shrugged on her jacket, started to pick up her folder of case notes, and then set it back down on the table. "And a burger. Feel like a road trip to the diner?"

"Well, you used the words 'burger,' 'road trip,' and 'diner' in the same sentence, so that's pretty much the sexiest thing anyone's ever said to me." Tala switched off the light in the war room and nodded toward the hall. "You driving, Chief?"

The crisp, chilled air seemed to sweep the heavy energy from them as they walked outside, and after they'd climbed into the Jeep, Wilder started it and rolled down all the windows, autumn leaves swirling in their wake as they blazed down the driveway toward town. The sky was soft violet, and the air had just started to frost around the edges. "Do you need me to roll up the windows?" Wilder glanced over at Tala in the passenger's seat, who was zipping up her black leather jacket to the top. She tucked a bright yellow scarf into the collar and stuffed her hands into the pockets, her nose already cherry red from the cold.

"No way. It's only about five minutes to town, and after going over every detail in there for hours, I need to feel the wind blowing some of it the hell away from me."

"Same." Wilder turned onto the main road and nodded at the officer parked on the side, one of the four stationed around the house after sunset. "So, who do you like for this?"

"Who do I have in mind as a suspect?" Tala shook her head, the last of the setting sun glinting across her dark eyes like a sheer wash of gold water. "I have some thoughts, but I need to just let them settle. I don't want to get my sights set on someone just because they're here in Salem. It could be anyone, and people are on edge and acting out of character because it's stressful." She exhaled, watching her breath crystallize to vapor. "It's stressful for everyone."

As they neared town and drove onto the square, everything felt different to Wilder, deserted somehow. Cars were still parked in front of a few shops, but most of them were dark, with *Closed* signs dangling off center against the glass front doors. Wilder had always loved autumn in Salem, and not just because of the crunchy, fiery leaves and cool bite to the air, but because town was bustling, bursting at the seams with people excited to be there. There were always special events in the park, the farmers' market on the weekends selling colorful produce along with lively local gossip, and just the warm, familiar feeling of community. The witch trials had ripped Salem to shreds once, and that cloud had never truly faded. The fact that this killer had managed to do it again just deepened the load on her shoulders with every breath.

The brass bell clanged against the glass door as Wilder held it open for Tala, and a waitress behind the counter nodded toward a row of booths by the window. The air was heavy with the homey scent of mashed potatoes via the steamy kitchen, and except for a couple of elderly regulars drinking coffee at the counter, it was unusually quiet. The waitress picked up a coffee pot and headed in their direction, silently filling their white ceramic cups and clinking them back down on the saucers. Tala picked up two menus from the stack behind the condiments and handed one to Wilder, who took it but dropped it back where it came from.

Tala smiled. "Know what you want already?"

"I've been eating here since I was ten." Wilder took a cautious sip of her steaming coffee. "I know."

"All right, hit me." Tala laid down her menu and folded her arms across the table. "How does one get the best burger in the place?"

"Ahh. You're smart enough to know it's all in the ordering." Wilder dumped sugar into her coffee from the glass canister and stirred, the clink of the spoon against the cup unusually loud in the quiet dining area. "Do you trust me?"

"Certainly not." Tala handed Wilder her menu. "But if you're asking me if you can order for me, that's a cautious yes."

Wilder laughed and raised one finger in the waitress's direction. "Excellent. That's good enough for me."

The waitress finished her conversation and walked over, no pen or paper in sight. A worn name tag dangled from her left shoulder by a thread. *Annie.*

"All right, Chief. What can I get ya?"

"Can we have a couple of sauce burgers flown on BB, with floppy onions and seasoned fries?"

She nodded. "What's the weather on those?"

"Mine is March, but I'll let you guess on hers." Wilder and the waitress turned to Tala, who crossed her arms in front of her and leaned back in her seat, one eyebrow raised.

"I'm going with May, unless you think August?" The waitress tilted her head and stepped back to give Tala a once-over. "Nah. She looks all right. I'll go with late May."

A slow smile spread across Tala's face as Annie walked away and draped an arm around one of the gentlemen at the counter as she refilled his coffee. "I get the feeling August wasn't ideal. I would've had to leave town before people got wind of it."

"You're not wrong." Wilder shrugged out of her jacket, holding her hand out for Tala's before carefully stashing them next to her on the booth. "It refers to the temperature of the meat. August is well done, and that just screams diner amateur."

"Damn. You guys don't pull any punches." Tala unrolled her silverware and folded the paper napkin beside the plate. "Lucky I'm with a local."

Wilder smiled and glanced over at the counter. "You have no idea how true that is."

The bell clanged dramatically against the door again, and Wilder saw Annie step back and lean against the counter, watching intently as if a fight was about to go down. Then she realized Miranda had walked in and stopped short when she'd seen them in the corner booth. Annie reached up to the kitchen window and rang the bell again to get her attention, holding up a white paper sack and motioning her over to the counter. Miranda's eyes were locked on Tala, and she snatched the bag from Annie and dropped a twenty on the counter in one motion. She started toward Wilder's booth and covered the distance in three long strides. Her hand was clamped over the top of the bag so tightly her fingers were white, with angry red splotches at the edges.

"So, what's the plan, Wilder? Are you just trying to humiliate me here?" She looked Tala up and down and turned back to Wilder. "Again?"

Wilder sighed, feeling the muscles in her jaw clench. "That's enough, Miranda."

Miranda's voice pitched up, strung tight and tense enough to break. "You owe me an explanation."

Her gaze hardened as she swished her ponytail over one shoulder. She was wearing her uniform, or at least that's what Wilder called it when they were married. Black yoga pants, a Lulumon sweatshirt, and expensive running shoes that were high-tech enough to win the Boston Marathon by themselves. They'd been married for years, and never once had she seen Miranda break into a jog, much less darken the door of a yoga studio.

"What were all those people doing in your house the other day?" She shifted her weight to her other foot and parked her hand on her hip. "Is that what you're doing now? Throwing lesbian sleepovers while a serial killer runs around Salem hanging innocent people in the park?"

Annie laughed so hard, the coffee she was drinking landed in an impressive spray across the Formica countertop. *Sorry*, she mouthed to Wilder, grabbing a towel from under the counter.

"I think you'll find I don't owe you anything," Wilder said, her pulse pounding in her temples while she silently contemplated how she could have ever been in love with Miranda. "But yes, I'm now offering free lesbian sleepovers at the cabin while a serial killer skips around Salem slicing and dicing." She made herself pause, drawing in a long, slow breath before she re-engaged. "Is that what you really think?"

"Well, you certainly seem to have made time to slum it in the dating pool." The words clattered across the table, and Wilder saw Tala steel herself. Miranda fixed her gaze back on Wilder. "Where'd you get her? The dishwashing station at that shitty Mexican restaurant down the road?"

Wilder jumped up before she'd even finished her sentence, but Annie beat her to the punch, grabbing Miranda's ponytail and jerking her away from the table. Miranda tried to wrench away, but Annie wrapped that ponytail around her fist and half dragged her to the door. "You talk to anyone in here like that again, and I'll string you up by that fake blond horsehair of yours. You've been gunning for it for years, and I've had it up to *here*—" Annie let her go with an impressive shove and opened the door. "With your holier-than-thou bullshit. Do we understand each other?"

Miranda looked back to Tala, and Wilder again started for the door until Annie held up her hand to stop her.

"Do we *understand* each other, Miranda?" Silence thickened and hung in the air, and the only remaining diner in the corner, an older woman in a cardigan, gleefully yanked out her phone and started filming. "And I'd suggest you don't make me ask you again."

Miranda nodded grudgingly, then walked out the door and crossed the street, disappearing around the corner with her take-out bag still crumpled in her fist. Annie slammed the door shut after her hard enough to dislodge the bell, which fell to the ground and rolled across the linoleum. Two plates appeared in the window, one stacked haphazardly against the other, and a large, hairy hand slammed down on the buzzer.

"Order up, boss!"

Wilder sank back against the seat, not quite meeting Tala's gaze. "Tala, I'm so sorry about not—"

Tala stopped her, tangling her fingers into Wilder's on the table. "You're sorry about what? About not losing your cool and jeopardizing the entire task force?" She smiled, catching Wilder's hand with her own and squeezing it. "I wouldn't have let you.

Besides, neither one of us needed to do anything anyway. Annie Oakley over there was just poetry to watch."

Annie appeared and dropped the plates down in front of them, along with a bottle of ketchup she pulled out of her apron, smacking the end of it against her hand as she spoke. "That ridiculous shit won't happen again, not in here at least. I'm sorry now I even let her get that far." She set the ketchup down and offered her hand to Tala. "I'm Annie Jackson. I own the place. And the shitty Mexican place down the road."

Tala took it with a wide smile. "Thanks, Annie. I owe you one."

"You owe me nothing. I'm sick of that racist bullshit mouth of hers." She glanced back at the kitchen as the bell dinged again. "Wilder, I know that's your ex, but she's lost her damn mind. Everyone knew her back when she was with you, and she wasn't like that, at least not that we could see. You got any clue what the hell happened to her?"

"Your guess is as good as mine." Wilder squeezed the ketchup into a small red lake on her plate before she looked up and smiled in Tala's direction. "This is Agent Tala Marshall, by the way, one of the most in-demand profilers in the country and the best of the best at Boston Headquarters."

"It's a pleasure, Agent Marshall." She crossed her arms, leaning back far enough to shoot another glance at the glass door, seemingly to make sure Miranda wasn't gunning for round two. "I assume you're here to help catch whoever's stacking up the bodies around here?"

"Just call me Tala, and that's right." She took a bite of her burger and swooned. "Although the trip to Salem would have been worth it just for this burger."

Annie smiled and looked back to the cook hanging out by the kitchen window.

Wilder pushed a wayward pickle back into her burger and lifted it cautiously in the direction of her mouth. "What the hell is going on around here, by the way? It looks like the entire town was abducted." She took an appreciative bite and went on. "I mean, I did finally get the gag order for the press to finally go through, but the judge approved only a short window of time." Wilder scooped up a generous trail of ketchup with a fry and looked back up at Annie. "But it still seems like everyone got the hell out of Dodge. Not that I blame them."

The bell dinged in the window again, and Annie answered back over her shoulder as she walked to the counter again. "Everyone's leaving Salem to stay with relatives in Boston or whatever. Might be smart. That last body at the high school put the fear of God in everyone, and it goes without saying that school is closed until further notice." She pulled the end of her apron string and retied it behind her back. "Didn't help when you had those checkpoints with cameras set up on all the roads in and out of town, but I get why you had to."

A teenage boy in a rumpled jacket wandered through the door, and Annie motioned him over behind the counter, taking the backpack he shrugged out of as he reached for the glass display of double-chocolate cookies.

"Yeah. I hate that the town is losing so much revenue during the busy season, but we have to be able to see who's coming in and out at this point." Wilder picked up her burger with one hand and grabbed a handful of paper napkins with the other, smiling at Tala's look of unabashed bliss. "What do you think of the burger?"

"Oh, this?" Tala lifted hers, already almost half gone. "The better-than-sex-burger? I love this thing." She examined it appreciatively and set it back down on her plate. "So, break down the secret order for me. What is it called again?"

"Better than sex, huh?" Wilder winked over the top of her burger. "I'll need to know more about that, but around here, we order it 'saucy' because they'll stuff a river of steak sauce and cheese into the center of the burger before it even goes on the grill, and the 'BB' you heard me ask for stands for brioche bun. The floppy onions are caramelized in cast iron, and they toss the finished fries in that wine-and-butter pan sauce the second before they serve them with flaky salt and parsley. It's heaven."

"Clearly it pays to know a local." Tala popped a fry into her mouth and examined the row of four unlabeled sauces in the small wire basket on the table.

Wilder's phone buzzed against the table, and she picked it up, cradling it between her shoulder and her ear as she grabbed her burger again. "What's up, Robinson?"

CHAPTER THIRTEEN

Tala took the keys from Wilder and started the Jeep, clearing a circle of frost from the windshield to keep an eye on Wilder as she attempted to wrap up the chaos they'd just come from. Robinson had called to let Wilder know that Roger Davis, Jessa's father, was setting up what he'd called a peaceful protest in the square, and by the time Wilder hung up the phone they were out of the diner and hurrying toward the center of the town, which suddenly now was packed with people. The protest was anything but peaceful, more like a public shaming of the police and their efforts to find the Salem serial killer, with bits of biblical rhetoric about Sodom and Gomorrah tossed in for shock value. Church hymns played on a loop from a makeshift speaker system behind the reverend, and Tala realized the gag order Wilder had gotten to keep the press out of Salem must have expired; by the time they got there, the place looked like the worst version of a televised tent revival. To make things even worse, someone had just started up a chainsaw down the beach to remove the branch used in the hanging.

Wilder had sprung into action with her officers, and between her, Tala, and Robinson they'd managed to quell the chaos after a few hours. Palpable fear still hung in the darkness at the edges of the park, chilling the air with the memory of Miriam, the midwife who was hanged not 150 feet from the makeshift pulpit Davis had erected in the gazebo. The aggressive reporter from the *Boston Globe* had been the worst of the press group and seemed to know too much about the last victim, or at least enough to catch Tala's attention. As she walked back to the Jeep, Tala made a mental note to call the medical examiner in the morning and ask her about the probability of a potential leak somewhere in the chain of custody.

She watched from her heated seat inside the Jeep as Wilder wrapped up the last of it, personally reassuring the locals and putting out the flames of fear Davis had flung like blazing torches into the crowd in hopes they'd catch. The pale crescent moon hung low and heavy behind the maples at the edges of the park, just visible through leaves that still held the colors of sunset. Darkness closed in slowly, like medieval iron gates coming together, and people shuffled down the sidewalks to their cars, the square emptying more because of the chill of memory than the brittle, icy air.

The air had just started to warm in the interior of the Jeep when Wilder finally turned and headed back, the wind ruffling the layers of her hair until she pulled out a police beanie and yanked it down over her ears. She walked differently somehow, her shoulders weighted and tense, and she kept sliding her hand around the back of her neck to squeeze the tension from her muscles. Wilder walked backward toward the Jeep, her eyes not leaving the square until the last glowing taillight disappeared and even the press had packed up and headed to the roadside motels at the edge of town. Tala watched as she finally turned and walked toward her, the cold air rushing into the cab like water when she opened the door of the Jeep.

Wilder slid in and leaned back against the seat. Her cheeks were ruddy from hours in the cold, and she closed her eyes too long before she opened them and laid her hand on Tala's knee. "Ready?"

Tala squeezed her icy hand with her warm one. "Almost."

She got out of the Jeep, opening Wilder's door and motioning her out without a word. Wilder hesitated, then slid over into the passenger's seat, rubbing the bridge of her nose with her fingers hard enough to leave red marks before she pulled the knit cap off her head. Tala put the Jeep into reverse and drove back to the cabin, passing houses with gold light spilling out of windows and into the black night. Broken streaks of bats crisscrossed the sky as she drove away from the village lights and turned down the long driveway toward Wilder's cabin, the only sound the low hiss of the heater warming the air around them with slow, undulating waves. By the time she'd slowed to a stop at the door, the first icy snowflakes had fallen, melting instantly against the windshield, and the air took on a dry, crisp edge as Tala got out and opened Wilder's door.

"Sorry. I guess I'm just—"

Tala smiled, glancing back at the door to make sure they didn't have an audience. "Shhh." She locked the door after Wilder slid out, double-checking it before slipping the keys into Wilder's pocket. "Someone told me once that having a normal reaction to a fucked-up situation was nothing to apologize for."

Wilder squeezed her hand, unlocked the door, and held it open for Tala after they'd climbed the icy porch steps. She sank to the bench inside and pulled off her boots, scooting over to the end to make room for Tala and handing her a pair of thick wool socks from the basket underneath. Tala lined up her boots beside Wilders and popped on the socks, taking Wilder's hand as they walked down the hall. The kitchen was dark as they passed it, although the rich, lingering scent of lasagna still hovered in the air, and even the embers in the fireplace were still glowing under a downy coat of silken ash.

Tala held her watch up to the pale light from the window, but it was still too dark to see it. "God. It feels like midnight."

"That's because it is." Wilder passed the staircase and slipped into the walk-in pantry in the hall, pulling Tala in and shutting the door behind them. "Everyone with any sense is asleep."

Tala started to ask, then thought better of it and waited as Wilder found a doorknob in the darkness and opened another door.

She flipped on a light that warmed the room they stepped into with a slow, amber glow. It felt instantly spacious and strangely warm, with thick, split-pine walls and an open shower area to her right. The focal point was the showerhead, antique rubbed bronze and as wide as a small umbrella, with rough wooden slabs to either side holding stacks of fluffy white towels, framed by two dove-gray robes hanging from iron hooks to either side. The wide stones with organic edges underfoot were distinctly different from the conventional hardwood floors in the rest of the house. Bracingly cool and satisfyingly uneven under Tala's feet, it felt almost as if she were walking down a stone path in the forest.

A glass wall the color of smoky quartz separated the area into two parts; they were standing in the smaller area that held the shower, with a dressing space opposite, but Tala could just make out another expansive space beyond. A warm glow was visible just beyond the glass, and Tala laid her fingertips against the cool, dark surface before she even realized she'd done it. It was alluringly beautiful, in a ghostly way. She glanced down for a handle but found nothing, almost as if she were looking into a dark crystal to another realm. She sensed Wilder's smile before she turned around.

"Looking for something?"

"What's in there?" She shaded the glass with her hands and looked again, but other than the flickering reflection of fire, it was too dark to see anything. "You know you have to tell me, or I'll just find a way to get in."

Wilder started unbuttoning her uniform shirt, leaving only a ribbed undershirt and white sports bra as she shrugged it off and folded it carefully onto a cedar bench by the door. "Think beyond what you'd expect to find in a typical white American person's house."

What the hell is Wilder talking about? Tala arched an eyebrow and turned back toward the glass. *She's about as white as it gets.*

She heard a click behind her, and then the room behind the dark glass began to warm with a hazy glow. It started with a flicker from the gas-flame sconces on the wall, then a glow from beneath the floorboards, which were set slightly farther apart than a traditional wooden floor. Two levels of wraparound cedar benches formed a central seating area along the walls, but it wasn't until she spotted the teak drain in the flooring that she suddenly realized what she was looking at.

"Is this what I think it is—"

"A sauna. I realize they're rare in houses here, but nearly everyone has a sauna in Finland. I'll never understand why Americans don't seem to see the magic."

By the time Tala turned around, Wilder had stripped down completely and had a towel wrapped around her waist. "I'd like to act modest here, but why?" The firelight from beyond the glass flickered in her eyes. "If I remember right, this is exactly how we woke up this morning."

"Correct." Tala smiled as she pulled off her sweater, then unbuckled her belt, the brass clinking against the silver cuff bracelet she always wore on her left wrist. "I'll assume I've been invited to join you."

Wilder laughed as she pressed a button on the wall. The glass wall split in the center and retreated to both sides with a soft *whoosh*. "Absolutely. Why do you think you're here?" She paused and looked past the dark glass. "But don't feel pressured to undress unless you want to. I'll be inside. Just come in whenever you're ready, and you'll find towels everywhere out here, so make yourself comfortable." She paused, her gaze dropping down Tala's body for just an instant before she met her eyes again. "Take as long as you like."

Tala nodded as Wilder disappeared behind the glass. A nearly opaque mist rose around Wilder as she tossed a ladleful of water on the rocks inside the sauna, and Tala stopped, focusing on the pitched log ceiling to slow her mind enough to feel the rise and fall of her breath. *Did Wilder know what it meant in Native American culture to be invited to sauna with someone?* She slipped out of her jeans and folded them carefully on the wood slab bench beside her. *And why did a random white person have a secret sauna that looked like it belonged in a magazine?* She scraped her hair into a bun and let her thoughts settle as she stacked the rest of her clothing on the benches by the doors and reached for a snowy white, oversized towel.

Tala pressed the button at the side of the glass and stepped in. Two levels of cedar-slat risers wrapped around the room, the first at floor level, then the next about three feet above, with deep-set stairs built into the wall for access. Sheer gold liquid light rose from between the slats and filtered the steam like sunlight, hovering between her and Wilder, who sat on the lower level across from a tall cast-iron woodstove. She was leaning back against the cedar planks with her eyes closed, the white towel wrapped around her waist, skin glistening under the soft lighting recessed into the raw plank ceiling. It was obvious that Wilder lifted, but naked, the cut lines of her broad shoulders were even more defined and beautiful. It seemed somehow appropriate that how strong she was wasn't visible to everyone. There was a quiet gentleness to Wilder's strength, a choice to whisper in a world that shouts.

Tala picked up the zinc bucket by the stove and threw a ladleful of water onto the stones. An iron rack held rough, angular stones stacked to the ceiling, and the water disappeared into moonstone steam as it hit them. Wilder opened her eyes and nodded to the bench beside her. Tala sat and melted back into the slats behind her, smiling as she felt Wilder sweep a stray lock of her hair behind her ear.

"Thank you." The words hovered between them as Wilder turned toward her. "For showing me this."

Wilder traced the line of Tala's shoulder with the tip of her finger, her touch as light as thought, trailing a fingertip down the inside of her arm to her wrist. "I had this built a few years ago, and I've never invited someone in." A slow hiss of silver steam escaped from behind the lower rocks and rose like temple incense to the ceiling. "You're the only one I've wanted here."

Tala stood, slowly unwrapped her towel, and lay down on the bench, this time with her head on Wilder's thigh. She felt Wilder's breath quicken in the silent room as she settled her open hand over Tala's heart and sat back again.

"So." Tala watched the silver layers of steam drift over them and settle like moonlight over the lines of her naked body. "Tell me about Finland."

Wilder smiled, her eyes still closed in the undulated heat. "My dad did a university semester abroad in Finland, where he met my mom in Helsinki. They fell in love, got married on a whim, and then came to the States when I was a baby. I think they always planned to return someday, but he took off with someone else when I was five."

"So, she was a single mom?"

Wilder tangled her fingers into Tala's and settled them again over Tala's heart. "She was the best single mom. I knew from when I was little that I wanted to be sure she could go back to Finland if she wanted to, and thankfully, I ended up being able to do that for her."

Tala gazed seriously up at Wilder. "Because of your glittering chess career?"

Wilder threw her head back and laughed, the sudden sound echoing around the log walls. "Not even close. I'd won quite a bit by the time I was done, but Mom never touched a penny of it. She just invested it, very well, then refused to give it to me until I was almost thirty."

"Smart woman." Tala got up and poured another ladle of water over the hot stones, then took her place on the bench. "So did she ever remarry?"

"I don't think she intended to, but I secretly signed her up for an international dating app a few years after high school, vetted her potential dates, and had almost given up when I met Hugo. I knew he'd be perfect for her. He's from Amsterdam but was living in Helsinki, and within a year of meeting, they were married. They live there in a town outside the capital, called Lahti, which is next to a gorgeous lake she literally can't get enough of. I go over two or three times a year to visit."

"It sounds beautiful. I've always wanted to live by a lake, even though I never learned to swim. I'm seriously scared of water in general." She looked up at Wilder. "They're still together?"

"Honestly." Wilder raked a hand through her hair and paused, her tone suddenly thoughtful. "I don't think I ever saw my mom truly happy until she was back in Finland. I was visiting there a few years after they moved, and Hugo had just built her this big, gorgeous dock that stretched out over the water. I was watching her from the kitchen window one morning when the steam was rising off the lake, and she was sitting in one of the blue Adirondack chairs at the very edge, as close as she could get to the water, with her coffee in her hand. She always drank it from the same Finnish-style wooden mug I carved for her in high school." Wilder paused, her fingers slipping through Tala's damp hair. "Maybe it was the sun rising over the mountain or maybe it was just her, but I'll never forget how her face just glowed." She stopped suddenly, and Tala waited, the silence heavy and soft between them. "She had a cancer scare a few years later, and I remember her saying that she hoped it was nothing, but that if it was her time, she wasn't afraid to die."

"Why did she say that?" Tala looked up at Wilder. "Did she ever tell you?"

"She did." Wilder's voice was quiet, almost lost in the steam. "She said she finally felt truly loved."

"What happened with her health?" The words were out before Tala could catch them.

"It turned out to be nothing. The scan that made things seem so bad initially was a false positive, thank God." Wilder pulled Tala closer and smiled. "She threw a party for herself in Helsinki when she found out and declared she intended to live to a hundred with Hugo, apparently so they could travel the world and make love in every country. I was there, and I remember laughing until

I cried and clapping with everyone else, thinking that if I never found my person…it was almost enough that my mother had."

Tala did some quick math in her head. "Wait. Weren't you married to Miranda then?"

"I was." Wilder nodded, her words slow, like a memory she didn't quite recognize. "She wasn't there." She got up to throw some water on the rocks, then stepped out, returning with two water bottles in a matter of seconds.

Tala smiled, reaching out for one of them. "You're kidding me. You have a built-in fridge out there somewhere?"

"I don't know what to tell you." Wilder sat back down and loosened the knot in the towel around her hips. "It's not my first time in a sauna." She turned and looked at Tala for a long moment. "How are you feeling? Are you okay to stay for a few more minutes?" She spun the cap on the water bottle and handed it to her.

"I'm—" Tala realized too late she'd been staring at Wilder's arms as she opened the water. "I'm good. I can go as long as you can."

Wilder smiled. The steam hovered both dense and translucent in the air. It smelled like seawater and desert at the same time and clung to Tala's hair as she pulled the length of it over one shoulder. Wilder, still staring into the flames flickering in the woodstove, reached for her hand and raised it to her mouth, kissing her palm, the touch wrapped with thought and memory.

"In about a minute, I'm going to ask you about your family." Wilder looked into her eyes and then back to the stove. "If it's not time, just don't answer, okay?"

Tala nodded, her heart suddenly racing. Wilder's tone was light when she laid her head back against the cedar slats and whispered, "Tell me something about little you, when you were a kid. About the reservation." She stopped and seemed to choose her final word carefully. "Anything."

Tala started to answer, then stood and slowly straddled Wilder's thighs. She leaned into her chest, her mouth soft against

Wilder's ear for a hundred silent breaths before she spoke. "I want to. But I don't know how."

Wilder rested her forehead against Tala's, tracing her lower lip with her thumb. It was forever before she kissed her, before Tala couldn't tell where her own breath began and Wilder's ended, before Wilder's hands were wrapped around her hips, pulling Tala tighter into her body. She felt Wilder's heartbeat against her chest, her arms strong and steady as her eyes locked onto Tala's in the hazy, flickering light. "Then it's not time. You'll know when it is."

Tala nodded, then took one of Wilder's fingertips into her mouth and swirled her tongue around the tip before she slowly took it deeper. Wilder groaned as she closed her eyes and leaned back against the cedar wall. Tala melted into her body as Wilder slid one hand up her waist, then lightly over her nipples to the base of her neck. Her thumb was gentle under Tala's chin, tipping her face up before she slid her tongue down the curve of Tala's neck to the hollow at the base of her throat.

The warmth of Wilder's breath was intense, and Tala closed her eyes, trailing her fingertips across Wilder's nipples. Every strong line of Wilder's body was beautiful, like a sculpture she wanted to memorize with her fingertips. She felt Wilder's hands span her waist and opened her eyes to see the fire flicker against the darkness of Wilder's eyes like a wildfire on a far-off mountain.

Wilder smiled. "I want to stay here all night with you, but this might get dangerous in hundred-degree heat. I'll shower upstairs so you can take your time down here, okay?"

She nodded as Wilder's hand slid warm over her heart, and Tala dropped her head softly onto Wilder's shoulder.

"You'll find cashmere robes on the wall in there, and a basket under the towel bench with soaps, lotion, anything you need."

Wilder stood with Tala's legs wrapped around her waist and set her gently back on the bench, then closed the stove, her gaze lingering for a long moment before she stepped out of the sauna and the smoked doors closed behind her.

❖

Wilder opened the door to their room upstairs to find a crackling fire in the fireplace and a bottle of white wine and glasses on the hearth. It was made only slightly less romantic by the wine bottle being stuffed into a stained oven mitt along with a random scoop of ice, then nearly toppling over on the uneven stone surface. Wilder pulled out a crumpled Post-it Note she found in the bottom of one of the glasses.

Hope the sauna fire was what you needed. That place is gorgeous by the way. Thanks for the invite, asshat.
PS. I lit this one too on my way back upstairs just in case.

Wilder made a mental note to thank Maren the next morning. The flames flickered against the brick walls of the fireplace and warmed the air as she turned on the shower, then poured the still-surprisingly chilled Cabernet Franc and settled the bottle with a little stone clink back on the mantel. The shower was sharp and hot, and Wilder turned up the pressure and let it pound her shoulders and the back of her neck until her muscles started to loosen and unfold onto her bones. She stayed until the water started to cool, but a mist of steam still hovered between her and the bathroom mirror as she heard Tala stirring around on the other side of the door. She pulled on a snug white tee and some navy flannel pants from the closet in the bathroom, running a quick hand through the damp warmth of her hair.

This was the moment—the tiny window of time in which she could choose to hit the pause button and rethink getting involved with someone while they were both supposed to be chasing a damn serial killer. Wilder swiped at the steam on the bathroom mirror with her palm and took a breath, staring back at her reflection. Tala had been right, that day in the diner. She'd married Miranda because she was chasing the happiness she'd seen her mother find.

Even on the morning of her wedding, she knew Miranda wasn't the one, but at some point after the divorce, it had just been safer to assume she'd never find the person that set her soul on fire. Now, every time she looked at Tala, she felt like she was standing in the wind on the edge of a crumbling cliff, the parched earth crumbling and sliding like slate under her feet, cracking to gray powder a thousand feet below.

The mirror had fogged over again before she finally opened the door to the bedroom, where Tala was sitting in the center of the bed, cashmere robe falling off one bare shoulder, staring into the fire.

"I just realized I poured two glasses of wine without thinking." Wilder walked over and ran her fingers through Tala's hair, her words as soft as the hiss of green pine in the hearth. "I'll go down and get you the cordial."

"No. It's okay." Tala's words seemed far away, and she didn't look up. "Wine seems like a better idea tonight."

Wilder hesitated, then handed her one of the glasses, the condensation clouding the glass like a frosted sunlit window, and joined her on the bed, tucking her legs underneath the edge of the duvet. The air was silent and heavy, as if it too were waiting.

"I think it's why I became a profiler." Tala pulled the robe back onto her shoulder and glanced up at Wilder. Her cheeks were flushed, her skin still dewy from the sauna. Wilder watched as she raised her glass, then lowered it slowly without drinking. Her gaze returned to the lazy flames climbing into the chimney with bright-blue fingers that twisted around themselves, then sank reluctantly back into the glowing coals below. "I should have known before it happened. That maybe I could have prevented the whole thing if I'd caught the signs."

It was a long moment before she raised the glass again, this time drinking half the wine before she remembered to breathe. Wilder put a gentle hand on her shoulder before she took the glass and set it on the nightstand beside them.

"Whatever it was, I can tell it was a lot." She slid a slow hand onto Tala's thigh, waiting until she knew the touch was okay before she spoke. "How old were you?"

"I was ten. My brother was three." Tala started to go on, then stopped, biting her lip. "You must think I'm crazy, talking about some memory I haven't even told you about."

"Listen." Wilder waited until Tala met her gaze. "If you cut down an enormous tree in the woods, you don't just grab a random branch and try to drag it out of the forest by yourself." Wilder laced her hands behind her head and leaned back into the pillows. "You cut it into pieces and carry them out one by one. And if they're too heavy, sometimes you have to just drop them and come back for them later, or chop them into smaller pieces to be able to carry them at all." She paused, brushing Tala's cheek gently with her thumb, letting the silence settle, watching her words drift together in the space between them. "What do you wish you would have seen back then?"

Wilder waited for her to go on, barely resisting the urge to throw words at the silence that stood like a glass wall between them. But the glass wasn't hers to break. The wind wrapped itself around the window to the left of the fireplace, pressing a branch against the black glass as it started to snow, the sound of the wood scraping against the windowpane slow and insistent. "Nothing, really." Tala drew a hesitant breath and looked up at Wilder. "I guess I always thought I could have done something if I'd just caught it before it happened. I know that isn't true, but the thought still lives in the back of your mind, you know?" She tightened her robe around her and hesitated. "Like seeing a ghost one day in the background of a dark photo. It's there every time you look, so you shove it into a box and bury it in the attic."

Wilder leaned over to the nightstand to put her own glass down by the lamp. Lingering woodsmoke made the air smell like warmth, and the flames had relaxed into a slow burn, embers cracking and falling under the grate. "But then one day you climb into the attic, and the sunlight is streaming through the windows."

Wilder smiled. "So, you dig it out, hold it up to the light, and there's nothing?"

"Yeah." Tala smiled, sinking back into the pillows and Wilder's arms. "And you realize that maybe there never was."

Wilder pulled her closer into her chest and whispered into the warmth of her hair. "It feels that way because you're trying to make sense of it now, as an adult. You have the tools for the job now, but back then, you didn't even know they existed." She held up her hand and waited until Tala held hers against it, fingertips gently meeting Wilder's. "Go easy on the ten-year-old you were. She was doing the best she could with the information she had then."

"I wish." Tala looked up at her, her dark eyes shimmering like lake water in the dim light. "Do you really think that's true?"

Wilder felt Tala exhale and soften into her arms as if she'd been holding the same breath since that day. "I know it is." She took a sip of her wine and set it back on the nightstand, closing her eyes when she felt Tala's hand move under her shirt and across her abs. "And if you're thinking about going to sleep anytime soon, that's not going to help."

"Wilder." Tala's fingertips grazed Wilder's nipples, and she leaned in, words moving like breath across her ear. "I'm definitely not thinking about going to sleep." Wilder slipped a hand around the back of her neck, then picked Tala up with one arm, flipping her underneath her body and slowly loosening the belt on the cashmere robe that slipped like water off her skin.

"Thank God." Wilder murmured the words into her neck, moving down slowly until she ran her tongue around Tala's nipple and pulled it into her mouth. She listened as Tala lost her breath and arched underneath her, working her fingers at the base of Wilder's neck, pulling her closer. Wilder stroked it with her tongue, slow and strong, until she heard Tala's breath catch, then pulled her own shirt over her head and tossed it over the side of the bed. "But I need to know that you feel safe, and that it's okay to change your mind." Wilder held her eyes. "You don't need a reason."

"Wilder, I know." Tala traced Wilder's bottom lip with the tip of her tongue. "You've never made me feel anything but safe."

Wilder kissed her as she lifted one of Tala's knees beside her and sank slowly between her thighs. Tala's fingers tightened at the back of her neck when Wilder pulled her nipple back into the warmth of her mouth, scraping it lightly through her teeth when she let her go.

"Just stay there." Tala's voice was low and intense. "Please."

Wilder edged up and leaned into the heat of Tala's body with her thigh as she worked her nipple, pulling it deep into her mouth, Tala's breath begging her for more intensity than she might have offered otherwise. Heat radiated off her skin as Tala lifted her arms and grabbed the pillow behind her, her hips restless against Wilder's thigh. Wilder watched her skin flush, the color of her mouth deepen as she bit her bottom lip, listening to her breath move from quiet to quick and hard in the span of a minute. She buried her fingers in Wilder's hair, mouth hot against her ear.

"Wilder."

Wilder smiled, working Tala's nipples between her fingers. "Tell me what you need, baby."

Tala tightened her fingers in Wilder's hair. "For you to take me." Her eyes shimmered with intensity as she looked up at Wilder, her voice a rough whisper. "Take me like I'm yours."

"Goddamn." Wilder traced the curve of her waist and slicked her tongue down the inside curve of one hip. She lifted Tala's thigh onto her shoulder and let herself sink into the heat of Tala's body. "That might be the sexiest thing I've ever heard."

Wilder sank down between her thighs, brushing her bare amber skin and straining clit with her breath until she saw Tala bite her lip again, her back arched, breasts glistening in the firelight. She paused for an endless moment, and then all at once, she gave Tala what she wanted. Wilder slicked the flat of her tongue over Tala's swollen clit, rolling it like water as she slid one hand under her hips. Her fingertips brushed lower as Tala's clit throbbed in her mouth, and she gently pulled it in, stroking the underside with her tongue as she slid two insistent fingers deep inside her.

"Fuck." Tala arched, her hips rocking, her hands pressed hard against the wall above her head. "Don't stop."

Wilder felt on the edge herself as she started fucking her slowly, turning her hand as she slipped a third finger inside. Tala moaned, a sheer mist of sweat glossing the curves of her breasts. Wilder lowered her mouth to Tala's clit again, rocking her hips with the hand she'd slipped underneath her, keeping her at a slow, steady rhythm that seemed to be making Tala come undone.

"Breathe." Wilder found the tense spot inside that was begging her to stroke harder and looked up, her gaze locked onto Tala's. "Just melt into me."

She felt Tala sink deeper into the pillows, her thighs opening for Wilder's shoulders. Wilder swirled her tongue across Tala's clit, increasing the pressure as she stroked her inside. Tala's thighs started to tremble, her fist twisting and crumpling the bedsheets beside them. Her back arched off the bed, and Wilder reached up and slid her wet fingers up and into Tala's mouth, nearly coming herself when Tala started working them with her tongue. Wilder looked into her eyes, her voice a hoarse whisper.

"Are you ready to come for me, baby?"

Tala nodded, whispering *please* until Wilder lowered her mouth to Tala's clit again, pulling it into her mouth, then rolling it under the flat of her tongue with a constant, intense rhythm. Tala's breath stopped, and she tightened around Wilder's fingers as she came, her nipples tense and straining as she cried out, gripping Wilder's shoulders, pulling her tighter, deeper inside. She came like fierce fire, slicking Wilder's hand to the wrist with lust that almost pushed Wilder over the edge in the moment. Tala's arms spread wide on the bed, every muscle in her tense and trembling as the orgasm visibly rolled through her body in crashing waves. Wilder reached up as they faded, placing a steady hand in the center of Tala's chest as her thighs slowly stopped shaking around her.

"Just breathe." Wilder slid out of her gently and crawled up her, pulling the duvet up and around them. She spooned Tala and pulled her back into her arms, whispering into her ear as her heartbeat finally started to settle under Wilder's hand. "I've got you."

Tala reached back and turned, looking deep into Wilder's eyes. "Say that again to me someday."

"When?"

"I don't know yet." She turned back, snuggling deeper into Wilder's arms, sleep already starting to fray the edges of her voice. "Just someday."

CHAPTER FOURTEEN

Wilder stirred in the bed, the sun unusually intense as it fell over her face and across the bed in a sheer, gold swath. She realized slowly she was coming out of a dream. Her heart pounded against her ribs in a desperate rhythm, and she still heard waves crashing all around a boat she hadn't been in. In the dream she'd been hanging onto the side, in pitch-black darkness, the only light a clear platinum-wash moonlight across the top of the waves, and something was knocking hard against the boat, making a deep, hollow, thumping sound as the saltwater rushed around her.

"*Mate.*"

Wilder sat up in bed, realizing suddenly that the knocking was on the other side of their bedroom door.

"There's more brass downstairs than a shooting-range floor." Maren's voice was an intense hiss. "And every one of them wants to know where you are."

Wilder bolted out of bed and looked down at the parking area in front of the cabin. Patrol cars and black undercovers were parked as if someone had thrown them down the drive, and she could see Robinson on the porch steps, cell phone pressed against his ear. Wilder glanced at Tala, still sleeping soundly with her arm draped across her face, as she wrapped the robe around herself and stepped into the hall, pulling the door shut behind her.

"Dude, you gotta get your ass downstairs." Maren stepped to the railing and peered over the staircase. Wilder heard people down there, and more than one cell-phone alert pinging. "Your boss and your bosses' boss are all over shit in the war room. Apparently, they've been calling you since just after midnight. They saw news coverage of some protest on social media and flipped out."

"What the hell?" Wilder paused when she heard Hooper below, then lowered her voice. "I literally never turn my phone off, and we heard nothing."

Maren pulled a cell phone out of the pocket of her jacket. "That's because I just found this on one of the benches outside the sauna." She handed over Wilder's phone and clicked on the ringer. "You must have left it there last night."

"Shit. How long have they been there?"

"Not long. They just pulled up. Your Jeep is here, so I lied and said the power went out last night, and your phone had probably died." She nodded toward the door. "Get your ass dressed and get down there. I'll try to smooth it over. Hooper and Trobaugh are schmoozing them right now, and it's actually working."

"How pissed are they?"

"I'd give it a nine out of ten, mate. When they got here, they looked like they wanted to melt our badges down and make cock rings out of them, but I think they were just worried. Once I assured them you were here, they started to relax, but they still sent my ass up here to lay eyes on ya."

"Fucking fantastic." Wilder ran a tense hand through her hair and opened the door behind her. "I'll be there in two minutes. Where's everyone else?"

"I'm throwing some brekkie together with Darcy, Trobaugh and Hooper are already present, and well, maybe we should just check where—" Maren made a joking play for the doorknob behind Wilder.

"Yeah, yeah. I know where Tala is."

"I mean, it's only fair to tell me all the juicy details since I saved your ass and all." Maren jokingly glanced at the door. "Just type up the full report with some photos maybe and leave it under my door by the end of the day."

"Fat chance." Wilder play-punched Maren's shoulder as she backed down the hall. "But I do owe you for all the romantic fire and shit you set up for me." She dropped her voice to a whisper. "I didn't waste it."

"Yeah. I bet you didn't." Maren started down the stairs. "Get your ass in gear. I'll try to put together some kitchen magic to calm them the fuck down."

"Hey, Maren."

Maren stopped on the stairs. "What?"

"I owe you. For real." Wilder paused and looked back through the crack in the door. "Thanks for saving my ass."

Maren flashed her a smile and tromped down the stairs, open Hawaiian shirt billowing in the breeze.

❖

Wilder rounded the corner of the stairs several minutes later and stopped at the kitchen, where Darcy and Maren were plating up a tray of muffins and breakfast rolls. The quickest cold shower of her life and a mad dash to find her uniform and badge had left her only slightly out of breath by the time she reached the bottom of the staircase. "It's quieter than I thought it would be. Where did they all go?"

"Turns out they thought you might have been a potential victim because no one could find you, so they called everyone in, but once I told them I'd laid eyes on you, almost all of them fucked off back to Boston."

"Except for Police Commissioner Hill. That's your big boss, right?" Darcy swiped at frosting threatening to drop from the side of one of the rolls and nodded down the hall. "He says he needs to see you, like, yesterday."

"Where is he?"

"War room with Trobaugh and Hooper."

"No pressure, Jesus." Wilder checked the top button of her shirt and disappeared into the hall, only to pop her head back through the open doorframe. "Hey, Darcy. Would you mind sending one of those rolls up for Tala? We decided it wouldn't be such a good look for her to walk in with me, and I think she might be starving."

"Of course." Darcy reached into the cupboard for a saucer. "They said they only needed you and Trobaugh and Hooper at the moment, so I'll take it to her."

"And dude," Maren caught her as she started to leave again, "when they ask you if you've seen the paper, just say yes."

"Christ. What the hell am I saying yes to?"

"Remember that pushy reporter from the *Boston Globe*? Howard Banyon?"

"Yes. Unfortunately."

"Well, somehow he got the scoop on Fardulis being involved with some high school girls and named the source you and Darcy spoke to, Jessa, in the article. But he must not want anyone to know it's him, because it's credited to a 'staff writer.'"

"What a load of bullshit. I knew he was there for a reason, and it has to have been him. No one else got anything." Wilder raked a hand through her hair. She walked down the hall to the war room, wishing the sound of her boots on the hardwood sounded a little less like cannons firing. Trobaugh was pouring a cup of coffee from the carafe on the table and pushed it toward her as Wilder walked through the door.

"Commissioner Hill." Wilder stuck out her hand, and Hill shook it with a friendlier energy than she was expecting. She glanced down at the table where a stack of *Boston Globe* newspapers lay. "I'm sure you've seen the paper?"

"I just filled the commissioner in on the background of the museum robbery connected to the last victim." Trobaugh held Wilder's gaze. "And a few of the details of your visit with the young woman he was allegedly involved with."

Wilder thanked her and nodded. "First, let me apologize for worrying you, Commissioner. I didn't realize there was an issue with my phone." Wilder took a seat and reached for one of the papers. "Thank you for your patience."

"Agent James explained the problem, at least as much as I could understand through that crazy accent, and we were all just glad you were accounted for. I was concerned you might be missing and called in the troops."

"I appreciate the concern, Commissioner." Wilder smiled. "I would have done the same."

Maren came through the door just then carrying a long wooden tray, heaped with cinnamon rolls and muffins, as well as ramekins of extra icing and a sweet orange glaze that smelled like heaven.

"I'm not here to stay." Maren flashed a smile that looked like sunshine as she set down a small stack of saucers next to the tray. "But no one can work on an empty stomach, and I had this prepped last night anyway, so they were easy to just toss in the oven."

The commissioner lit up like someone had just handed him a winning lottery ticket and jumped to his feet, reaching for a saucer. "Now you're speaking my language. What can you tell me about these little beauties?"

Maren winked discreetly in Wilder's direction as he looked over the pastries. "First, we've got a raspberry crème fraiche muffin, laced with just a bit of brandy, as well as a cinnamon-burnt sugar roll with bitter-orange sauce."

The commissioner managed to pull his eyes away from the pastries long enough to glance up at Maren. "Agent James, I looked into your credentials a bit when this whole thing was coming together, which were impressive." He rubbed his palms together and eagerly took the refill for his coffee cup that Trobaugh offered. "But you've outdone yourself here. Don't go too far. I want you and Agent Norse to weigh in on some developments for us in a few minutes."

Maren put both on a plate for him, added a touch of sauce to each, and handed it over, ducking out and down the hall as quickly as she'd appeared. The clink of ceramic saucers blended with the toasty warmth of fresh coffee in the air seemed to take the edge off everything and gave Wilder a chance to glance over the article on the front page of the paper as her boss dug into the treats. Banyon had reached someone who knew the situation between Jessa and Fardulis and wasn't afraid to talk about it. The source was noted as "confidential," of course, but whoever it was seemed to know more than even Jessa had disclosed to Darcy when they were at her house. Wilder's mind spun, trying to remember who Jessa had said even knew about her and her teacher, but all she could remember was a max of two people she might have confided in: a friend at her college and someone at her church here in Salem. She shook her head at the roll Hooper tried to push in her direction and took a sip of her coffee. Whoever Jessa told her secrets to, they needed to find them. They might have even more information than what had landed on the front page, and at this point, they needed every advantage they could get.

"Well, let's get to it, shall we?" The commissioner dug into his second roll with a devotion that almost brought a smile to Wilder's face. "Tell me about your little visit to the good reverend's daughter."

Tala had just buttoned her jeans and pulled on a sky-blue cashmere sweater when she heard a knock at the door. She ran her fingers lightly through her still-damp hair and opened the door, motioning Darcy in with a sigh of relief.

"God. I'm so glad you're here. I'm dying to know what's happening, but I didn't know whether to go down there or not." She leaned to look down the hall before she pulled Darcy inside and the door shut behind them. "Where's Maren?"

"She's in our room studying that amended profile you put together for us. She's been obsessed lately, convinced she's missing something." She looked around suddenly, her gaze settling on the cooling coals in the fireplace. "That's why you always smell like woodsmoke. You guys have a fireplace in here."

"Yeah. I usually light a fire in the mornings, just to take the chill out of the air." Tala nodded in the direction of the couch, noticing for the first time that Darcy had brought her a plate. "That looks amazing. Are those cinnamon rolls?"

Another knock startled them, the echo obscenely loud in the quiet room. Maren didn't bother with pleasantries as she stuck her head around the door and handed Tala a steaming mug of coffee, then ducked out without a word.

"It's not like her to miss a chance to say something." Tala sipped the coffee, watching the dark macadamia-nut steam rise to her nose as she looked down appreciatively. "Is she okay?"

"You know, the more we hang out, the more respect I have for that weirdo." Darcy leaned back into the sofa and tucked her legs underneath her. "At first, she comes off as…" Darcy tried not to laugh but looked at Tala, and it was a lost cause. "Well, you know how she comes off. But more than once she's really surprised me. At any given point in the day, she's going over everything we know and a few things we don't about this case."

"I get what you mean there." Tala sank back down on the sofa and reached for her cinnamon roll, pulling apart the buttery brioche layers, a sweet swirl of toffee-scented cinnamon glaze dripping languidly onto her fingers. "There's a lot to her that isn't immediately obvious, but I think that's her secret weapon: she knows what she's doing. I walked down to the kitchen in the middle of the night to get some water a few days ago, and she was sitting on the counter going through a pile of her notes. It looked like she'd been there for hours." Tala dropped the first bite into her mouth with a contented sigh. "Anyway, I trust her. And I don't say that about many people." Tala set her saucer down on the coffee table and picked up her coffee, a smile sweeping across her face. "You guys look like you're getting along well."

"We are," Darcy said with a sudden interest in her shirt cuff. "And that's all I'm saying for now."

"Fine. We'll save it for later." Tala reached for another corner of her roll. "Did everything smooth out downstairs, though? Did Wilder's boss calm down?"

"Yeah. Of course. Trobaugh and Hooper got him laughing, and Maren fed him. It's a hard combination to resist."

Tala smiled. "For anyone, I'd imagine."

Darcy smiled, and Tala resisted the urge to press for details. For now, it was enough that she looked happy. She set her cup down on the table and grabbed one of the pillows, wrapping her arms around it, and told herself not to talk about what had been lurking at the back of her mind since their visit to the medical examiner. She glanced over at Darcy and made herself take a sip of coffee. Unfortunately, knowing when to leave things alone had never been her strong suit.

"Just ask." Darcy scooted Tala's plate over to the end of the coffee table and propped her feet up on the edge. "I don't know if I'll have an answer, but at this point, we've lived together, checked out some dead bodies together, and might even know a couple of each other's secrets." She smiled. "So why not?"

Tala had to laugh, at the same time trying to ignore the burn of the stupid tears behind her eyes. She picked at a loose thread on the pillow in her lap, her coffee forgotten. She looked up to the ceiling, choosing the words, then turning them over in her mind before she let them fall together.

"My mother." A tear fell onto Tala's cheek, and she looked again at the ceiling, too overwhelmed to care. "What did she...?"

Darcy pulled tissues from the box on the side table, then offered them carefully, as if she knew somehow a sudden movement in this moment might be too much. She waited for her to go on, but Tala felt frozen, afraid of the answers to the only questions she had.

"It seems like you might not know what to ask." Darcy's voice was soft and calm. "Is that right?"

Tala nodded, but she couldn't make herself look at Darcy. It was just too much. "I'm sorry. I'm not trying to be rude. I just—"

"You don't have to explain." Darcy's voice was gentler than her words. "Just say what you need to say."

She paused then, turning around so that her back was to Tala on the couch. Tala wordlessly turned around as well, and the painfully rigid muscles in her shoulders started to relax as she leaned into the slow warmth of Darcy's slender back. She stared into the fireplace as a cloud passed over the sun. They sat in silence and watched it cast the room in a violet-gray haze, almost as if evening had suddenly replaced morning.

"I feel like I should have all these questions." Tala whispered the words as if they were a secret. Because they were. The room seemed to grow warmer suddenly as she dragged her sleeve across her cheek to catch the tears. "I guess I've always needed to know…" She paused. "That she's—"

Tala felt a faint whoosh rush past the couch. She opened her eyes as Darcy turned around slowly to look at the fireplace, where a small fire was suddenly dancing, hovering just above the cooled, ash-covered coals.

"That she's still here?" Darcy smiled, then gently turned so they were back-to-back again. The fire crackled in the hearth, red-gold sparks spiraling up the chimney at the moment the words fell together in Tala's heart, like the ragged edges of a broken stone clicking back together.

"What does *she* need me to know?"

The only sounds in the room were the climbing flames, the crack and hiss of the burning wood that wasn't there, and Tala's heartbeat, the same heartbeat that had sounded so loudly in her ears in the hall that night. The scent of burning pinyon bark and reservation dust drifted by her, dense and acrid, and Tala squeezed her eyes shut against the memory of the empty hall and the chipped paint of the edge of her mother's bedroom door, cool and sharp under her fingertips. She made herself breathe it in, to feel the pounding of blood in her head, to be willing to open that door. She filled her lungs with breath like armor and held it. She couldn't do anything to help her mother then, but she could stop herself from running now.

"She's proud, Tala." Darcy's words jerked her back to the present, and the palpable warmth in the room intensified. A tear dropped from Tala's chin to her wrist and slid into her palm like an offering. She held her breath and waited for Darcy to speak again. "She wants you to know she's sorry she couldn't be there to give it to you herself." Darcy stopped. "But…" She hesitated, as if listening, then started again. "Sky… Willow."

A sob clutched Tala's chest, but for the first time since that day, the grief was lifting, like a trapped willow branch released from the ground. It was changing, shapeshifting with every word that hovered in the darkened room. "Why?" Tala asked as she watched the shadows of the flames flickering against the log walls.

Darcy was quiet for a long time. Tala held her breath.

"She says you already know."

"She's right." Tala smiled into the fire, closing her eyes as the warmth in the room intensified, then settled over her heart. "I do."

Chapter Fifteen

A re you sure you're okay here?"
Hooper jammed a huge bite of peanut-butter-and-banana sandwich into her mouth as she pulled on her boots by the door. Wilder leaned over and looked out the window. Everyone else was already outside on the porch, waiting to head to the coroner's office.

"I'm fine. We need to make sure we have all the documentation on the victims, and I'd like one of you to just have a chat with Dr. Ard in case she's run across anything else we can use. She left me a message about having found something with the Fardulis autopsy overnight, and at this point we need all the damn clues we can get. I'm staying because I've got to do some paperwork or I'm going to drown."

Hooper crumpled the paper towel she had wrapped around her sandwich into a ball and shoved it into her pocket. "Can do. I'll talk to her myself."

"And hey, my ex has a shop on the square on the other side of the museum, so steer clear." Wilder smiled as Tala walked past the window, laughing with Darcy and scraping her hair into a ponytail. "I don't want her to see Tala for even a second. She's surprised me with how vicious she's been about the possibility of someone else in my life, and I've gotten some really nasty texts from her lately."

"About Tala?"

"Yes, indirectly." Wilder tossed her keys to Hooper, who caught them with one hand and dropped them into her shirt pocket. "So, I'm counting on you to intervene if she runs into you guys and gets in Tala's face. I was so angry when we saw her in the diner, I almost decked her." She paused, catching sight of Tala examining a birds' nest built into one corner of the porch roof. "Not that I don't think she can take care of herself—"

"But you don't want her to have to?"

"Exactly."

"I'll have my eye on the situation. No worries. Tala's too good to have to deal with that bullshit, if you ask me." Hooper pulled a Babe Ruth candy-bar wrapper out of her pocket and handed it to Wilder, then added the paper towel ball for good measure. "Didn't the scary blonde wonder leave *you*? Why all the fire and brimstone now?"

"She did leave me, and for a man. But she went right-wing after we split up, in a major way, and frankly, I can't really predict what she's capable of now."

Trobaugh stuck her head in the door and held out her hand. "Maren wants to drive, so I'm going to head that off at the pass." She winked at Wilder. "I'll say no, so you don't have to. I'd like to make it to retirement in one piece."

Hooper handed her the keys and zipped up her jacket. "Everyone has their phones on, so keep us posted if you happen to see a random serial killer wandering around the place." She opened the door, sticking her head back just before it closed. "Sure you don't want to have Robinson send a patrol car to sit out here?"

"Right, and have one less in town managing the chaos? No, thanks."

"Fine, but if you're dead and can't cook tonight, I'm gonna throw a fit." Hooper winked as she shut the door, and Wilder watched everyone pile into the Jeep, where Trobaugh was already in the driver's seat, blasting Joan Jett.

Wilder wandered into the kitchen and poured the last of the coffee, leaning back against the sink as she took a moment to savor the memory of the night before. Flashes of Tala's amber skin, the deep flush across her chest as she arched her back…it all had been playing on a loop in Wilder's mind since her feet hit the floor in the morning. Not that it did her much good. It was nearly two in the afternoon by the time the commissioner felt up to speed and finally left the cabin to go back to Boston.

The doorbell rang suddenly, followed by a knock hard enough to rattle the coffee in her cup. Wilder looked at her watch. It had only been about five minutes since the rest of the task force pulled out of the drive, and even if they'd forgotten something, every one of them had a key. She pulled on her boots before she checked the peephole and opened the door.

"Reverend Davis." She paused, taking note of the dented Toyota Camry parked behind him. No one else was in it. "How can I help you?"

"I think it's about time we had a little chat, don't you?" The reverend pushed past Wilder and started down the hall, then stopped when he finally seemed to realize he didn't know where he was going. Wilder pointed toward the den. Sunlight hovered in the empty space as they walked in, the silence amplified by the absence of fire in the fireplace, but the room was warm and inviting, and the scent of coffee still hung in the air from earlier that morning.

"Roger, I'm afraid we're out of java, but can I get you some bottled water, or perhaps start a new pot? It only takes a couple of minutes to brew."

"Never mind about that." He sat on the leather chair across from the couch, carefully taking off his jacket and folding it into thirds before placing it on his lap. "We'd better just get to the matter at hand."

The reverend was short, with yellowing gray hair that he combed back with a wide-tooth comb and a greasy product. Or at least Wilder hoped it was product. His face was round, with too-small dark eyes and thin lips he licked far too often. His clothes had that stuffy scent that every secondhand store seemed to be drenched in, and it filled the room within seconds.

"And what is the matter at hand?" Wilder settled onto the couch, wishing she could open a window. "How can I help you today?"

"Let's be honest, son. You don't give a good goddamn how you can help me." White spittle gathered into the corners of his mouth almost instantly, and Wilder watched as he leaned forward in the chair. "You force your way into my home without my knowledge, separate my daughter from her mother, and accuse her of sleeping with her *teacher*? What kind of a perverted mind do you have to even suggest that?"

Wilder tensed, suddenly aware of her service weapon on her hip. The reverend's energy was different than she'd ever seen. He was right on the edge of something, and Wilder had no interest in finding out what.

"First of all, you know I'm a woman, and your wife willingly invited us in that morning. I didn't accuse your daughter of anything. She's a victim, plain and simple, and we needed to talk to her because she might have had information that we needed at that point." Wilder lowered her tone and took a breath. "Believe me, the last thing I wanted to do is upset your wife or your daughter, but she was kind enough to talk to us about an issue that happened while she was still at Salem High, an issue we believe was ongoing and may be relevant to current events."

"You mean the dead drama teacher whose name you're now dragging through the mud as some molester of young girls?"

"Yes, sir. The relationships he allegedly engaged in were illegal, and had he not been killed, I would have personally made sure he was held accountable."

"Come on. You really think the blame lies with the man here?" The reverend threw his head back and laughed, although the sound fell flat quickly. "He had to work with oversexed teenage girls all day, and it's only a matter of time before he made a mistake, if you can even call it that. I know how they are these days. They offer it up on a silver platter." The reverend flexed his hands and pulled them back into the fists Wilder guessed he didn't even know he was making. "With all the distractions these days, young girls aren't interested in living a godly Christian life anymore. All they want to do is flaunt their flesh on the TikToks and try to seduce men of God to stray from their convictions." He paused, which seemed to amplify his anger rather than the other way around. "I've focused on leading my flock back to God and the righteous path like never before in the last few years, but whorish young women on the devil's payroll are one of the biggest obstacles."

Wilder held his eyes and took a measured breath. She didn't like where this was headed, but changing his repugnant belief system wasn't on her to-do list for the day. "Roger, can you tell me when you found out about the relationship between your daughter and Mr. Fardulis?"

"I've known for a couple of years now, since she was a junior in high school, although this was a shock to her mother, thanks to your little impromptu visit the other morning. I'd hoped he'd take a more serious interest in her, and I think it would've headed that way, but then she insisted on flitting off to college instead of finding a husband."

"What was happening," Wilder fixed her gaze on the reverend and leaned forward, elbows firmly on her knees, "if indeed it happened, and I believe your daughter that it did, was a crime. She bears zero responsibility for it, for the record." Wilder looked at the dark mirror of cold coffee in her hand to refocus. "You should have reported it, but we're beyond that now. We believe Mr. Fardulis was killed sometime during the night on Thursday. Where were you during that time period?"

"I was at the church, all night, going over this week's sermon."

"Were you alone?" Roger nodded, and Wilder went on, keeping her voice even. "Can anyone corroborate that allegation for us? For example, is the church equipped with video surveillance of any kind?"

The pools of spittle at the corner of the reverend's mouth grew to foam, and his face started to reflect the fires of Revelation. He started to speak, sputtered, then got up and unfolded his jacket, jamming his arms through the sleeves so hard they caught at the elbow and threw him off balance. "If you're accusing me of murder, you're wasting your time and the time of the entire village." He paused to slip into full sermon mode, with the same sing-song cadence of every preacher that has ever stepped behind a pulpit he considered a throne. "With all the sin and iniquity our community is drowning in these days, with rampant abortion, men parading around as women, and the collapse of the godly home as we all know it... You're insinuating that I, a man of God, may have had something to do with it?"

Wilder followed as he led them back down the hall and opened the front door for himself, stepping onto the porch. He turned around slowly, his face dripping in derision. "And, might I add, that you might want to remove the plank from your own eye before you look for the speck in *mine*, of all people. It would be a shame if this killer was suddenly on your doorstep."

Wilder stood in the door and watched as he fired up his car and gunned it so hard the back wheels spun the gravel into a spitting fan as he pulled out onto the road. Wilder noticed him staring into the rearview as he disappeared, but once he was finally out of sight, she pulled her phone from her shirt pocket, hit *pause* on the active recording, then punched the dial button for one of her contacts. She answered after only two rings.

"Mrs. Davis?" She walked back into the house and clicked the deadbolt in place behind her. "I hope I haven't caught you at a bad time. I have a couple of questions I was hoping you could help me with."

❖

"They pulled *what* out of his throat?"

Wilder dropped her fork onto her plate and shook her head as she watched Hooper gleefully pouring sausage gravy over a split biscuit and following it with a drizzle of maple syrup. She'd subbed in and volunteered to cook tonight, deciding with no one's approval that Breakfast for Dinner was the theme of the night, and that a box of rice crispies, a case of lager, and a couple of pounds of bacon were going to cut it. Tala and Trobaugh had stepped in, thank God, and they'd ended up with fluffy sweet-potato pancakes, biscuits and cream gravy, and crispy fried eggs over smoky, seared country ham to round out the selections.

"It was wild, man." Hooper folded the last slice of bacon into her mouth with a satisfied look of bliss. "Dr. Ard showed us a video of her pulling it out with these long tweezers. It was rolled up, and the words were burned into waxed paper."

"Which was smart, I gotta give it to our guy, despite not being in the business of handing out scout badges to serial killers." Trobaugh handed the plate of biscuits to Tala, grabbing one for herself on the way. "The wax was just waterproof enough to keep the writing legible."

Darcy looked up from her Rice Krispies. "What was the verse again?"

"Revelations 21:8. *The immoral will be consigned to burn forever in a lake of burning sulfur.*" Hooper looked up, the next bite of ham suspended on her fork. "Whatever that is."

"We have the photos from the autopsy, so I'll look it up, but what's your take on this?" Wilder glanced around the table, and everyone turned to Tala.

"What?" Tala said, coffee cup dangling from her fingers. "It's not like I have him on speed dial or something."

"Close enough." Darcy shot a smile in her direction. "Let's hear it."

Tala pushed her plate toward the center of the table and leaned back in her chair. "Look, I know we touched on this before, but I think our killer is goading us with a very specific purpose. Remember how no body was associated with the number two?" She paused, glancing around the table. "Take a closer look at our bible verse there."

Wilder got up and grabbed a dry-erase marker, nudging the whiteboard out of the corner and writing *Revelations 21:8* at the top. She looked for a moment, head tilted to the side at the same angle as the rest of the table. "Okay. Somebody jump in here. I got nothing."

Tala stayed where she was and looked at Darcy, who was staring at the whiteboard.

"I might have it." Darcy walked over to Wilder and took the marker out of her hand. "Take the chapter number, 21. Two plus one is three, right? Then add three to eight, which is the verse number, and what do you get?"

Trobaugh studied the board like every word was written in a different language. "Eleven?"

"Exactly." Darcy continued writing. "Then break that down to single numbers, and we have one plus one, correct?"

"What a clever bastard." Wilder took the marker and wrote the number two across the top of the board. "There's our missing body number two."

"Well, slap my ass and call me Martha!" Maren smacked the table with her hand for emphasis, which unfortunately still contained half a biscuit. "But doesn't that mean that…"

"Yeah." Tala leaned back in her chair and picked up her coffee. "That's exactly what it means."

Trobaugh looked pointedly into her empty coffee cup, then slid it over to Hooper to fill from the carafe next to her. "Am I just under-caffeinated? What the hell are you guys talking about?"

Wilder recapped the pen and joined everyone at the table, brushing her fingertips lightly over Tala's shoulder as she passed. "It means that the killer is sending us a message. The first victim had that vertical cut down her palm, that we couldn't be sure wasn't an accident, the second victim had four scratches on her lower abdomen, and we had the same problem there. The third victim had her tongue cut into three pieces, but again, that number could have been symbolic or random."

Trobaugh tapped her pen on the table. "So we had representations of the numbers one, four, and three, if indeed that's what it was, but we were missing—"

"The number two." Wilder nodded. "I think with that element added, we're looking at a killer who's numbering his bodies and intends to continue. And unless I'm way off, I think he's challenging us. From this point it's a race to stop him from recreating the body count of the witch trials."

"Maybe more importantly, the fact that it was a bible verse condemning immorality ties the motive up pretty nicely," Tala said, reaching for the carafe and nearly knocking over Hooper's water in the process.

Trobaugh grabbed a notebook from the stack on the table behind her. "How so?"

"This killer is taking out people he thinks are exhibiting immoral behavior." Tala paused. "Our first victim, Chesney, had a charge for solicitation, correct? So, she possibly dabbled in sex work, although we don't know that for sure, and she was trans, which, given the killer's assumed motivations, no doubt felt like a call to action."

"But what about the second victim, Miriam, the midwife?" Trobaugh jotted in the notebook as she spoke. "She sounds like an all-around saint."

"I mean, it depends on your perspective, but she did have that affair recently that everyone in town knew about." Wilder cut in. "Most people wouldn't even give it a thought, but something about our killer and that bible verse makes me think they noticed."

"And then we have Gillian Thomas, the Boston University student who was home on break." Tala tapped her pen on the table and spun it slowly through her fingers. "Wasn't she known at BU for her activism supporting women's rights and her political aspirations?"

"And she was an out lesbian." Wilder nodded, running a hand through her hair. "All of our victims have reasons the killer might find them morally—"

The doorbell rang and then rang again. Everyone looked in Wilder's direction, and Wilder looked at her watch. "What the hell? It's after eight."

"Listen. It ain't easy being Salem's lesbian superhero." Maren winked as she gathered up the dishes, hooking the syrup pitcher with her pinky as she headed for the kitchen. "I'd imagine the women of this town have you on speed dial."

Wilder laughed and walked down the hall, looking through the peephole before she opened the door.

"Wilder Mason? Chief of police?" The speaker barely waited for Wilder to nod before he continued, words falling over each other like a handful of stones scattered across the porch. "Howard Banyon from the *Boston Globe*. We met at the last crime scene?"

"You're aware the gag order for the press has been reinstated, right?"

"I do realize that."

Wilder stepped out on the porch and closed the door behind her. "How can I help you? If you can tell me what it's about, that might help."

"I've done a little digging myself." Banyon cleared his throat, glancing at the closest window when Hooper moved the curtains back and peeked out. "I just want to know if you think there's a correlation between the Salem Witch Trials of 1692 and the current murders." He waited for Wilder to answer. She did not. "I mean, the evidence does seem to support that theory."

Wilder paused before she answered. Anything she said could and would be public, but if he knew something, this was her chance to get it. She motioned them from the door over to the porch railing and leaned against it.

"And what evidence are you talking about?"

Howard looked slightly thrown off. Wilder watched him pat his shirt pocket for what she assumed was his notebook or his cigarettes but then seemed to remember he had neither. Wilder also noticed a scrap of toilet paper stuck to the heel of his loafer and a lone toothpick peeking out of his polyester trouser pocket.

"Well, I just think the correlations are there. Everyone does." He paused, shoving his hands into his pockets and colliding with the toothpick. He winced and flicked the toothpick off the railing. "So, is this a road of investigation that you're actively pursuing?"

Wilder waited a couple of beats longer than necessary before she replied. "And are you asking me this off the record? Because I happen to know you live in Boston, not Salem, so it doesn't affect your safety personally, correct?"

"That doesn't mean I don't care about the people who live here." Howard sniffed and seemed to have trouble meeting Wilder's eyes. The white plastic buttons of his thin, button-up shirt strained over his belly as he shifted his weight. "I happen to be dating someone who lives here."

"And who is that?"

"I don't have to tell you, but I think I've made it clear that the good of this community is my concern." He paused, clearing his throat again. "So, are you actively pursuing that line of investigation, or not?"

Wilder crossed her arms and leaned farther back against the railing. A bird swooped into the birdhouse above her head and flitted right back out again, the rush of air lifting the edges of her hair. "Why don't you give me a little insight into what you're talking about, and I can tell you if it's a priority right now."

"It's not rocket science, Mason." Banyon's patience seemed to be waning, and his voice hardened to a brittle tone. "You're really not seeing the similarities between the witch trials of 1692 with the goddamn pileup of bodies in 2023? I mean, the last victim was found with the actual rope used to hang the first victims of the witch hunt." He shook his head. "What more do you need?"

Wilder was silent, her gaze not wavering from his. He looked down finally, jingling his keys in his pocket. "I just think you owe it to the citizens of Salem to think about it."

"I'll keep that in mind, Howard." Wilder pushed off the railing and offered her hand. "Thanks for stopping by. I'm sure you'll be keeping an eye on our progress."

Howard shuffled down the steps and got into his dusty Kia Sorento, revving it a bit harder than necessary before he drove off. Wilder watched until the car was out of view and stared at the stars until the dust settled in the drive. Then, she opened the door and walked back in.

❖

Trobaugh and Hooper were in the kitchen cleaning up when Wilder walked by. Well, Trobaugh was, anyway. Hooper was leaning against the counter eating a bowl of mint-chip ice cream. She looked up when she saw Wilder, spoon still dangling from her mouth. "Hey. What was that all about? Harold confessing his undying love for dykes in uniform again?"

"Something like that. He asked me to be his leather daddy, and I told him I was already booked up for the month." Wilder got a glass from the cabinet and filled it with ice. "Did you guys recognize him from Salem High?"

Trobaugh started the dishwasher and dried her hands on a tea towel. "Well, I didn't like that guy the first time I saw him, in the gym, and you mentioned not seeing him on the surveillance tapes the other day, so Hoop here decided to run his plates while you guys were out there flirting."

"And?"

Hooper grinned and dropped her spoon back into the bowl. "Looks like your stalker out there is as far away from a legit reporter as it gets. More like a night manager for a low-rent motel on the wrong side of Boston, and—"

"Let me guess. The *Boston Globe* has never heard of him?"

"Bingo." Trobaugh snatched the empty ice-cream container just as Hooper was about to put it in the freezer, then tossed it in the trash. "But just to be sure, I did a quick Google search to find any bylines, and all I got back were crickets."

Wilder filled her glass with water and turned back around. "Jesus. Maybe this should be whiskey." She kneaded the back of her neck with her other hand. "I can't say I'm shocked, though. That guy had a smarmy feel about him from the get-go."

"Why he'd bother, though?" Trobaugh clicked the stove on, lowered the flame, and filled the copper kettle. "I mean, I know everyone in town is concerned, or downright freaked out and running for the damn hills, but he doesn't even live here. Why the hell does he care? You'd think he'd be headed in the opposite direction, not taking a casual Sunday drive to the police chief's house to have a chinwag about it over some iced tea."

Wilder nodded. "He did say he's dating someone in Salem. If that's actually true."

"The dating pool must be grim if they're having to import stock." Hooper handed her wife a tea bag and the little pot of sugar on the opposite counter. "Or maybe you're just tied up at the moment, and the female population is having to improvise."

Trobaugh arched an eyebrow. "You and Tala are looking pretty cozy."

Wilder tried not to smile and failed miserably. "I mean, who wouldn't be attracted to her? She's gorgeous, brilliant, and makes me feel..." She paused, searching for words to describe a feeling she'd never felt. "I can't describe it. When I'm with her, I just feel calm."

Trobaugh glanced at Hooper and bumped shoulders with her. "That's what I said when I met this one."

"And you guys have been married like, how long?" Wilder winked and stepped back. "Since the actual witch trials?"

Trobaugh nodded. "You better keep walking back there, Junior." She grinned and set her teacup in the sink. "But since you owe us now, do you mind if we use your Jeep to grab some backup ice cream? I don't want someone coming down here in the middle of the night and having a breakdown because there's no mint chip."

Hooper narrowed her eyebrows. "You're talking about me, aren't you?"

"Absolutely." Wilder smiled. "The keys are on the hook by the door."

Trobaugh glanced toward the upstairs as they headed for the door. "I almost forgot. Tala said right before you stepped outside that she was going for a shower and then for you to meet her in the sweat lodge, whatever the hell that means."

Wilder relaxed at the thought, and she nodded, filling her glass with more ice before she headed to the sauna.

CHAPTER SIXTEEN

Tala looked through the smoky glass as she heard Wilder in the doorway. She'd just gotten the fire hot enough to heat the rocks above, and the steam was perfect: delicate, silky, and meltingly soft. She relaxed against the cedar bench as Wilder took a quick shower, the shape of the slats pressing into her naked body through the towel underneath her. She was bathed in the steam, shimmering under a wash of desert-sunset tint from the fire.

Wilder opened the door with a white towel wrapped low on her waist. "Jesus Christ. You're beautiful."

Tala smiled and patted the bench by her head. Wilder sat down slowly, one hand squeezing the back of her neck. "This was such a perfect idea, and your fire looks amazing. I'm impressed. Lighting a sauna fire and keeping it at the right temp is a whole different ballgame."

"Your neck is still bothering you, isn't it?" Tala looked up from the bench and watched her kneading it with her hand. "Do you think you injured it?"

"No. It's not that." Wilder lifted Tala's head and put it on her thigh as she sat down, trailing her fingertips down the center of Tala's chest as she settled back on the bench. "At first I thought it might be the couch, but that wasn't it either."

"What do you think it is?"

"Honestly, since I was a kid it's been the part of my body that warned me when something wasn't right, when there's danger around me, so it worries me that it's been so constant. I can't figure out if it's about the case…"

"Or just about you?" Tala opened her eyes and looked up. "When's the last time you felt this way?"

Wilder laughed and rubbed her temples as if trying to push the thought out of her head. "That would be the day of my wedding to Miranda."

"Oh, that's not good." Tala reached up and brought Wilder's head down for a kiss. "Well, try to keep from marrying anyone in the next few days, for sure, but we need to figure out what's going on there sooner rather than later."

Wilder smiled and leaned back against the slats. "Do you remember that reporter that caught me going into the gym the day we found Fardulis?"

"Yeah. I think you said later he was from the *Boston Globe* or something?"

"That's him." Wilder picked up a white linen towel from the stack beside her on the bench and patted her face dry. "Well, he showed up here at the house a few minutes ago and wanted to chat."

"He wanted to *chat*?" Tala sat up, folding her legs underneath her on the bench. "He knows there's a gag order on the press right now."

"Exactly. Apparently, he wanted to know off the record whether we were looking into the connection between the original witch trials of 1692 and the serial murders now." Wilder looked over at her, her mind spinning. "He said the evidence 'supports' that line of investigation, and then he mentioned that Fardulis was found with the rope that was stolen from the museum."

Tala shook her head. "I know for a fact that we didn't make that information public. And no one would have known that was what was taken from the museum except the owner—"

"And she hasn't been back in town to even find out. I'm the only one she's spoken to about the details, and I intentionally didn't tell her." Wilder leaned back against the slats and stretched her shoulders, one by one. "I informed her the next day that an exhibit had been broken into, but I didn't even tell her which one it was. She also told me she's staying in Boston with her daughter until we find this guy. I'll look into it tomorrow and see if maybe she returned without letting us know, but that just doesn't sound like something she'd do."

"So if it wasn't her, and it certainly wasn't us that let it leak, how does your reporter know about it?" Tala sounded thoughtful. "Maybe he was digging to see what information we had so he could determine how close we are to identifying the suspect. But that still doesn't come close to explaining how he knows about the rope."

"And when I didn't jump in and confirm his theory, or even acknowledge it as something we were looking at, he seemed annoyed. Like he wasn't getting the information that he came for."

"Or he wasn't getting the admiration he came for." Tala pulled her hair up into a bun and secured it with the elastic around her wrist. "Serial killers are proud of their work, and when they aren't being recognized for it, they start to get antsy."

Tala got up and threw another ladleful of water on the hot stones, which sizzled instantly into steam and rose into a shifting silver cloud. She turned around and lay back down on the towel, pulling Wilder's hand to her chest to cover hers.

Wilder drew in the steam and smoothed a stray wisp of hair out of Tala's face with her other hand. "The crazy thing is, he's not even a reporter. Trobaugh and Hooper ran his plates and did a quick check on him, and it turns out he manages some seedy motel on the wrong side of the tracks in Boston. They even double-checked with the *Boston Globe*, but he's never worked there."

Tala rolled her eyes. "Why am I not surprised?" She was quiet for a second and then looked up at Wilder. "Do you like him for this?"

"He's way too invested and shady not to have something to do with it, even if he's not our guy. I'm going to see if I can get a judge to sign a warrant for his cell-phone records first thing in the morning. If we can track his locations using the cell towers, then we can see if he was near where the bodies were discovered." Wilder ran her fingers up and down Tala's arm as she spoke. "It's somewhere to start, at least."

"And we have eyes literally everywhere right now, so we might just get a break and not run into another body. I've never seen so many cruisers in one small town."

"Boston PD has been great." Wilder nodded. "And the interim chief they sent is used to working with these officers and seems to be getting along well with our little crew as well. It's been awesome not to have to manage the station while I'm trying to track this guy down."

After a shower and a return to the cashmere robes, Tala and Wilder headed upstairs. Tala passed the window on the landing halfway up and stopped, pressing her face almost into the glass.

"Hey. There's a light in the treehouse." Wilder leaned in to look, but she already had a pretty good idea who was out there. She'd seen Maren making a cheeseboard and tucking a bottle of wine into a picnic basket earlier that day. Sure enough, Darcy passed the window in the treehouse a few seconds later, holding a wineglass and laughing.

"Ah. I thought it was them!" Tala smiled and followed Wilder up the stairs. "There's just something about them that I love as a couple, if that's what's happening. It's like Darcy was this iceberg, and she's been melting underneath Maren's sun since she met her."

Wilder held the bedroom door open for Tala. "That's a perfect description. I didn't see it coming, but Maren seems like the perfect amount of crazy for her."

Tala walked in, saw a bottle and two whiskey glasses on her nightstand, and picked it up, turning it in her hand. "Sour cherry cordial." She smiled over at Wilder. "Thank you for this."

"I got it for you earlier today, but that one is a love-it-or-hate-it variety. It's my personal favorite, but it's not for everyone, so don't feel bad if it's too tart. I'll drink it if you don't, and there's still some of your last bottle downstairs."

Wilder started a fire while Tala pulled on some red-plaid pajamas. The crackling green pine warmed up the room before the flames erupted, and Wilder broke the seal on the cordial after she changed into her sweats and a hoodie. She handed Tala her glass and poured her own, settling down on the bed. "We've got to be careful. This could get to be a habit."

Tala smiled, clinking her glass to Wilder's. "You can drink whatever you like, you know. You don't have to drink the non-alcoholic stuff just because I do."

"I'm sure I will occasionally." Wilder pulled the quilted flannel throw off the foot of the bed and tucked it around Tala. A log shifted in the fire and sent up a shower of sparks as Wilder looked back at her. "Look, this is none of my damn business." Wilder glanced up, her dark eyes soft. "But is there a reason you don't drink?"

Tala clapped her hand over her mouth suddenly and handed her glass to Wilder, shaking her head.

"I tried to warn you." Wilder bit her lip to keep from laughing. "They're not kidding when they say it's sour."

Tala swallowed, gave a little shiver, then slowly took her glass back. "It's delicious. I just wasn't prepared for the blinding intensity of that." She took a long breath and let it out. "I'm not giving up. I've got this." She took a smaller sip and swallowed it without too much trouble, then leaned in and kissed Wilder on the cheek.

"Thank you," she said, letting her hand linger on the warmth of Wilder's inner thigh. "That first night in front of the fire, when you brought out the bottle you'd gotten for me, that was really special." She turned the glass in her hand, watching the firelight sparkle against the cut glass. "I don't date much, but when I do, my girlfriends hate that I don't drink." She paused. "I'm not an alcoholic. I've just seen too much of what it does to people, especially on the reservation. I wanted more for myself."

"I understand that." Wilder stroked Tala's cheek with her thumb. "Why play with fire?"

"I've told you about how my little brother sank into that world after high school." She took a longer sip and looked into her glass as if the memory of it was playing on the surface like a movie screen. "I'll be damned if I was going to let him go down like that."

"So what happened?" Wilder leaned back against the headboard, cradling her glass in her hand. "Where is he now?"

"Anchorage, Alaska." Pride surged through her as she looked up at Wilder. "He's stationed at Elmendorf Air Force Base and almost done with his degree."

She reached over to the nightstand and picked up her phone, clicked through her photos until she found the one she wanted, and handed it to Wilder. It was her favorite picture of the two of them, the day he graduated from basic training. His eyes were bright and glittering in the sun, the wind blowing her hair around them both.

"After he finished basic training, I saw a light come on in his eyes that I'd never seen before. He loves the military, and now he's just—"

"Happy?"

"Exactly." Tala laughed, taking her phone back and setting it on the nightstand again. "And suddenly, he was really okay. And I was free to concentrate on my career. But I'm aware things could have turned out very differently. We're both sober, and we've never talked about it, but I'm guessing the reasons are similar."

Wilder got up and stacked two more logs on the fire, turning out the overhead light and leaving just the amber mica lamp glowing by the sofa. "So, I have a question." She climbed back onto the bed and refilled their glasses, handing Tala hers with a slow kiss.

"Hit me," Tala said, then reconsidered. "Doesn't mean I'm going to answer it, though."

"The first day I met you, you gave me your on-the-fly profile, which was scarily accurate, although one part of it was off."

"Ah." Tala smiled. "I said you weren't a top." She tapped her finger lightly against her glass. "That wasn't actually the whole story."

"I'm all ears." Wilder held up the duvet, and Tala crawled in beside her. "It stuck in my head because it's the only thing I've heard you say that wasn't spot-on."

"I tend to date girls who let me lead." Tala smiled. "In a few different ways. So I think I may see everyone through that lens if I don't know them."

Wilder laughed, setting her glass and Tala's on the nightstand. "So, you're the boss in bed because you haven't met someone who could handle the job?" The first button on Tala's pajama top slipped through her fingers. "Or you didn't give them a chance?"

"In hindsight, maybe I didn't give them a chance." Tala watched as the rest of her buttons gave way. "Why? You think you can handle it?"

"I think you'll find I can handle all of you, Ms. Marshall." Wilder traced the slope of her shoulder with the heat of her mouth, then pulled her own hoodie over her head and the rest of her clothes off the side of the bed. She slid Tala underneath her and closed her eyes hard when Tala took one of her nipples into her mouth, swirling it with her tongue. Wilder's voice was lower this time, a scrape. "God. You're so beautiful." She hooked Tala's pajama bottoms with her thumb and dropped them off the side of the bed as she flipped Tala over in the darkness so she was sitting across her hips, the fire vibrant and sparkling behind her.

Wilder's hand slipped underneath her, and she tipped her hips forward until Tala's clit was slicked against the heel of Wilder's hand. Tala closed her eyes, biting her lip as Wilder started to move and slipped two fingers inside, her hips rocking against Tala's, keeping the heel of her hand softly against her clit.

"Oh, God." Tala's voice was more breath than words as she met Wilder's rhythm. Wilder held her eyes, the muscles in her shoulders tense and just starting to glow with a soft sheen of effort. Wilder shifted so the back of the hand inside Tala was also sliding over her own clit. She slowed to a stop, then placed her other hand in the center of Tala's chest. "Put your hands on my wrist, baby. Just ride me."

Tala held Wilder's wrist, leaning into her, and Wilder met every soft circle of her hips with her own. Tala's hair fell forward and brushed Wilder's abs, and she felt herself letting go, just letting Wilder move her. Wilder's arms flexed, creating their own rhythm, and her thighs began to tremble around Wilder's hips. Tala rode more intensely, watching Wilder's muscles ripple from shoulder to abs, her breath suddenly deeper and faster. She bit her lip, watching as Wilder neared the edge, as she arched her hips, her hand still strong in the center of Tala's chest, and came underneath her with the intensity of the earth cracking open. Every muscle pulled taut at the same second, and Tala watched the orgasm roll through her body before she closed her eyes and slipped dangerously toward the edge herself.

"Keep riding me, baby." Wilder stroked the tense spot inside her as her hips started to move again. "Let me watch you come for me."

Tala leaned back, her hands behind her on Wilder's thighs, losing her breath when Wilder started working Tala's clit with her thumb. Her body took on its own rhythm, slicking back and forth against Wilder's hand, her clit swollen and straining against Wilder's touch. She always held herself back at this point, never felt safe enough to let someone push her over the edge, but with Wilder, she had no choice. She started to come, felt it wash over her like an ocean wave, pulling and pushing until she was trembling all over as she sank onto Wilder's chest.

"Breathe, baby." Wilder said as she pulled her into her arms. It was a few long moments before Tala stopped trembling and Wilder pulled the duvet up over them both. "You're safe with me."

❖

When Wilder woke up the next morning, Tala was already gone, the scent of fresh coffee wafting up the stairs. She checked her watch and reluctantly rolled out of bed, thankful she'd woken up in time for a shower, then paused at the window to check for the light in the barn that meant Tala and Hooper would be almost done with yoga.

By the time she got downstairs, only Trobaugh was in the kitchen, holding what looked like an empty carton of pumpkin-spice creamer in front of an open refrigerator. She stared into the open carton as if there might be a hidden stash in one of the corners. "Goddamn it. The only thing I told Maren to stay out of and she comes down here and chugs it in the middle of the night like some kind of stoned frat boi." She tossed the carton into the trash a touch harder than necessary. "I love the communal-living thing, but I can't catch a serial killer without coffee, and we're all supposed to be in the war room in fifteen."

Wilder smiled, moving some frozen vegetables around in the freezer. "Isn't that Tala's thing, too? I don't know how you two drink that kind of a sugar bomb in the morning, but whatever." She handed her what looked like a foil-covered brick and shut the freezer door. "The minute I met Maren I thought that might happen, so I invested in a backup."

Trobaugh peeled off the foil to reveal a carton identical to the one she'd just thrown away. "Are you telling me you stockpiled and disguised emergency reserves of pumpkin-spice creamer?" Trobaugh almost laughed and caught herself just in time. "You're in love, and this proves it." She popped the carton into the microwave and clicked through a few buttons as the front door flew open and Hooper loped into the kitchen.

"Hey. I know I'm late. I just need to change clothes, and I'll be ready." She looked around and grabbed a coffee cup. "Where is everyone?"

"Maren and Darcy are already in the war room, and according to Darcy, Maren went back there last night after their date and stayed until around three in the morning. This Harold guy is throwing her for a loop, and she's convinced we've missed something."

"She just has a bad feeling about him?" Hooper heaped a spoon with sugar, spilling most of it onto the counter before it made it into her coffee cup. "Or what?"

"I get it." Trobaugh glanced over at Wilder. "That thing last night was just strange, so I think she's right. He's involved somehow. We just have to find out how."

Hooper hooked a finger into the handle of her coffee cup and headed for the stairs, pausing to look back over her shoulder. "Where's Tala, by the way? I waited to start this morning, but she never showed up in the barn for yoga."

Wilder's stomach dropped. "She wasn't out there with you this morning?"

"No. I haven't seen her since last night."

Wilder met Trobaugh's gaze, and they rushed down the hall at the same time, but Wilder could tell from the voices that only Maren and Darcy were in the war room. Tala's chair was empty, her favorite pen crossed over her case folder in front of it.

Trobaugh got the words out first. "Have either one of you seen Tala this morning?"

Maren ran a hand through her hair, and Wilder noticed for the first time that the strain was starting to show on her face. "Nah, mate. We figured she was still upstairs with you."

Wilder's heart was pounding as she ran up the stairs. If Tala wasn't upstairs, she wasn't in the house. And if she wasn't in the house—Wilder raced around the corner into their room, where silence hung like dust motes in the air, sliced through with a wide swath of winter sunlight.

Chapter Seventeen

"Just sit for a second and breathe, mate." Maren held a cell phone to one ear with one hand, the other resting on Wilder's shoulder as she sat frozen on the bed. "You're frantic, that's understandable. But you crazy bastards had guns on me once when I came back after being gone for twenty minutes, so we can hope it's just something like that. When is the last time we saw her?"

"Last night. When I woke up, she was gone."

"What was she wearing?"

Wilder gave her a look and rolled her eyes.

"Sorry. Force of habit."

Heavy footsteps clomped up the stairs, and Hooper rounded the corner of Wilder's bedroom. She looked serious and was pale. "Guys, we found something. You need to come downstairs."

Wilder looked at Maren, then punched the doorframe as she walked through it. She followed Maren downstairs and into the hall, shaking the pain out of her fingers. *How could this have happened to someone I love, on my watch, in my own damn house?*

The front door was standing open, and she could see Robinson's car pulling up in the drive. Trobaugh stood guard on the porch, her shoulders braced in a way that showed Wilder she wasn't going to want to see whatever Trobaugh, obviously in detective mode, was guarding. The feeling in the air as Wilder walked out was like nothing she'd experienced before, like present at the scene of a crime yet trapped in a nightmare at the same time.

Trobaugh pointed to the left of the door, on the porch floorboards. It was Tala's cell phone and two small drops of blood. Wilder leaned on the railing and stared like this was happening to someone else, while Robinson climbed the porch stairs and instantly stepped into action, taping off the porch as he radioed in for additional units. Trobaugh and Hooper were stoic as they led her inside to the war room, followed by Maren.

"Look, mate," Maren said, her voice more serious than Wilder even knew was possible. "This looks bad. I'm not going to sugarcoat it for you, but let's examine the facts and just go from here, okay? You've got all of us with you, and whoever this bastard is, we're going to find him and take him down before anything happens to your girl."

"Why would she even be down here?" Tears burned the back of Wilder's eyelids, and she willed them away, steadying her voice. "I woke up this morning before dawn, and she was asleep beside me, so whatever happened, it was in the last few hours."

"Wilder." Darcy's voice was even as she walked into the room, holding Tala's phone in her gloved hand. "I know this is a long shot, but do you know the password to get into her phone?"

"I have no idea." Wilder raked a hand through her hair. "She's hardly ever on it anyway. Is it even locked?"

"Yeah." Darcy set the phone on the table and stepped back. "It's locked. That's the first thing I checked."

"Would you have heard her leave?" Maren looked over her shoulder at Wilder. "Like, I'm a stone-cold sleeper. When I'm out, I'm out—"

"Same here." Wilder took the glove Trobaugh offered her and picked up the phone. "She very easily could have left without waking me." She took a deep breath and looked at Trobaugh. "How fresh is the blood? Give it to me straight."

"Visually, I'd say two to three hours."

"What the hell?" Panic rose in Wilder's chest. "I know she's always up first to get the coffee going before yoga, but she and Hoop go out the back door and across the grass to the barn. Why would she be on the front porch that early in the morning?"

"Us all being here together might have given us a sense of safety that we shouldn't have assumed we had." Maren looked out the window at the additional units pulling into the drive. "Listen. I'm going to get Robinson and your guys on the smaller shit so we can get a head start on tracking her the hell down." She pulled on her jacket and zipped it up. "Tell me you have a home security system. I remember seeing a camera on the right of the main door."

"I do." Wilder looked up and tried to focus. "You can access it through the pantry. There's a smaller door to the left of the sauna entrance. It's an unlocked alcove, and the footage should be rolling and easily accessible. It's a standard system, so have them back it up a few hours."

Trobaugh looked at Hooper, who nodded after a long pause. "Actually, Maren, if you can get them started patrolling the grounds, taping off anything they find, we'll go over the footage together rather than have the officers do it."

Wilder rubbed her temples and looked up. "Except for Robinson, if we could just keep the officers outside the house for the time being…" She paused, unsure how to wrap words around how she was feeling. "We don't know who we can trust, and I want people looking for Tala who know her and care about her."

"That's us, mate. Copy that." Maren ran a hand through her hair and headed for the door. "I'll update Robinson so he can get the officers and CSI started. Then I'll meet you guys in the alcove."

Wilder joined Maren and Hooper as they headed for the door, looking back over her shoulder just in time to see Trobaugh ask a silent question and Darcy almost imperceptibly shake her head.

❖

"God, I wish the lighting was better across the front of the house." Wilder tapped on the small alcove table and leaned over Trobaugh's shoulder as she backed up the footage from that morning. "Nothing ever happens here, so I never watch it. And call me crazy, but I assumed my house would be the last fucking place the serial would hit."

"Nah. I thought that too." Hooper watched intently as she rolled a pen through her fingers. "We all could have been more vigilant."

Trobaugh looked up at Wilder. "What time did you wake up with her beside you?"

"Around four this morning, and she was asleep, so whatever went down had to have happened after then."

Hooper leaned in to check the spinning clock on the bottom edge of the video. "And you have no interior cameras, correct?"

"Nothing. Just the motion detectors over the entrances."

Trobaugh stopped the tape at four a.m. and started fast-forwarding it. Time seemed to slow, thicken, and wind itself around Wilder like a snake as she tried to push away the awareness of how quickly the killer had done away with his victims in the past. *Tala's an agent, though. She has years of instinct and skills in her back pocket.* She pressed back the tears burning behind her eyelids. *This had to be different.*

"Hang on. Go back." Hooper leaned in, and Trobaugh halted the tape. "I think I saw something at 6:01 a.m." Trobaugh put it on a slow rewind, and Hooper kept her fingertip pointed at the lower right quadrant of the screen. "Look. Do you see the gravel moving there?" She paused, then clicked the tape to a halt again. "And then this." She pointed to a slice of something black on the very edge of the frame. "Doesn't that look like a bumper to you? And the corner of a plate?"

"Son of a bitch." Wilder dropped her head and leaned on the back of Trobaugh's chair, her elbows locked, every muscle in her body tensed. "He parked right out of frame. I can see the last three digits of the plate, but they're too blurry to make out."

"We'll send it to headquarters and see if they can enhance it. If those last three match, that may be enough to get a warrant." Hooper leaned closer to the screen and took a photo with her phone. "He might have gotten lucky there. But I'm inclined to think he might have known just where to park."

All three were silent for a few seconds, and then Hooper showed Wilder her phone at the same moment Wilder picked up hers and clicked it on.

"Robinson." She listened for a few seconds, then replied. "And you've made the interim chief aware of the situation?" She took a long breath. "Listen. I want you to do something for me. I need you to put out an APB for Salem and Boston Southside and get a couple of unis out on the street looking for this license plate for me." She squinted at the phone Hooper was holding up for her. Plate number Charlie-Three-Tango." She paused, looking closer. "Sierra-India-Seven. Name is Harold Banyon. Just let me know the minute you see that plate, and we'll take it from there."

"Okay. Roll tape." Wilder clicked off her phone and dropped it into her pocket. "Let's see if we can get something else. Anything."

They went through the next nine minutes of tape on the slowest speed, looking for literally anything else that came into frame, but the only other movement was what they could only assume was the same bumper leaving exactly nine minutes and three seconds after arriving.

"Well, that did fuck all." Wilder rubbed her forehead with the heel of her hand, frustration coloring her words. "All we know is that someone was here, and that was a given. Tala wouldn't have walked off on her own."

"Or left drops of her blood on the porch if there wasn't some sort of a struggle." Hooper opened the door to the alcove and held it for Trobaugh and Wilder. "This was bold as hell to just snatch one of ours right off the front fucking porch. He's making a statement with this, which may buy us some time. We just have to use every second of it to get closer to Tala."

Wilder led them down the hall and back toward the front door just as Robinson was coming through it. Brittle morning cold still clung to the air around him, and frost had slicked the sides of his black boots. He dropped his phone into his pocket and unwound the scarf from around his neck.

"Chief, we've got the APB out here in Salem and a BOLO in progress on southside Boston, as well as a detective en route to Banyon's residential address. If we hear anything, I'll let you know the second it happens."

Trobaugh and Hooper excused themselves to grab their jackets from upstairs, and Robinson laid a hand on Wilder's shoulder. "I know this is rough. I'll be here. I'm not going anywhere." He held Wilder's gaze, which felt strangely like a comforting anchor amid the chaos. "We'll catch this bastard and get her back to you, okay?"

Tala came to slowly, like being shoved though a tight, black tunnel, with every bump in the road her face bouncing against what felt like a mattress. Her hands were tied behind her back and her feet bound, but whoever did it shouldn't have bothered. Her head felt like it was being crushed from the inside out, and everything was moving in slow motion, or maybe that was her thoughts, which felt like they had an anchor dragging them underwater back into unconsciousness. After a few minutes, she realized that the cloth they'd tied over her eyes had slipped just enough for her to see a sliver of light that faded and flashed back to life again, as if being blocked by passing trees and buildings, but even that amount of light felt like too much.

She concentrated on not panicking by taking note of the few sensations she could identify within her surroundings. Her neck was aching, and the air smelled heavy, almost like a cloying candle at a Christmas party. She moved her face across the surface of what they'd dumped her on, which she could tell instantly from the texture was a cold mattress, which probably meant she was in a van, just because of its size. She heard occasional cars passing them for what seemed like hours, but after they turned off a paved road to something that sounded like dirt or gravel, the crunching of the rocks under the tires took over, and she didn't hear anyone else pass them. Someone was driving the vehicle she was in, but other than that, she was alone.

She'd felt this alone only one other time in her life. Tala turned her face deeper into the mattress and let herself fall in slow motion backward into the black abyss she'd emerged from.

❖

Wilder glanced at the rearview window as they pulled up to Roger and Marjorie Davis's home, watching as one, then two patrol cars arrived and parked silently behind her. One car was in the driveway of the house, a beat-up eighties station wagon with faux wood-paneled sides and a *Taylor Swift for President* bumper sticker adorning the rust-covered chrome bumper.

"Well, my money's on that being Jessa's car." Hooper got out first, followed by Trobaugh and Wilder. She shaded her eyes from the sun and lowered her voice, directing her question to Wilder. "How do you want to play this?"

"Quickly and cleanly, if at all possible. We don't have a warrant, so we're just hoping we can find out where the reverend is and where he was last night, if at all possible."

"And Darcy and Robinson are getting the warrants for Banyon's phone records ASAP?"

"Yeah, but we know that might take a goddamn minute. Hopefully, the fact that it's law enforcement in danger will speed up the process."

"I'm sure it will." Trobaugh looked at her watch. "No one wants anyone to get hurt, but when one of our own has clearly been abducted, I think they'll come through for us as soon as possible."

Wilder laced her fingers behind her head and looked up into the powder-blue sky. "I know you're right. I'm just—"

"You're stressed as hell, man, and we all would feel the exact same way." Hooper met her gaze. "I'd be shooting the place up if Trobaugh was in danger. You've got nothing to feel bad about."

"What about them?" Trobaugh glanced over at the patrol cars behind the Jeep. "Do they know how you want this to go down?"

"I spoke to them before we left. Two cars are front and center, with one in the back, in case he tries to flee. And I've got my radio on." Wilder had thrown on her chief's uniform, strapping on her gun holster and radio right before they raced out the door. "I need Marjorie to know this isn't a social call if she's inclined to cover for her husband."

Wilder did a test call on her radio, then all three walked carefully to the front door, keeping every window and visible exit in sight. A pendulous heaviness filled the air, and Marjorie opened the door just as they climbed the front steps, as if she'd been watching them.

"Wilder. This is unexpected." She took a step back and glanced behind her down the hallway. "May I ask what this is about?"

"Marjorie, I know it's early, but we have some questions we'd like to ask your husband. May we come in?"

Marjorie shoved her hands deep into the pockets of her pale-pink cardigan. Faded plastic buttons shaped like strawberries strained at the front, and the bottom one had been left undone. "He's not here." She faltered. "Jessa's here. She's decided to take the rest of the school semester off." It was a long few seconds before she continued, and clearly she was choosing her words carefully and using the fewest possible. She straightened her shoulders and glanced down. "But Roger left early this morning on a fishing trip."

Trobaugh stepped in and gently introduced herself and Hooper. "Mrs. Davis, this is of the utmost importance. Can we come in and speak with you about some details?"

She looked behind her again and hesitated. "I don't know. My daughter is having a bit of a hard time at the moment. Can we maybe schedule a time to sit down in a few days?"

"No." Hooper cut in, her voice deep and resonant. "You can invite us inside so we can discuss this privately, or you can come down to the station. Those are your options."

Marjorie looked across the street at her neighbor, who had just stepped out, presumably to see why police cars were parked across from her house. Marjorie hesitated, then backed up and held the door open. Jessa was coming down the stairs just as they were walking in and looked at her mother with wide eyes. "What's wrong?" She took two steps back up the staircase, suddenly sounding unsure. "Am I in trouble?"

"Jessa, it's important, but you're not in trouble." Wilder tried to keep her voice even and soothing, although she felt like breaking through every door in the house looking for Tala. "We just need to speak with you and your mother for a few minutes in the living room."

All five filed through the doorway, and Marjorie offered to make some coffee, but Wilder politely declined.

"Every second counts here, and someone could be in danger. So I'm going to ask you some questions, and I need you to tell me the truth, okay?" She paused. "Where is your husband now? Do you know what time he left?"

"I didn't hear anything." Jessa looked over at her mom. "I didn't even know he was gone until this morning when Mom told me."

Trobaugh leaned forward, her elbows on her knees, and directed her question to Marjorie. "Mrs. Davis, think carefully about this. Was this trip planned, or was it spur-of-the-moment?"

Marjorie stiffened and glanced to the right, not moving her head. Hooper picked up on the cue and asked Jessa if she might be able to go over what she remembered from the previous night out in the hall. They left, and Wilder heard Hooper direct Jessa down the hall and closer to the front door so she'd have some privacy.

"It wasn't planned." Marjorie pulled the cuffs of her cardigan down over her hands and crossed her arms in front of her. "We had a fight last night."

Trobaugh nodded. "What was the fight about, Mrs. Davis?"

"Ordinarily I don't speak up about anything, but Jessa finally told me what happened to her with that teacher." Her pale-gray eyes filled with tears, and she looked up at them for the first time. "And when I told my husband, he informed me that he *knew*. That he'd known since it started, when she was a sophomore at Salem High." She hesitated, as if unsure if she should go on. A tear dropped down the side of her nose, and she caught it with the edge of her sleeve. "Apparently, he was in the habit of reading her diary back then."

Wilder softened her voice, hoping she'd continue. "And what happened then?"

"He told me he'd been to your house to see you. And that he'd threatened you." Wilder felt Trobaugh's eyes on her but stayed focused on Marjorie. "And I told him that he couldn't just control everyone the way he's always done with me. I told him that he shouldn't have done that, and he flew into...this rage. He kept talking about how women are straying from their God-given purpose, and it's destroying the men of this town." Her voice dropped to almost a whisper. "I've never seen him like that. There was just nothing behind his eyes. And then he left. He said he knew exactly what needed to be done."

"Marjorie, if he *is* in the house, you need to tell us that now." Wilder listened for the sounds she'd heard coming from downstairs the last time she was there and didn't hear anything. "Did he hurt you or Jessa?"

"He's not here." Marjorie met her gaze. "I wouldn't lie to you, Wilder."

Wilder smiled for the first time. "I know that. And I'm going to do my best to keep you safe. I promise."

Trobaugh cut in, almost as if she'd been waiting to ask the question. "Mrs. Davis, where were you when you had this fight with the reverend?"

"We were sitting right there, where you are now. And it was around two-fifteen in the morning. I remember because the grandfather clock in the corner had gone off just a few minutes before."

"And when he left," Wilder said, "did he take anything with him? Or did he just walk out the front door?"

Marjorie shook her head. "I watched him leave, taking only the keys off the hook and the car."

"And it's registered in his name? You don't happen to know the plate number, do you?"

"Both our names." Marjorie got up and rifled around in one of the desk drawers behind her chair. Finally, she pulled out a photocopy and handed it to Trobaugh. "I always keep a copy of the registration in the desk here. Just in case. And I wrote the address of his fishing cabin on the bottom there. It's on the other side of Beverly Harbor, on Dead Horse Beach. I hope that helps."

Trobaugh and Wilder stood at the same time as Hooper rounded the corner and walked back into the living room. "Mrs. Davis, I appreciate your kindness this morning. Your daughter decided to head back upstairs, but she was very helpful."

She walked them to the door, hesitating before she opened it. She glanced up the stairs. "We bought this house a few years ago, because of some unwise choices my husband made. This one is in only my name because I used my inheritance to buy it."

"Now," Hooper smiled, "that's what I'm talking about, Mrs. Davis."

Just a hint of a smile flashed across Marjorie's face. "So, I guess my question is, do I have to let him in the house if he comes back and is being awful?"

"No, ma'am," Wilder filed out the door with Trobaugh and Hooper as she opened it. "And if you need help explaining that fact, call us at the station, and we'll gladly take that job off your hands."

"Wilder." The sun washed across Marjorie's face as she stood on the stoop, and Wilder realized she was starting to look more relaxed than she'd seen her in years. "My husband told me what you said, and how you stood up for Jessa. Thank you. It gave me the courage to do the same thing."

"Of course." Wilder smiled. "And I'll be checking in on you both soon."

Wilder started the Jeep and pulled out on the road, glancing into the rearview mirror at Hooper. "Will you call in that plate for me?"

"Already done. Did it while you were talking to the good reverend's wife."

"What did Jessa have to say?"

"We're under the gun, so I'll tell you the long version later, but her father's prone to depressive episodes and sounds like an abusive bastard. Jessa hopes he doesn't come back. He's been so on the edge the last few days she was afraid to leave her mom on her own with him, which is the real reason she hit pause on college. I also got her to take me on a little tour of the house, and I even went down into the basement and checked it out thoroughly, with her help."

Trobaugh turned around in her seat. "No signs of Tala? Or a struggle?"

"Nah, nothing, and to be honest, it would be hard to hide anything down there. It's all just an open space. The attic is only a crawl space, but I got Jessa to show me that too. She even handed me her dad's flashlight. No way she's up there."

"Goddamn it." Wilder slammed her hand against the steering wheel so hard the air vibrated around them. "We've got to find that son of a bitch."

Chapter Eighteen

Tala woke up again when the van lurched to a stop so violently it propelled her forward almost to a sitting position. Her hands and feet were still bound, but the cloth around her eyes had fallen around her neck. She looked slowly around for an escape route or something to use as a weapon but saw nothing, not that she could have utilized either even if there had been. The zip ties around her wrists and ankles were starting to cut into the skin, and the tie on her left ankle was pulled so tight her skin had swollen around it. She could hear her driver on the other side of the wall but had no chance of getting a look at him; the van was a built-out like a box, with a sheet-metal wall separating the cargo area from the driver and blacked-out windows.

The driver's side door slammed shut, and one set of heavy footfalls crunched on what sounded like gravel. The van door slid open and hit the stop with a metallic *thunk*, but the sudden sunlight behind the person standing in the door blinded her instantly. She pressed her arm over her face and lifted it slowly to let her eyes adjust.

"Well, good morning, Agent Marshall." The voice registered before the face, and her heart sank like an anchor to concrete. "It's about time to pay for your sins, isn't it?"

❖

"Are we headed for the cabin?" Hooper sat forward on her seat. "What's the plan?"

"Absolutely." Wilder flipped on her lights and sirens, turning onto an access road to give them the best chance of getting out of town quickly. "Will you guys punch that address into the GPS and tell me what you come up with? Let's see if we can get a Google Earth pic of that cabin. I think I know which one it is, but I want to be sure before we go busting in there, and some of those more remote cabins don't have visible numbers."

Hooper's fingers were already clicking over her phone screen behind Wilder. "I'm on it."

"And I have the directions pulled up." Trobaugh connected her phone to Wilder's dash display system, and the route popped up with an overview of Beverly Harbor along the Atlantic coastline and directions at the bottom of the screen. "It looks like it'll take about seventeen minutes to get there, give or take, but the roads look clear as far as the traffic report."

Eastern white pine trees and sunlight-dappled red maples lined the winding road as they headed out of town, the silence falling heavy and dense around them. The hardest part was not knowing if Tala was okay and trying not to let herself think of the very real fact that they might already be too late. Trobaugh lowered her window as they started up the winding road leading to the north edge of Beverly Harbor, the roads nearly empty, and the cold air swept through the cabin, doing nothing to budge the tension.

Wilder's phone rang, and she jumped, then clicked it through the Jeep's speaker system. "Robinson?" She took a sharp left curve as the road started climbing toward the north shore. "Tell me some good news."

"Boss, every possible unit is out in Boston, including the FBI. We've been to Banyon's house and workplace and interviewed every available person in surrounding houses. By all accounts, no one has seen him for over a month, and the mail and newspapers piled up are telling us the same thing. According to his neighbors, no one has seen his vehicle for about that amount of time, or any movement or lights in the actual residence."

"So, he's been in Salem the whole time?"

"That's my guess, but if he hasn't, he certainly hasn't been in Boston."

Hooper leaned forward between the seats and cut in. "What about his place of employment? What did they say?"

"He's been AWOL for about the same length of time, and his last check was mailed two weeks ago. We found it in his mailbox at his residence, unopened."

Wilder looked at Trobaugh and Hooper, then cleared her throat. "Let's call the DA and see if we can get a warrant expedited for that motel."

"I'm actually here now. I wanted to be sure his residence was cleared, so agents went there first, and I visited the motel myself. The owner has been completely cooperative and even gave us a master key to search all the unoccupied rooms and outbuildings. We had several units here by the time I arrived, as well as agents, so it took us less than fifteen minutes."

"How big is the place?" Wilder tapped her thumb on the steering wheel and tried to put together the next logical move. "And how many rooms are occupied?"

"It's just a small, run-down place on the southside. Only four rooms were occupied, and all of those guests allowed us to search. We cleared every room beyond that."

Trobaugh squeezed Wilder's arm, glancing back at Hooper. "And the owner didn't think Banyon had been on the property recently?"

"He did have keys that he didn't return, but she was positive. And it's such a small place, I get what she's saying. She would have seen his vehicle even if she didn't see him."

"That's good news, I think." Wilder gripped the wheel and stared straight ahead. "Let's see if the BPD will park a uni outside his residence until we find Tala, just in case. And thanks, Robinson. For going out there yourself."

"Chief, we're going to find her. It's only a matter of time." Wilder listened to him take a breath and remembered he was as tired as she was. "I'm headed back to Salem now, and I think that bastard is somewhere in town. I'll keep you posted. If he's there, we'll drag him out from whatever rock he's hiding under."

The call clicked off, and Wilder shook her head. "I can't get over the feeling she's here somewhere. If Banyon is responsible, I can't see him taking her to Boston. Ultimately, he just wants attention, and the killer has been building that momentum in Salem since this whole shitshow started."

"Hey." Hooper leaned forward between the seats again. "What the hell is that?" She pointed straight ahead at the tracks that veered off the road and disappeared sharply down an incline to the right.

Wilder pulled over slowly and flicked on her hazard lights. "Is this the only route to the cabin?"

Trobaugh scrolled back to the map on her phone. "Correct."

Wilder grabbed her flashlight and opened the door. "Well, whatever it is, we can't go past it. It's possible it's just a car that ran off the road, but we've got to find out and at least call it in."

The three of them got out and looked over the ridge to see a crumpled gray car half wrapped around the base of a tree like a frozen ocean wave. A single blinker on the right side flashed on and off like a heartbeat, and as they watched, a jagged corner of window fell out of the rear window and clinked onto the mangled chrome bumper.

"I'll make the initial call-in." They walked back the short distance to the main road, where Hooper got in and pulled up the radio, then clicked it off with her thumb and slowly climbed back out. Wilder turned around, took another look at the car that was nearly wrapped around a thirty-foot pine, and elbowed Trobaugh.

"Holy shit." Trobaugh hurried back to the edge of the ridge, snapped a picture of the license plate, and held it up, magnifying the image until Hooper compared it to the sheet of paper with the reverend's plate number. "Hoop, call it in, and get a bus on the way, but we need to get down there and see if he needs medical attention."

Wilder stepped back, raking both hands through her hair. "That car has a trunk. What if Tala is—"

"She's *not*." Trobaugh grabbed both of Wilder's shoulders and pulled her gaze forward. "She's not in the car, but we've got to work the scene. He might be alive."

Wilder nodded, and after Hooper had called it in and locked the Jeep, the three of them hiked down the ridge to the vehicle. A thin curl of gray steam was still rising from the engine, leaking through the hood that now resembled a *V*. Trobaugh had Wilder and Hooper step back while she carefully approached the driver's side of the vehicle.

"Is it him?"

Trobaugh didn't answer, just reached through the half-open window to check the driver's vitals, then leaned in far enough to grab the keys from the ignition. "It's him," she said finally, walking to the back of the vehicle. "I recognize him from the photographs in the living room this morning. And we're too late." Wilder took one step toward the car, and she held up her hand. "Wilder, just let me do this for you, okay?"

Hooper discreetly stepped between Wilder and her line of vision, but Wilder had already looked down, barely suppressing the urge to run to the crumpled sedan. She heard the trunk open, followed by a few endless seconds of silence, then a terrifying screech from an eagle soaring overhead.

"It's empty, man." Hooper squeezed her shoulder. "Davis is dead, and Tala's been nowhere near that car."

Wilder nodded, walking off the tears that threatened to spill over. She looked over the ridge, listening to the sirens in the distance, barely resisting the urge to scream. *Why would someone take Tala?* She wove her fingers through her hair and turned away from Trobaugh and Hooper, staring into the steep drop-off under the ridge edge. *If anyone, I should be the target. Why wasn't it me?*

❖

"So we have permission to go inside?"

Hooper spoke with her head nearly inside Wilder's glove box, where she was painstakingly selecting a handful of protein bars to line up carefully on the dash, apparently in order of desirability. After she'd switched up the order at least twice, she left them balancing on the edge of the dash, leaned back in her seat, and tore the wrapper off the winner with her teeth.

"We do." Wilder glanced down at the GPS display and back up to the winding road that dropped dramatically off the left side with only a few patches of rickety, rust-covered guardrails. "Robinson went over personally to deliver the death notification to Marjorie and got verbal permission to search the place. There's a spare key over the door."

"Geez. That's original." Hooper grudgingly passed the last bar in the row back to Trobaugh and straightened the remainder before returning to the conversation. "What's your feeling on this? Do you think Tala's there?"

Wilder accelerated past the speed limit and glanced again at the ETA on the display. Four minutes. "Nah, but we have to check. He was heading to the cabin, not from it, based on his direction, so he most likely didn't even get there."

"This might be too much information, but based on the blood pooling in his face when he was slumped over the steering wheel, that's almost a certainty." Wilder watched Trobaugh look suspiciously at the bar in her hand and set it back on the console, where Hooper snatched it and put it back in its assigned location. "And that may have been what he meant when he told his wife 'he knew what needed to be done.'"

"I agree." Wilder turned left off the main highway onto a gravel county road. "I think it was more about fear that if someone knew about Fardulis, he might be next, as far as being exposed for abusive behavior, so he took the easy way out. There were tracks in the grass shoulder where he went off the road, but he had to be going over eighty to cause that much structural damage to the car, and I didn't see a single brake track or even a swerve to indicate he'd tried to avoid the collision."

"I agree. He just went right for it." Trobaugh leaned forward and pointed to the left of the gravel road, at a small, grayed, cedar-plank cabin with a dented black mailbox marking the drive. "Correct me if I'm wrong, but doesn't that say 'Davis'?"

"It does." Wilder pulled up too fast and left skid marks as she parked the Jeep. "Let's get in there. If Tala's not here, I want to get to wherever she is."

"Let's look, but this isn't it. There's only a concrete-slab foundation," Hooper said as they walked up to the slanted, wood-plank porch. "And it's max 250 square feet with no attic space. Let's just get in and out."

Trobaugh called out Tala's name as they turned the rusty key in the lock, and the bent hinges groaned as the door swung open. The violet early evening light was all they needed to see that she was nowhere in the one-room cabin, and a search that constituted a quick look behind the curtain separating the toilet from the rest of the living space took them less than a minute.

"And no outbuildings," Wilder said, opening the back door and scanning the small, fenced, back property. "No storm cellar, and the dust pattern in front of the door was undisturbed."

Wilder took a final look as Trobaugh picked up a call, then locked the door as she walked back into the cabin. She wanted to tear the place apart out of sheer frustration, but that wouldn't help them find Tala. Why had someone taken Tala specifically? Was she simply downstairs at the time?

"Wilder." Trobaugh's voice was low and controlled, and by the time Wilder had even looked up, she was already heading for the door. She held it open as she continued. "They enhanced the license plate from the footage outside your house this morning enough to match the numbers to Banyon's vehicle. They also got the warrant to ping Banyon's phone, but it turns out they didn't even need it." Wilder and Hooper were out the door before she even finished her sentence. "Robinson was headed back to the station after delivering the death notification, and he spotted Banyon's car parked at a residence. We don't have an arrest warrant yet, but they're working on that. He just texted me the address."

❖

Wilder pulled up just down the street from the address and double-checked the numbers. She saw Banyon's car in the drive and Robinson's unmarked car down half a block on the other side. She signaled him with her lights, and he silently responded in kind. She'd spoken to the FBI agents on the scene, who had arrived earlier. At this point they were only backup, but there were enough of them to sweep a house in five minutes should they see probable cause.

"Do you know who lives there?" Hooper said, zipping up her jacket against the black winter air just on the other side of the Jeep windows.

"No. It's one of the nicer parts of town, and we don't get many calls up here. The owner's name that dispatch sent over didn't ring a bell either, but I sure as hell know it wasn't Banyon." She glanced out at the house again and checked once more that she had her firearm, cuffs, and radio. Tension hung thick in the air, the street unusually quiet. Not one person was outside, and the only motion came from the flickering amber glow of the Halloween displays on the stoops of the homes. Not even the wind was stirring.

The air was crisp and cold as they got out of the Jeep, and brittle leaves crunched under their feet on the street as they started walking toward the home. Robinson followed suit, and they met where the road intersected the walkway to the house. It was a brick, three-story colonial, with beveled white columns and a perfect stone walkway. Motion-detection lights clicked on and lit the path as they approached the steps leading to the door, and gold light glowed from every window through sheer, white curtains. Three pumpkins and a selection of seasonal gourds were arranged on each step, and a garland of glittery yellow and crimson leaves was draped across the double front door.

"I gotta say, this is not what I was expecting." Hooper scanned the front of the house and stepped behind Wilder and Trobaugh as they reached the door. She glanced back at Robinson, who was standing at the bottom of the steps. "He's either got accounts in the Cayman Islands or a sugar mama, and my money's on the second option."

Wilder pressed the doorbell twice and waited. After what seemed forever, heavy footsteps made it to the door, and Banyon opened one of the two doors, dressed in boxers, a plaid robe, and a shrunken NASCAR tee shirt that had crept just above his belly.

"What the hell are you doing here?"

"Mr. Banyon, these are Special Agents Trobough and Hooper, and we're investigating the abduction of an FBI agent, Tala Marshall. We have reason to believe she might be on the premises, and we need you to answer some questions about her disappearance."

Banyon leaned out the door and watched as armed agents stepped out of no fewer than six unmarked cars, and more cruisers turned down the road, slowing as they approached the house. He looked back to them, his eyes glazed with either fear or panic, Wilder couldn't tell which. He didn't say anything, just seemed to be frozen, squeezing the cellophane-wrapped chocolate muffin he'd been carrying into an entirely different shape. Wilder waited for a response that didn't happen, then went on.

"We are already in the process of getting a search warrant, but we'd like to have your permission. We can wait, but you're just delaying the inevitable. If you cooperate, this will go down a lot easier."

Banyon said nothing, just looked down in shock as he urinated down the front of his boxers onto the expensive tile entryway floor.

"Mr. Banyon, we need your permission to search the premises."

He finally nodded, sinking to a sitting position on the floor as they passed him and left him with Robinson, who was calling in the troops to search for Tala.

After a preliminary search that turned up nothing, they left it to the other agents to complete and sat down with Banyon in the expansive dining room. The house was full of officers, FBI agents, detectives, and SWAT, every possible light was on, and it sounded like it was being torn apart. Because it was.

Two officers were posted at each entrance to the room, and Banyon, who'd seemed to find a pair of sweatpants, sat handcuffed at the end of the long oak table. Trobaugh, Hooper, and Wilder sat as close as possible to him and leaned close. He wilted under the intensity of their presence and started sweating, long droplets rolling down his forehead and splashing onto the table.

"Banyon, I'm going to cut the bullshit here and get right to it because an FBI Agent is missing, and we tend to take that very personally." Wilder took a breath. "I know you were at my house this morning when she was abducted, because we have videotape of your every move."

"I don't know what the hell you're even talking about. I've spent the whole damn day right here on the couch."

"Well, that's clearly not true." Hooper's voice dropped to a low, threatening timbre. "And if you think we're going to hold your hand and sort through a thousand lies while one of our own is out there somewhere, you're just dumber than you look."

"Look. I'd tell you something if I could, but I really don't know what you're talking about." Harold looked on the verge of tears. "If I had taken an agent hostage, do you really think I'd answer the door in my robe and wet myself?"

"Let's start with what the hell you're doing at this address." Trobaugh scooted her chair even closer to Banyon's. "We know this house doesn't have your name anywhere on it, so why don't you start with telling me who owns it."

"It's my girlfriend's, or my girlfriend's husband's, maybe? I don't know. We've been going out for about six weeks, and I stay here sometimes. He has a place in Boston too. They're separated."

"So, your new lady has a husband that doesn't mind you hanging out in your boxers in his expensive-ass house rent-free and doing his wife whenever you feel like it?" Hooper was clearly in no mood to entertain Banyon's bullshit. "Try again. The truth, this time."

Robinson stuck his head around the doorframe. "Chief, we found a gun display case upstairs in the master bedroom. It's locked, but a space for a pistol is empty."

Wilder nodded and kept her eyes on Banyon as Robinson disappeared around the corner again. "Know anything about that?"

"Look. I don't know anything at all about a missing agent." He looked up to the ceiling, the stress pounding in the purple veins crawling up his forehead. "But one thing I know for sure is that you don't have me on video at your house this morning. If you don't believe me, you can check the security cameras in this place."

"I'm sure they're pulling those up as we speak." Trobaugh narrowed her eyes. "Why would you go to Chief Mason's house last night if you're not involved? Those two things were separated by only a few hours, so I'd say that's a big coincidence, wouldn't you?"

"I didn't even want to go to your house last night. My girlfriend wanted to know what information you had on the serial psycho. She said it made her nervous and she couldn't ask herself."

"Why not?" Wilder tapped her thumb on the table to keep from throwing something. "That makes no sense."

"That's a stupid question." Banyon rolled his eyes. "You know that as well as I do. You're barking up the wrong tree here. The second I got back last night she asked me what you'd said and then asked to borrow my car. I haven't seen her since. She dropped off my car and took her rig. She's probably at their lake house or something." Banyon spit out the words and nodded toward the upstairs. "Look it up on the cameras. You'll see."

"Harold." Wilder lifted her head, her tone making Trobaugh and Hooper look at her instead of Banyon for the first time since they'd sat down. "Who is your girlfriend?"

"You don't already know that?" Banyon rolled her eyes. "Miranda. Your ex-wife."

CHAPTER NINETEEN

Two minutes later, in what seemed like a sea of flashing blue and white lights, yellow tape, and confusion, Wilder pulled her phone out of her jacket pocket and walked across the front lawn to make a call.

The first ring didn't even make a dent before Maren snatched it up. "Bout fuckin' time, mate. What can I do?"

"Dude, I need some shit, and I don't even have the energy to make it sound pretty." She rubbed her eyes with the heel of her hand and went on. "But I'm going to do whatever it takes to find Tala." Wilder suddenly felt like she didn't even have the energy to form the words. "I need to borrow your girl because my skills aren't cutting it, and what we have to do might get us all fired." She closed her eyes against the flashing lights of yet another patrol car pulling up. "You in?"

There was a long silence on the line, followed by a dramatic sniff from Maren. Then another. "I mean, I can't believe you felt like that was even a question, but I'm willing to overlook that if you're buying celebration drinks after we get Tala the fuck back where she belongs." After a pause, the line came to life again. "Darcy said it's about damn time. Where do you need us?"

Wilder had to lower the phone and look at the stars glittering in the inky sky for a few seconds before she answered. It was the first rush of relief she'd had since she realized Tala was missing, and she was overwhelmed by a sense of sudden gratitude for the people who had somehow become family without any of them noticing.

❖

"It's right around the corner there, about a mile, it looks like."

Trobaugh pointed to the arrow on the GPS display, but Wilder knew the SWAT unit was already there. Every available officer and most of the agents sent over from Boston had immediately jumped into their cars when Banyon dropped the Miranda bomb, but the three of them had stayed a few more minutes to get the most information they could from Harold before they followed.

"So, you had no idea where Miranda was living?" Hooper unbuckled her seat belt to lean up between Trobaugh and Wilder. "How is that even possible in a town this small?"

"Look. I don't want any more contact with her than I have to. I've met her husband once or twice, and he actually seems like a nice guy, but that's it. He owns a chain of veterinary hospitals across Boston. I thought they still lived in the house she bought after we split up, and he was commuting to Boston during the week." Wilder spun the wheel to take a right turn she'd almost missed. "But now they're separated, according to Banyon, anyway."

Hooper snorted from the back. "If you ask me, Banyon's more employee than boyfriend. It sounds like she sent him out to get information, so she didn't have to do it herself and attract attention."

Trobaugh popped on her glasses and looked across at Wilder. "I remember you saying that she went a little crazy the last couple of years you two were together. Can you see her being our killer? Did she have *that* big of an ax to grind about ridding Salem of sinners?"

"She's always been obsessed with the witch trials, although she's never even once been on my radar. It started with her deciding that being gay was an 'abomination,' and then one day she just left." Wilder shook her head. "According to her friends and people in town, she just got more and more radical and went off the deep end about women's reproductive rights, race, trans rights, all the hot-button issues. It makes sense now. I can't believe I didn't see it before."

Wilder started to speak, but a number she didn't recognize was calling, and she clicked it through to the car speaker system. "This is Wilder Mason. How can I help you?"

"Wilder?" The voice on the other end of the line was smooth and resonant. "This is Dr. Garrison Wheeler. I'm Miranda's husband."

Wilder looked at Hooper and Trobaugh, then shifted her concentration back to the road. "Garrison, good to hear from you again. Do you have any idea where Miranda is at the moment?"

"That's what I was calling to tell you." A long pause seemed to stretch on forever. "Based on a voice mail I got a few minutes ago, she may be planning to harm someone. She didn't say who."

"Did she say where she is right now? Or do you have an idea where that might be?"

"I honestly don't know. But she's dangerous, Wilder. I think we both know that by now."

"That's the understatement of the year." She took a breath and steadied her voice. "We got a tip about your lake house, and we're on our way there now. Do we have your permission to enter and search the premises?"

"Absolutely. Do whatever you need to do to handle the situation." The line broke up to static for just a few seconds, then came back. "About the theft from my medical practice to Boston authorities a few months ago. It was quite a bit of powerful horse tranquilizer."

"You're saying that tranquilizers were stolen from your practice?" Wilder met Hooper's gaze in the rearview window.

"Yes, and now I think Miranda might have been responsible. I'd imagine that news didn't get to you in Salem, so I'm telling you now in case it's relevant."

Trobaugh's phone dinged just as Wilder was hanging up with Garrison through the crackling static. Ominous gray clouds were rolling in over the stars, and the wind ran its fingertips through bare aspen trees on either side of the road, the branches scraping the sky that seemed low and heavy, hovering just above the ground. The ocean was restless, the top of the waves glossed with pale, silver moonlight.

"It's Maren. She and Darcy just got there." The phone dinged again as she went to set it back on the console. "She says Darcy needs to talk to you."

Hooper pointed through the seats at the vehicles lined up on both sides as they turned left and down a murky drive that ended at a rocky, deserted beach. "That must be the lake house." She squinted and leaned closer. "Could be worse, I guess. At least no other houses are around."

"How long do you think before people start noticing?"

"Not long." Trobaugh clicked off her seat belt and zipped up her jacket, looking up at the Cape Cod style beach house set back from the shore. They watched as the FBI and officers started mobilizing, several of them jumping out of the open back of the SWAT van that had pulled up just before them. "And once they do, this place will be flooded with press. If she's there, we need to go in and find her as quickly as possible."

"Copy that." Wilder got out as the wind whipped up from the water and blew her jacket open. She zipped it up and nodded as Trobaugh and Hooper ran up the drive to the other units and Maren walked toward her, her hair blowing around her face. Rain was beginning to drift in on the wind, slicking her skin with the scent of seawater.

Maren hugged her hard and stepped back. "Listen. We'll talk later. Go get Tala."

"Yeah." Wilder shook her head, trying to fight off the feeling of dread sweeping across the dunes and circling her. "Where's Darcy?"

Maren nodded at the beach, and Wilder caught just a streak of light across her blond hair. She was standing by the water in a dark FBI jacket, her arms folded in front of her.

"Why isn't she up with everyone else?"

"She didn't tell me shit, except that Tala isn't up there." Maren glanced back at the lake house. "You've got to go talk to her. I'll handle what's going on up here."

Wilder nodded, giving Maren a quick hug before she walked the opposite direction down the beach. It took a few minutes to reach Darcy, who didn't look at her when she got there. She was just staring out to sea, hair blowing around her face. Wilder stopped and stood beside her, looking out over the water.

"She's out there, Wilder."

Wilder dropped her head into her hands. Everything seemed to slow around her, and she felt like sinking into the sand.

"She's alive. But Miranda is out there too." She stopped, shrugging off her jacket into the sand and unbuckling her holster. She looked over at Wilder as she unlaced her boots. "Are you just going to stand there? Let's go."

Wilder gazed out over the water, and a swath of pale moonlight shifted through the clouds just enough to show her what the hell Darcy was talking about. And then she saw it. A small yacht was bobbing up and down on the waves, about fifty yards from the shoreline. Not a single light was on, not even navigation lights.

"They're out there, Wilder." Darcy nodded toward the lake house. It was up the beach and around a sharp corner, so after Wilder had walked down to Darcy, it was out of sight. "Because the house is around the bend of the beach, it's possible she hasn't seen the lights at the lake house, but if we go out there all guns blazing, she'll just kill both Tala and herself sooner. She's planning to do both."

"But she's alive right now. If there's even a chance, I'm going to get her." Wilder dropped her jacket and holster on the sand, unbuttoning her uniform shirt as she spoke. "Go back up to the house."

"Fuck that. I'm going with you." Darcy dropped her phone into her boot. "I can feel both of them, Wilder. You have a lot better chance of saving her with me than without me."

"Fuck." Wilder stood on the beach beside her, the wind wrapping itself around them, waves breaking at their feet. The wind was on the rise, but experience told her the waves were small enough at this point that it was possible to swim out to the boat. Not safe, but possible. She balled up her shirt and dropped it on the sand. "You're there only for guidance. If someone's going to put themselves in danger, it's me. Do you understand?"

A glassed-in portion of the very center of the boat suddenly glowed to life.

"Miranda just turned on the lights." Wilder looked over at Darcy. "What does that mean?"

"It means she feels safe, that she thinks no one knows where they are. Either that or she's so close to the end of her plan that it doesn't matter anymore." Darcy squeezed Wilder's hand. "Either way, we've got to get out there."

Darcy glanced up to the lake house that was just out of view, then waded out and dove under the waves. Wilder followed, keeping a close eye on Darcy for signs of fatigue, but at the halfway point, she was still swimming ahead of her when she stopped suddenly, treading just above the surface in the black, swirling water.

"Tala is at the bow, the very front of the ship. I don't know anything other than that." She hesitated, spitting out a mouthful of seawater. "I don't know exactly what's happening, but we don't have much time. You've got to go get her." She pointed to the opposite end of the boat. "There's a ladder that leads to a small platform at the stern, or at least there should be. My family had a similar boat when I was a kid. I'll come from that direction. That way we have the best chance of taking her down."

"Darcy, I'm not leaving you." Wilder tried to steady her voice, but fear had wrapped itself around it. "If we go, we go together."

"Our only chance," Darcy nodded toward the front of the boat bobbing in the distance, "is to have me at the other end to create a distraction if we need it. She needs you more than I do."

"We're coming back alive." Wilder held Darcy's cheek briefly in her hand and met her eyes. "All three of us, do you hear me?"

"Yes, ma'am." Darcy nodded. "Let's get this done."

❖

Tala let her head drop forward onto her chest. The wind whipped through her hair, eventually loosening it from the braid it had been in. A smattering of rain melted into her skin as she watched Miranda in the glassed-in center living area of the yacht, working on her computer at the small captain's desk next to the couch. No lights had been on since sunset. She hadn't even known where Miranda was on the boat until suddenly it had blazed to life a few seconds earlier, like a ghost ship coming alive.

Miranda's speech about paying for her sins was the last thing she'd said to her. She was silent as she walked her through the house and onto a small dock at the back, then up the aluminum plankway and onto the yacht. After a few hours, she'd shoved her to the front of the boat, then made her stand in front of the short guardrail that came up just under the small of her back. The sun was setting in the distance, the whitecaps rising and falling on the dark ocean surface beneath her. She thought about talking to Miranda, trying to reason with her, but the thick, black energy of hate was so dense whenever Miranda looked at her, she figured it would only make things worse.

"Don't worry. I didn't use all the rope on the child molester." She'd tied Tala's hands behind her back with the thick, stiff rope from the museum display. "I saved some for you." She laughed then, a mirthless, fake laugh that gave Tala the chills. "The trouble with you and Wilder is that you're front and center in town, making your sexual immorality seem almost *normal*." She yanked the rope tighter with one hand, trying to get enough length for an additional knot. "Someone had to do something about the perversion taking over Salem." She jerked a few more times before she gave up on the second knot and just yanked the first as tight as possible, then stepped back to admire her work. When she did, Tala saw the pistol tucked into her waistband. "I was just planning to eliminate Wilder, but then you arrived on the scene, which was even better. She'll remember this lesson longer."

Her wrists and ankles were still zip-tied, but now she was roped onto the guardrail. That had been just after sunset, and Miranda had disappeared again until the lights came on in the central cabin. The fact that the psycho bitch was just inside the glassed-in room, working calmly at the computer like it was a normal evening, almost made Tala laugh out loud. She tried, but she felt tears on her cheeks instead and looked away, steeling herself and returning to loosening the aged rope around her wrists. There had been just enough rain to wet her skin, which had allowed her to finally be able to slip out of it, although she had trouble keeping the pain from showing on her face. The brittle rope had rubbed her wrists raw, but Tala stayed as still as possible, her hands behind her back as if nothing had changed.

Miranda had looked up from her computer every few minutes, had even come to the door once to be sure she was still there, but seemed strangely absorbed in whatever she was doing on the screen. The pistol lay on the desk beside her. Tala had felt a surge of hope when the rope had loosened around her wrists, but the zip ties were still cutting into her wrists and ankles. Miranda had removed them from her ankles briefly to walk her out to the dock and onto the boat, but she seemed to know Tala was still too weak from the shot to have the strength to fight back. The second they'd boarded she'd put new ties around her ankles. Tala finally let a tear fall as a brightly lit plane cut through the black sky and clusters of angry clouds overhead. She knew the truth. She might not be tied to the guardrail anymore, but if she tried to jump, she'd drown.

She'd just raised her head to look again when she realized that Miranda was now standing on the deck, sloshing it with water. The gentle movement of the waves tilted the boat just enough to roll the liquid toward her, and when it got close enough, the smell rose into her nose like powdered fire. Gasoline.

Miranda kept serenely smiling as she emptied the container of gasoline and walked slowly back to Tala at the guardrail, a box of matches in her hand.

"Did you happen to look on the other side of the boat, dear?" She laughed, but the smile didn't register in the eyes made of black ice. "Of course not. You couldn't. Silly me. I'll just have to describe the lifeboat waiting for me. It's usually strapped to the side, of course, for emergencies, but I'd say this qualifies, wouldn't you? I have more work to do after I end your sorry little life with the fires of hell. Have you ever heard the verse that tells us that the wages of sin are death?"

"Miranda, I—"

Miranda slapped the words out of her mouth, leaning in so close to Tala she could smell the sweat on her skin. "Don't you ever say my name. You're lucky I've let you live this long, but eventually, the earth shall be cleansed of all iniquity, and you're the one I want to see disappear next."

That was the moment she saw her. As Miranda stepped back, Tala saw Darcy on the other end of the boat, dripping wet, her finger up to her lips as she ducked into the lighted cabin. Tala snapped her eyes back to center and said the first thing that came to her mind.

"Fuck you, Miranda."

Miranda's face blazed red rage, and she drew back to slap Tala again when she clearly heard something behind her. Miranda stepped away and turned toward Darcy slowly, the matches clutched in her fist. When the words finally came, they were so brittle with hate they seemed to fall and clatter across the wooden deck. "Well, well. I guess one of your little friends showed up after all."

Darcy slowly raised Miranda's pistol that Tala had seen her snatch off the desk where Miranda had left it.

"Miranda, this can still end without anyone getting hurt."

"That's cute." Miranda threw her head back and laughed, looking back at Tala, then to Darcy again. "You think this is going to end without anyone getting hurt?"

She looked Darcy up and down, then took a step backward toward Tala. "You think that because you have my gun, I'm just going to let this little bitch go free and run back to Wilder?" Miranda stepped back until she was standing slightly to the side of Tala, facing Darcy. Almost close enough to touch.

Darcy focused her gaze on Tala. Miranda was screaming now, infuriated at not being the center of attention, but Tala couldn't hear her. Silence sifted into the space between Tala and Darcy, and she heard the words as clearly as if Darcy had whispered them into her ear.

Fall back, Sky Willow.

Miranda turned back to look at Tala, furious spittle flying from her mouth. The air was still and silent as Tala launched her forehead into Miranda's nose, knocking her to her knees as blood spurted so violently it filled the space between them with a fine red mist. The second she felt Miranda crumple onto the deck, Tala lifted herself onto the railing and leaned back, letting herself fall slowly into the dark grip of the ocean.

CHAPTER TWENTY

Tala finally opened her eyes as Wilder held her face above the surface of the water.

"Breathe, baby."

Wilder waited for what seemed like forever for Tala to draw a breath that sounded like knives slicing through her lungs, and her heart exploded with relief. She held one hand still firm and steady at the back of her neck, but Tala suddenly started to panic, no doubt remembering the zip-ties around her hands and feet. "You're safe." Tala looked into her eyes for the first time, and Wilder smiled. "I've got you."

Wilder looked up and kept looking at the railing, gently treading water and moving them both away from the boat. "I want you to slip your arms over my head and just rest on me, okay?" Wilder ducked her head, sliding under Tala's wrists so she was balanced on her back. "I'm going to get you to shore and go back for Darcy."

Wilder pulled them through the rough water as quickly as possible, but it felt like hours before she heard a shout go up from the beach when someone finally spotted them. Several agents rushed into the water and swam out to them, and she felt Tala being lifted off her. Robinson had been the first to reach them. He handed Tala off to the agents behind him and helped Wilder to solid ground. She stood and immediately looked over his shoulder to see Maren running down the beach toward them.

"Boss, what about Agent Norse?" Robinson's voice was low as he looked behind them and then back to Wilder. "Maren has been losing her *mind*."

Wilder shook her head. "I know she got onto the boat. After that I—"

A deafening explosion literally shook the beach and the water around them, launching debris and flaming boards into the glittering night sky. Everyone ducked as the initial boom reverberated over the water, then stood slowly and stared out to sea as the angry shades of crimson and yellow flames blazed into the sky. Wilder heard agents start to call it in behind her, heard the shouting about getting a rescue boat to the shore, but she scrambled back to her feet and reached Maren just as she crumpled into the sand.

"Maren, get up. We've got to go out there."

"What do ya mean, mate?" Maren's anguish was palpable as she stared at the burning slice of hell rising from the black, churning sea. "She was on that *boat*."

Wilder crouched down on the sand at eye level and gripped Maren's shoulders hard.

"Get the fuck *up*, dude. I believe in her, and we are not letting shit go down like this. She saved Tala's life." She stopped to steady the emotion in her voice. "And now we need to save hers."

Maren met her eyes, then jumped to her feet and ran into the water, throwing her shirt off behind her. Every law-enforcement agent on the beach was shouting at Maren to come back, but Wilder stopped just long enough to lock eyes with Trobaugh and Hooper, who had just run up the waterline. Trobaugh nodded toward the water, and Wilder dove in, pacing Maren in seconds. They swam until they were about halfway out before they came up for air. Maren's eyes were locked on the towering fire ahead and was just taking a deep breath to start again when Wilder's hand landed on her shoulder. Maren looked back at her, but Wilder smiled and nodded to their left.

"I hate to say anything, here." Darcy smiled, treading water, the blond slick of her hair reflecting the light of the flames. "But isn't the shore in the other direction?"

Maren launched herself toward Darcy, but Wilder hung back, letting them have their moment before mentioning that unless being hit by sparks and burning debris was the plan for the night, they might want to start swimming to shore. By this time, glowing floodlights were being set up and turned out to sea, and rescue vehicles were racing down the beach. The reflection of that unfolding activity across the water and the fire still burning behind them as they swam to shore made everything seem surreal. Except for Darcy, apparently, who nearly punched an EMT attempting to transfer her to a rescue bodyboard.

"I've got this one." Maren waved them off, then pulled Darcy into her arms again the second her feet hit the sand. She smiled as Darcy melted against her, whispering the next words softly against her wet cheek. "And I'm not letting her go."

Wilder walked past them and to the shore looking for Tala, only to be instantly lost in a sea of flashing ambulance lights. Hooper walked up behind her and wrapped a blanket around her shoulders. "She's in the last bus in the row, man." Her voice caught and she smiled. "She may have a mild concussion, and they're going to keep her overnight for observation, but she's going to be fine, thanks to you guys." She laughed, looking back at Trobaugh with a thumbs-up. "Also, my wife says you're fired."

Wilder laughed and ran to the ambulance just as they were lifting Tala's gurney into the back. Wilder jumped in, her hands warm around Tala's face. Tala looked up at her, her wet hair falling over the side of the gurney, and smiled. "You remembered."

"Of course I remembered." Wilder kissed Tala gently and stroked her cheek with her thumb. "You told me to tell you again that I had you, someday." Wilder braced herself as the EMTs got into the front of the ambulance and the motion rocked the vehicle already parked precariously on the sand. "And I'd like to make that official when we get the hell out of this shitshow."

"Ask me again." Tala smiled. "When I'm not in the back of an ambulance."

"Sorry to interrupt guys, but we've gotta go." A younger EMT with a red beard smiled up at them, the back doors in his hands. He looked up at Wilder. "Are you family?"

"Yes." Tala said, tangling her fingers into Wilder's. "She is."

❖

Wilder woke up the next morning to a knock, followed by Sergeant Robinson's long beard and his wife Sophie peeking around the hospital door.

"Feeling up to a few visitors?" Robinson winked at Tala, who looked instantly thrilled and reached out for the plate of brownies Sophie was carrying. Sophie pulled a chair up beside the bed and hugged Tala, peppering her with what sounded like a million questions at once. Robinson smiled as he handed Wilder one of the two black coffees he was carrying.

"God, you're saving my life here." Wilder lifted the lid and blew on the surface, then breathed in the rich, dark steam for a long moment before she took a sip. "Tala slept like a baby, although she's gunning to get the hell out of here now, but I slept with one eye open."

"That's why we're here so early. I wanted to give you the official word myself." Robinson paused and cleared his throat, sounding suddenly unsure how to deliver what was, essentially, a death notification. "The coast guard did get out there in time to put out the fire before it completely sank the boat frame, and they found enough of her remains to know that Miranda is deceased."

"Thanks for being the one to tell me." Wilder's voice was low as she glanced over at Tala, who had taken a hair tie from Sophie and laughed as she tried and failed twice to corral the wild length of her hair into it. "So, what the hell happened after Tala fell into the water?" Wilder pushed up the sleeves of a hot-pink hoodie one of the nurses was nice enough to let her borrow when she saw her come in shivering and soaking wet. Unfortunately, because the back of the hoodie also said JUICY in silver sequined letters, she knew she'd never hear the end of it if she had to get out of that chair. "I rode with Tala in the ambulance right after, so I never heard the story."

"It's not a long one." Robinson stopped abruptly with a wide smile to accept the brownies Sophie offered them before she went back to visit with Tala. "Anyway, when Miranda realized that Tala was really gone and Darcy had her gun, she pulled out a box of matches, struck one, and tossed it onto the deck that had already been sloshed in gasoline. It created an instant wall of fire, and Darcy literally couldn't do anything but try to save herself." He shook his head, taking back the rest of Wilder's brownie she couldn't finish. "The coast guard did find a drifting lifeboat about fifty meters out to sea, so it's not clear if blowing herself up was Miranda's Plan B, but having read her manifesto, I'd say it's more likely it was Plan A."

"Her *what?*" Wilder shook her head, rubbing her temples in tense, slow circles. "I'd ask what was in it, but I'm afraid you'll tell me."

"She wrote a rambling seventeen pages and emailed it to all the news stations about the 'legacy of salvation leadership' she expected to have after she'd ridded Salem of its modern-day witches." He popped the last bite into his mouth and rolled his eyes. "Fortunately she took credit for all four murders, so she's our killer. But you should know that it did list Tala as a victim as well, so it's clear she intended to blow up that boat with Tala on it."

The door opened again, and Hooper and Trobaugh came in, followed by Darcy and Maren, who was carrying a backpack of snacks and sandwiches she promptly passed out to everyone until there wasn't an empty hand in the room. After everyone got a chance to compare notes on the details of the previous night, Wilder got up and whispered in Tala's ear, then got everyone's attention.

"I think it's safe to say that we suddenly have some time on our hands, and Thanksgiving is just a few days away. Tala and I were wondering if you'd like to spend it in the cabin." She paused, running a hand through her hair. She felt strangely emotional, looking around the room at the people who'd become so important in her life in a way she knew would only get deeper and richer. "With us."

"Well." Hooper looked around the room, then cleared her throat. "I think I speak for all of us when I say that we'd already invited ourselves. In fact, I'm a little offended you think we planned to leave before we do some epic feasting in the war room."

Maren bit into one of Sophie's brownies, swooned, then reverted to the task at hand. "Also, we're gonna need you to wear that hoodie, like, all day, every day, mate."

Robinson nodded, stroking his beard. "I've been thinking lately that I'm feeling a little 'juicy.' Where did you get that masterpiece?"

"Turn around. We need photos from every angle." Trobaugh took out her phone and attempted to get behind Wilder to photograph the logo. "Sequins are definitely your color. Who knew?"

Everyone dissolved into laughter as Darcy hugged Tala. "Just get home. We'll do the rest. None of us are letting you out of our sight for a while."

"Darcy." Tala closed her eyes against the cold, sharp memory of the wind wrapping itself around her as she'd spotted Darcy at the other end of the boat the previous night. Everything had fallen silent as she'd locked her gaze on Tala. Something in that moment had been totally different, something intensely powerful she hadn't been able to wrap words around. "Thank you for knowing what to say to me last night."

"Tala." Darcy squeezed her hand. "I don't know what Aponi Standing Deer said to you. I felt her there, but she didn't need to speak through me. I just watched it happen." She gave her a quick hug and looked toward the door when she realized everyone was leaving. "Just get home and we'll talk, okay?"

Tala nodded, watching everyone file out, the silence suddenly light and still in the room. Wilder leaned over and kissed her like she never wanted to let her go, then touched Tala's forehead to hers as she spoke. "They'll probably wait a couple of weeks before they clear you to go back to work, right?"

"Based on what the doctor said, they'll want me out for at least ten days or so." Tala looked up at Wilder, who was now holding her face in her hands. "Why?"

"Perfect. That will give us plenty of time to move you home to the cabin." Wilder smiled. "If you say yes, of course."

"I can't think of anywhere I'd rather be," Tala said, her eyes sparkling, "than home in Salem with you."

About the Author

Patricia Evans splits her time between the US and Ireland, searching for the perfect whiskey and cigar combination and the perfect seaside pub to sit by the fire and enjoy them.

www.tomboyinkslinger.com
@tomboyinkslinger

Books Available from Bold Strokes Books

A Wolf in Stone by Jane Fletcher. Though Cassilania is an experienced player in the dirty, dangerous game of imperial Kavillian politics, even she is caught out when a murderer raises the stakes. (978-1-63679-640-6)

New Horizons by Shia Woods. When Quinn Collins meets Alex Anders, Horizon Theater's enigmatic managing director, a passionate connection ignites, but amidst the complex backdrop of theater politics, their budding romance faces a formidable challenge. (978-1-63679-683-3)

One Last Summer by Kristin Keppler. Emerson Fields didn't think anything could keep her from her dream of interning at Bardot Design Studio in Paris, until an unexpected choice at a North Carolina beach has her questioning what it is she really wants. (978-1-63679-638-3)

StreamLine by Lauren Melissa Ellzey. When Lune crosses paths with the legendary girl gamer Nocht, she may have found the key that will boost her to the upper echelon of streamers and unravel all Lune thought she knew about gaming, friendship, and love. (978-1-63679-655-0)

The Devil You Know by Ali Vali. As threats come at the Casey family from both the feds and enemies set to destroy them, Cain Casey does whatever is necessary with Emma at her side to bury every single one. (978-1-63679-471-6)

The Meaning of Liberty by Sage Donnell. When TJ and Bailey get caught in the political crossfire of the ultraconservative Crusade of the Redeemer Church, escape is the only plan. On the run and fighting for their lives is not the time to be falling for each other. (978-1-63679-624-6)

Undercurrent by Patricia Evans. Can Tala and Wilder catch a serial killer in Salem before another body washes up on the shore? (978-1-636790669-7)

And Then There Was One by Michele Castleman. Plagued by strange memories and drowning in the guilt she tried to leave behind, Lyla Smith escapes her small Ohio town to work as a nanny and becomes trapped with an unknown killer. (978-1-63679-688-8)

Digging for Destiny by Jenna Jarvis. The war between nations forces Litz to make a choice. Her country, career, and family, or the chance of making a better world with the woman she can't forget. (978-1-63679-575-1)

Hot Hires by Nan Campbell, Alaina Erdell, Jesse J. Thoma. In these three romance novellas, when business turns to pleasure, romance ignites. (978-1-63679-651-2)

McCall by Patricia Evans. Sam and Sara found love on the water, but can they build a future amid the ghosts of the past that surround them on dry land? (978-1-63679-769-4)

One and Done by Fredrick Smith. One day can lead to a night of passion...and possibly a chance at love. (978-1-63679-564-5)

Promises to Protect by Jo Hemmingwood. Park ranger Maxine Ward's commitment to protect Tree City is put to the test when social worker Skylar Austen takes a special interest in the commune and in Max. (978-1-63679-626-0)

Sacred Ground by Missouri Vaun. Jordan Price, a conflicted demon hunter, falls for Grace Jameson who has no idea she's been bitten by a vampire. (978-1-63679-485-3)

The Land of Death and Devil's Club by Bailey Bridgewater. Special Liaison to the FBI Louisa Linebach may have defied all odds by identifying the bodies of three missing men in the Kenai Peninsula, but she won't be satisfied until the man she's sure is responsible for their murders is behind bars. (978-1-63679-659-8)

When You Smile by Melissa Brayden. Taryn Ross never thought the babysitter she once crushed on would show up as a grad student at the same university she attends. (978-1-63679-671-0)

A Heart Divided by Angie Williams. Emma is the most beautiful woman Jackson has ever seen, but being a veteran of the Confederate army that killed her husband isn't the only thing keeping them apart. (978-1-63679-537-9)

Adrift by Sam Ledel. Two women whose lives are anchored by guilt and obligation find romance amidst the tumultuous Prohibition movement in 1920s California. (978-1-63679-577-5)

Cabin Fever by Tagan Shepard. The longer Morgan and Shelby are stranded together, the more their feelings grow, but is it real, or just cabin fever? (978-1-63679-632-1)

Clean Kill by Anne Laughlin. When someone starts killing people she knows in the recovery world, former detective Nicky Sullivan must race to stop the killer and keep herself from being arrested for the crimes. (978-1-63679-634-5)

Only a Bridesmaid by Haley Donnell. A fake bridesmaid, a socially anxious bride, and an unexpected love—what could go wrong? (978-1-63679-642-0)

Primal Hunt by L.L. Raand. Anya, a young wolf warrior, finds herself paired with Rafe, one of the most powerful Vampires in the Americas, in an erotic union of blood and sex. (978-1-63679-561-4)

Puzzles Can Be Deadly by David S. Pederson. Skip loves a good puzzle. Little does he know that a simple phone call will lead him and his boyfriend Henry to the deadliest puzzle he's ever encountered. (978-1-63679-615-4)

Snake Charming by Genevieve McCluer. Playgirl vampire Freddie is on the run and a chance encounter with lamia Phoebe makes them both realize that they may have found the love they'd given up on. (978-1-63679-628-4)

Spirits and Sirens by Kelly and Tana Fireside. When rumored ghost whisperer Elena Murphy and very skeptical assistant fire chief Allison Jones have to work together to solve a 70-year-old mystery, sparks fly—will it be enough to melt the ice between them and let love ignite? (978-1-63679-607-9)

A Case for Discretion by Ashley Moore. Will Gwen, a prominent Atlanta attorney, choose Etta, the law student she's clandestinely dating, or is her political future too important to sacrifice? (978-1-63679-617-8)

Aubrey McFadden Is Never Getting Married by Georgia Beers. Aubrey McFadden is never getting married, but she does have five weddings to attend, and she'll be avoiding Monica Wallace, the woman who ruined her happily ever after, at every single one. (978-1-63679-613-0)

Flowers for Dead Girls by Abigail Collins. Isla might be just the right kind of girl to bring Astra out of her shell—and maybe more. The only problem? She's dead. (978-1-63679-584-3)

Good Bones by Aurora Rey. Designer and contractor Logan Barrow can give Kathleen Kenney the house of her dreams, but can she convince the cynical romance writer to take a chance on love? (978-1-63679-589-8)

Leather, Lace, and Locs by Anne Shade. Three friends, each on their own path in life, with one obstacle…finding room in their busy lives for a love that will give them their happily ever afters. (978-1-63679-529-4)

Rainbow Overalls by Maggie Fortuna. Arriving in Vermont for her first year of college, an introverted bookworm forms a friendship with an outgoing artist and finds what comes after the classic coming out story: a being out story. (978-1-63679-606-2)

Revisiting Summer Nights by Ashley Bartlett. PJ Addison and Wylie Parsons have been called back to film the most recent Dangerous Summer Nights installment. Only this time they're not in love and it's going to stay that way. (978-1-63679-551-5)

The Broken Lines of Us by Shia Woods. Charlie Dawson returns to the city she left behind and she meets an unexpected stranger on her first night back, discovering that coming home might not be as hard as she thought. (978-1-63679-585-0)

Triad Magic by 'Nathan Burgoine. Face-to-face against forces set in motion hundreds of years ago, Luc, Anders, and Curtis—vampire, demon, and wizard—must draw on the power of blood, soul, and magic to stop a killer. (978-1-63679-505-8)